GRACE

The Daughters of Allamont Hall
Book 5

A Regency Romance

by Mary Kingswood

Grace: The Daughters of Allamont Hall Book 5

Published by Sutors Publishing

ISBN: 978-1-912167-16-6 (revised paperback)

Cover design by: Shayne Rutherford of Darkmoon Graphics

A traditional Regency romance, drawing room rather than bedroom.

Grace's four older sisters have married and moved away, and life is very quiet and boring. It's so stifling being female, occupying herself with her tapestry or painting, when she'd much rather have been a soldier, galloping about with a sword in her hand. She wouldn't mind marrying, because who wants to be an old maid? But all her suitors are dullards who are only interested in her dowry. If only something exciting would happen!

George Graham is at a loose end, too, now that his Oxford cronies are settling into boring domesticity. But when he learns that a valuable diamond necklace may have been hidden somewhere in his parent's house, he's fired with enthusiasm for the search, and lively Grace Allamont is just the girl to help him. Along the way, they find plenty of adventure, lots of trouble — and a most unexpected love.

The Daughters of Allamont Hall is a series featuring the six unmarried daughters of Mr William and Lady Sara Allamont. Each book is a complete story, but there are also background threads running from book to book as a bonus for series readers.

Book 1: Amy
Book 2: Belle
Book 3: Connie
Book 4: Dulcie
Book 4.5: Mary (a novella, free for mailing list subscribers)
Book 5: Grace
Book 6: Hope

Table of Contents

1: Diamonds

Grace sat with her head demurely lowered. Her feet were placed neatly together, her hands resting in her lap. She said nothing, allowing the impassioned young man to have his say. She had received enough proposals of marriage now to understand the proper form.

The drawing room was spacious, for Allamont Hall was a fine building in the generous style of the previous century, and he strode about it, hands gesturing to emphasise his points, like an actor on a stage. He told her of his delightful manor house in Wiltshire, and the hunting lodge — not his, precisely, but his uncle allowed him the use of it — and the rich farm lands whose rents paid for a most elegant and stylish manner of living, according to his description of it. He mentioned the two carriages he intended to have and the several more horses to add to his stable, and he hoped that, when she was his wife, she would have no fewer than twenty-three servants at her command, and wear diamonds and silk, and sit down to two full courses at dinner every day. He dined with twenty families regularly in his own neighbourhood, he said, and more in Bath, and counted some great names among his acquaintance — he mentioned one or two, in an overly casual manner. There was a living in his gift, if she should have any clergymen in the family. She should want for nothing, he assured her, nothing at all.

Except for love, of course. Of *that* he made no mention, only respect, esteem, companionship.

When he had exhausted his eloquence, she lifted her head and made the little speech which repetition had rendered fluent. Most obliged — such a great honour — very sensible of the innumerable advantages of the match — the greatest regret — impossible to accept — so very sorry to be the cause of disappointment.

He grunted in surprise, eyebrows raised. Leaning one arm against the mantelpiece, he stared at her in bewilderment. He was a solid young man, dressed with more flamboyance than elegance, his cravat an impressively overwrought arrangement. "You do not wish to be mistress of Darrowhall, Miss Allamont?" His tone was full of astonishment, as if he could conceive of no greater happiness in life.

"I have no wish to be mistress of *any* establishment," Grace said. "I have not the least intention of marrying at present, as I have expressed to you many times before."

"Indeed you have professed something of the sort, but naturally you were not serious. All young ladies aspire to marriage, when the right offer is made."

Grace said nothing, hoping he would draw the obvious conclusion from her refusal— that this was *not* the right offer.

The young man had too elevated an opinion of himself, however. "I must beg you to consider your answer most carefully. It would be foolish to expect a man, once rebuffed, to continue to press his suit, and who can say how many more offers you might receive? If I may speak with the utmost frankness, Miss Allamont, your age is against you, nor have you enjoyed the advantage of a season in London to prepare you for a role in the highest echelons of society, such as would make you attractive to the nobility. Viewed in this light, I do not believe I flatter myself in supposing that you will not receive a better offer than mine."

This presumption was too much for Grace. Straightening her back and lifting her chin, she said carefully, "You do indeed flatter yourself, sir. I shall never lack suitors, for it seems *impoverished* gentlemen are drawn to my dowry like bees to clover."

This was a little too close to the mark, for the young man's lips compressed. "There is no more to be said," he snapped. "I hope you do not live to regret this day, Miss Allamont. Pray give my regards to Lady Sara and Miss Hope. I bid you good day."

He swept out of the room. She waited, listening to the murmur of voices in the hall, as he reclaimed his hat, gloves and greatcoat from the footman. Then steps crossing the hall, the front door creaking open and footsteps crunching on the gravel, disappearing round the side of the house to the stables, for he was too impatient to wait for his horse to be brought round.

When all was quiet again, she picked up her skirts and skipped out of the drawing room and across the hall to the book room, banging open the door. Here she found her youngest sister, Hope, giggling over a journal with their cousin, Hugo. Hope was the prettiest of the sisters, and Hugo was a broodingly handsome man. As they bent over the pages, their dark heads almost touching, an observer might take them for brother and sister instead of distant cousins.

In a corner, Miss Bellows huddled with a book. Poor Miss Bellows! Once the governess to the six Allamont sisters, as they had left their lessons behind her role had dwindled over the years to companion and chaperon. Now, with only Grace and Hope yet unmarried, Miss Bellows had added the role of matchmaker to her repertoire. She looked up with hopeful eyes.

"Grace, dear! Well? What did you say to him? May we wish you happy?"

"I trust you will always wish me happy, Lavinia, but not, I hope, as the wife of such a grasping man as that. Who asked him to come all the way from Wiltshire to pay court to me anyway?"

"Oh!" Miss Bellows' face fell. "You turned him down, I collect. Poor man! I hope he will not be too disappointed."

"He will not repine for long," Grace said. "He has such a high opinion of himself that he will soon be pursuing some other heiress to grace his precious Darrowhall, and to pay for his diamonds and his twenty-three servants and two full courses every evening. He will not feel my loss for long, I assure you."

Miss Bellows sighed. "Yet such an *eligible* young man, and a very agreeable manner. A most pleasing countenance, too, and so obligingly civil to me, always, and devoted to you, Grace."

"Oh, stuff!" Grace said. "His devotion was entirely to my dowry. They are always so devoted to my dowry, these ardent young men. I know we are very fortunate to have such large portions, and it was generous of Papa, when he was quite miserly in other respects, but sometimes I wish he had not set up that mysterious account for us in Shropshire. At least then I would not be plagued with fortune-hunters like this Wiltshire fellow, with all his airs. You are too romantic altogether, Lavinia, if you see anything of affection in his manner towards me."

"Well, I never liked him," Hugo said. "He is not going to hang about and have another pop at you, is he?"

"Lord, I hope not!" Grace said. "I have no idea why he stayed so long. Not because of any encouragement on my part, you may be sure. If I told him once I had no wish to marry, I must have told him a hundred times, but he would never take the hint."

"They never do, these fellows," Hugo said. "Always think they will be the one to turn your head. How many have there been now? Must be a dozen at least."

"Seventeen," Hope said in anguished tones. "Grace has had *seventeen* offers, although the elder Mr Cranford proposed three times before he gave it up and went away quite broken-hearted, so perhaps two of those do not count. And I have had five, and none of them the least bit interested in anything but our money."

"Now, now, Hope, I believe there may be just a little exaggeration," Miss Bellows said. "Mr Dawson is certainly rich enough not to care about your dowry."

"Oh, *him*!" Hope cried. "I do not regard him as a serious suitor, for he is old enough to be my grandfather, or almost so. As if I could ever consider such a match. I daresay we shall never marry, sister. We shall be old maids together, and take comfort only in each other as we grow old, and be buried side by side in the churchyard."

"Well, that sounds very dull," Grace said. "I have not found anyone who suits me yet, but I suppose we shall both marry eventually. We must, for the alternative is far worse, and I do *not* want to be an old maid like Miss Endercott, and be laughed at by the village children. I wish I had been a boy, and then I might have gone into the army. Think how exciting that would be, galloping into battle with my sword! I should like it of all things. But no, I must sit with my tapestry or my paintbrush, or practise upon the pianoforte, and hope for an eligible man to rescue me from such tedium. It is so boring to be a lady! If only Mama would allow us to go to London. Just think how exciting that would be, and that is also where all the most eligible men are to be found. We could have our pick of them, I daresay, and surely one or two would be tolerable."

"But we are so *old*!" wailed Hope. "I am one and twenty already, and you are *three* and twenty! Who will want us when we have been out for years and years?"

"You refine too much upon it," Miss Bellows said firmly. "Although it is a pity Lady Sara will not permit you to stay with your sister now and then. The Marchioness would soon find husbands for you, I am certain of it. Look how splendid a match she managed for Miss Graham, when even her own mama despaired of finding anyone suitable for her."

The sisters were silent, not liking to contradict Miss Bellows, but not quite agreeing that becoming the third wife of a gouty Viscount with a string of children and grandchildren could be described as a splendid match.

"You could always marry me," Hugo said, grinning. "Either one of you would do the trick, for then the Hall would be mine, you know, and I should like that tremendously. I was exceedingly put out when Papa suggested I take a look at the accounts for you and sort things out, but it has been excellent fun."

"You just like galloping about the countryside talking to the tenants," Grace said. "And to be sure, that *does* sound like fun. But Hugo, you will not be offended if I say that I should not like to marry you."

"Nor I!" Hope said. "For that would make you just as bad as any of the others — marrying for the sake of the Hall is no different from marrying for a dowry. Oh, how I *wish* Papa had not left everything so awkwardly! Such a strange will, insisting that we all marry in turn by age, and then, if Ernest and Frank cannot be found, the Hall goes to James or Mark or Hugo, but only if they marry one of us, and if *that* fails, it will go to the church and we shall be cast out of our home, and what will become of us then?"

Grace rolled her eyes, for she had heard it all a thousand times before. She was fond of Hope, as she must always be of a sister, but the dear girl always imagined the worst.

"Now, now, Hope, it will not come to that," Miss Bellows said soothingly. "There is still plenty of time for Ernest and Frank to be found, for I daresay they are far away and news is slow to reach them. Even if they are not, you will both be married before then, I wager, so it will not affect you, and if not, you will always have a home with your mama. Lady Sara will have the Dower House, and a comfortable income of her own, so you need not fear to starve, or need to seek employment."

"No, indeed!" Grace said. "That would be dreadful, to be forced to become a governess or some such. Oh, Lavinia, I beg your pardon! I did not mean... it is only that we are not suited to such work, you know. Not like you, so kind and patient as you are."

Miss Bellows smiled thinly. "I am not offended, Grace, dear. I know better than most the disadvantages of my situation, which is why I urge you both to marry as soon as you can. Being a wife, and mistress of your own establishment, and enjoying your own dear children — it is a far more pleasant life, I do assure you."

A discreet knock at the door of the book room was followed by the portly figure of Young, the butler. "Mr Graham is here, Miss Allamont," he said to Grace. "Shall I show him into the drawing room? The fire can be lit in a moment."

"Oh, if it is only George Graham, we need not stand on ceremony. Show him in here."

Young threw a glance at Miss Bellows, but with the slightest lift of one shoulder, she acceded to the arrangement.

George Graham was the only son of Sir Matthew Graham, a close neighbour and family friend. He strode into the book room with an impish grin on his face.

"How very cosy, I declare! This is treating me very much as one of the family. Miss Bellows, I trust you are well? Hope. Hugo. Oh, I say, Grace, I like this new way you have with your hair. You look just like a boy!"

"This shorter style is all the fashion amongst the *ton*, or so Connie said. Hers is even shorter. Her maid cut it for me when she was here last."

"Very daring of you," George said, winking at her. "I'll wager your mama did not approve, eh? But never mind that, for as I rode over here, I passed that dreary friend of the Donboroughs and he had a face like a wet week in Bath. What did you do to him?"

"She refused him!" Hope said, in a melodramatic whisper.

"I should hope so!" George said. "Can't have Grace marrying such a dullard, can we? She can do better than that, I vow. Much, much better."

~~~~~

George rode home in a pleasant frame of mind. The Allamont sisters always cheered him up — well, not Hope so much, for she could be unspeakably miserable when the mood took her — but Grace was a lively girl, and always good fun.

There was another cause for good cheer, too — Miss Dilworthy would by now be ensconced in her travelling carriage, together with her snooty mama, her maid and a parrot in a cage, which accompanied her everywhere, well on their way back to whatever God-forsaken county they hailed from. Lancashire, he rather thought. Or was it Yorkshire? Well, good riddance to her. He wished the girl no harm, but he was not about to become leg-shackled to so spineless a creature. "Yes, Mama. No, Mama. Of course, Mama. At once, Mama." Never a thought in her head that hadn't been put there by the formidable Mrs Dilworthy. He could not imagine what his mother had been thinking of, to suppose for more than three seconds that he would be enticed to marry such a feeble specimen.

Unfortunately, now that Lizzie was safely wed and well-placed to launch her sisters into society when their time came, Lady Graham had turned her attentions to the matrimonial prospects of her son. George was determined that it would avail her nothing. No matter how many Miss Dilworthys she paraded in front of him, he had no intention of being caught. Not yet! He was barely five and twenty. Another five years, and then, perhaps he would consider it, for he knew his duty as the heir to a baronetcy, but not yet.

He turned in at the gates of Graham House, pondering whether it was worth the effort of taking a gun out that afternoon, or whether the day was too far gone, only to pull up with an exclamation of dismay. A carriage was drawing to a halt before the front door. His immediate fear was that the Dilworthys had returned, but a cursory glance confirmed that it was a different carriage. Besides, it was a man descending from it, and mounting the steps to the entrance.

Hastily, George rode round to the stables, slid from his horse, and tore into the house, striding through the twisting passages from the rear and into the capacious hall, to hear voices from the saloon. Both his parents, and a third — the mystery man. Without ceremony, he burst into the room. Three faces turned to him as one, his mother tutting in vexation, his father trying not to laugh, and the visitor smiling.

"George! How delightful!"

"Uncle Jasper! What are you doing here?"

His uncle smiled, but Lady Graham said, "Really, George! Must you come in here smelling of horse? And where are your manners? Greet your uncle properly."

"Ah, no need for formality, Julia. I am glad you are here, George, for this is a family matter, and you should know of it. Your great-grand-mama's will has finally been located—"

"Good Lord!" George said. "After all this time! Wherever was it?"

"Behind a loose brick in the stables, would you believe."

George gave a bark of laughter. "I would believe anything of great-granny. That is just like her, to hide it away somewhere it would likely never be found."

"Indeed. It was fortunate that my new hunter took exception to one of the grooms, and lashed out with a hoof in just the right place, else we might never have found it. But it confirms what you have said all along, Julia, that the necklace is to go to you."

Lady Graham inclined her head graciously. "She always said so, but of course without a will... But I imagine that Lilian will say she was not of sound mind when she wrote it?"

Her brother had the grace to look embarrassed. "Lilian did say something of the sort, I confess. She set her heart on that necklace long ago, and heaven knows she deserves it, given what she has had to put up with from the old lady. My wife has the patience of a saint. But the law is clear, and the necklace is yours."

"The famous diamonds — shall you wear them?" George said gleefully. "How splendid you will look!"

"Regrettably, no one will wear them," his uncle said. "The diamonds have disappeared. Lilian has scoured the house from attic to cellar, as you may imagine, but without the slightest success. The maid has insisted all along that they were lost, and the worst of it is, she says that the last time she recalls seeing them was here in this very house."

"Really?" Lady Graham said calmly. "I cannot say when I last saw her wear them."

"Do you mean," George said breathlessly, "that the Durmaston Diamonds may be somewhere in this house? Or behind a brick in *our* stables?"

"It is entirely possible," his uncle said.

"Famous! We must begin a search at once!" George said, with a wide grin. "A treasure hunt — what could possibly be more amusing?"

"Oh, George," his mother said, shaking her head sorrowfully. "So frivolous! Sometimes I despair of you. When will you ever grow up?"

His father raised an eyebrow languidly. "It will do no harm. Let the boy search if he wishes. He must be bored now that all his friends are occupied elsewhere."

"Occupied?" George said. "Tied down, I should rather say. Dragged off to the continent, like old Wilson, or worse, to Scotland, like Macintyre. Poor Lannington is to be fitted up for a cleric's coat, and never was a man less suited to the profession. And the rest of them married, or as good as. Leg-shackled, and at only twenty-five. Desperate indeed."

His father smiled fondly at his wife. "It is not so terrible a fate, being leg-shackled, as you will find out one of these days, George. But by all means look for the diamonds if you will. I daresay you will find nothing but a great deal of dust."

"There is no dust in this house, you may be sure of that," his wife said, bridling. "Nor is there any corner neglected by the servants where a diamond necklace may be hiding."

"Then George will be disappointed," her husband said. "But it must not be said that we failed to look for the necklace, knowing it to be missing."

"Exactly!" George said gleefully. "I shall start at once — in the attics, I think."

He raced off to begin, his mother's protestations fading into the distance behind him.

2: Searching

Two days of scrabbling round in the attics left George with no very pleasing impression of his mother's housekeeping.

"Do you never throw *anything* away?" he asked her as he joined them in the saloon before dinner. "Furniture with woodworm, gowns that went out of fashion a hundred years ago, samplers whose creators must surely be long dead and the most appalling thing I have ever seen — all feathers, quite hideous! It made me sneeze so hard I thought my head would fall off."

"Oh, that must be the cloak that dear old Uncle Samuel brought back from — well now, I forget where. Some island or other. He was in the navy, you know, working his way up from Midshipman. He became something very grand at the Admiralty eventually, until a runaway fish cart finished him off. But he went all over the place when he was younger, and acquired some amazing things from the natives."

"Amazingly hideous, if you ask my opinion," George said. "Which you did not, of course," he added hastily, seeing his mother's face darken.

"So have you found any sign of the necklace?" his father said, his lips quirking in amusement.

"Not so much as a single glass bauble to raise my hopes," George said gloomily. "But I have not the least idea what I am looking for. What is it like, this necklace?"

"It was a monstrous ugly thing, in all honesty," his mother said. "A high choker, not at all fashionable these days. I should never wear such a dreadful piece. But the diamonds were worth a fortune, and I never brought much money of my own to the marriage. Your papa has never reproached me for the lack, but I always felt it keenly. Not for your sake, of course, but it is pleasant for a mother to be able to leave something to her daughters."

"And you have no idea where it might be?"

"Do you not imagine that it would have been found by now, if it is indeed here, or anywhere else?" Sir Matthew said. "A diamond necklace is a rather conspicuous item. It lay in a sizable wooden box, as I recall, not something that might slip into a pocket, or fall down the back of a dresser."

"I should not be at all surprised if Aunt Lilian had found it long since and hidden it away," George said. "That would be just like her! And then she would deny any knowledge of it, naturally."

"That is a scurrilous assertion, George," his father said, with a frown of disapproval. "But even if your aunt's morals may be open to question — and I do not say that they are, but let us make the assumption for the moment — your uncle's are not. If the will gifts the necklace to your mama, you may be quite certain that Jasper would abide by that. No, if he says the necklace is not to be found, then we must believe him, and knowing how well hidden the will was, it is to be supposed that every brick of the stables has been examined."

"But no one has examined every brick in *our* stables yet," George said. "The necklace could be anywhere, and great-granny was so forgetful, she would have had no notion where she had left it."

"Hmmm… it is possible, I suppose," his father said doubtfully.

"Really, George!" his mother said. "What are you planning to do, dismantle the stables brick by brick?"

"Not dismantle, no. That would be dreadfully inconvenient. But I might go and poke about a bit, perhaps."

His mother tutted at him, and shook her head.

~~~~~

The Allamont carriage slowed and then rolled gently to a halt. The groom jumped down to open the door and let down the steps for the occupants. Lady Sara emerged first, statuesque, serene, her gentle smile unwavering as she gazed about her, looking up and down the ivy-clad walls of Graham House, almost as if she had never seen it before. But then it was indeed many, many months since she had called on her neighbours. Grace jumped down from the carriage, tripped on the hem of her gown and almost tumbled over. Behind her, Hope giggled and descended more slowly by way of the steps. By this time the butler and footman had emerged, and the three ladies proceeded up the entrance steps and into the hall.

Graham House was very old, much added to by each successive generation, so that the exterior featured four different styles at least, and the interior was a warren of long passageways, unexpected stairs and rooms tucked away in half-forgotten wings. There were reputed to be secret passages and sealed-up rooms, but such was said of any house with the least degree of antiquity. Sir Matthew had inherited the house fifteen years earlier with the baronetcy, and apart from joining two rooms together to make a larger dining room, had made no changes.

Grace rather liked the place. It had so much more character than the blandly modern Allamont Hall. She and Hope had been intimate with Lizzie, the eldest daughter, before her marriage, and they had spent many a happy hour tapping the walls of this room or that. Sadly, they had never found a secret passage — only a long-forgotten broom cupboard, with a shelf full of fossilised blacking for the grates and brushes brittle with age.

But if the house was interesting, the residents were less so. Lizzie was gone, and the next sister, Alice, was not yet out, so there were only Sir Matthew and Lady Graham to talk to, and they were no fun. There was no fun to be had anywhere, Grace thought glumly. Her four older sisters were all married now, their thoughts entirely taken up with husbands and babies and difficulties with the servants and the price of wax candles and lace. Grace and Hope were quite left behind, with only Mama and Miss Bellows for company. It was too dreary for words. How Grace longed for a little excitement!

As if to complete Grace's misery, when the ladies were shown into the saloon, they found Mr and Mrs Wills already established there. Grace sighed inwardly, and fixed a false smile to her face. Mr Wills had once been a suitor to the eldest Allamont sister, Amy, but when that had not answered, he had gone to Bath and found himself a different sort of wife. Grace tried her best to be charitable, but Mrs Wills had neither face nor figure nor demeanour to please. Nor did she play or paint or sing or draw, for her fortune appeared to be her only accomplishment. Had she been blessed with children, perhaps her manner might have softened, but as it was, she saw it as her business to interest herself in the marriage prospects of every unmarried woman in the county. Grace had not taken two steps into the room before she was accosted by the lady in shrill tones.

"Ah, Miss Allamont! Just the person I'd hoped to see. What is this I hear about a certain person, who shall remain nameless but we all know who I speak of, I am sure!" She cackled gleefully. "Sent away without ceremony, or so a little bird told me, in the strictest confidence. Poor man, so fond of you and yet dispatched without a shred of hope. Do sit by me and tell me everything."

Grace would have done anything rather than comply, but she could think of no reasonable excuse for refusing. So she sat beside Mrs Wills, rather overpowering in puce bombazine, with a hat of many feathers which waved distractingly at the slightest movement, and tried very hard not to reveal any information about the young man that would denigrate him or herself.

Meanwhile, her mama was smiling happily, engaged in lively conversation with Lady Graham and almost — could it be possible? — flirting with Sir Matthew. Grace was too diverted to pay attention to Mrs Wills, answering more or less at random. Mama was strange these days. She went away so often, and when she returned home, there was no knowing whether she would be happy and relaxed, as now, or silent and withdrawn.

After a while, just as Grace was beginning to cast about in her mind for an excuse to change her seat to obtain more congenial company, George came in, looking rather dishevelled, with wisps of straw in his hair.

"Really, George!" his mother said. "Where are your manners? Could you not have changed to greet our guests? Look, here is Lady Sara returned from London, and you look like a goat herder."

"Do I? What does a goat herder look like exactly?"

She clucked impatiently. "Make your bow to Lady Sara." He did so, and a delicate little cough from the other side of the room directed him to Mrs Wills, who smiled benevolently and would have urged him to sit beside her, had George not spied Grace nearby.

"Grace! Just the person! We have had the most enormous fun here, you cannot imagine how exciting it is." He explained to her all about the famous Durmaston Diamonds, and his fruitless search.

"Where have you looked so far?" Grace said.

"The attics and the stables, but no luck in either. I shall start on the cellars next."

"The cellars? Was your great grand-mama accustomed to wander about the cellars?"

"Well, no, but—"

"Then she could hardly have left her diamonds there, could she? You should start with the rooms she used when she stayed here, and then widen the search to include all the public rooms she might have used."

"Oh. That makes sense," George said. "You are clever, Grace. I should have asked for your advice right from the start. Will you help me search? You can make sure I am looking in all the most likely places."

"I will, if I am allowed. Mama might not quite like it."

But Mama smiled and inclined her head graciously. "How kind in you to offer your help. Perhaps if Lady Graham does not dislike it, you may stay here for a while? I can send the carriage for you at... five o'clock? Would that suit?"

"We would be delighted to send Miss Allamont home in our carriage," Sir Matthew said affably. "No need to take your horses out twice."

Amidst the smiles and little speeches of gratitude and obligation between her mama and the Grahams, Grace slipped out of the room with George.

"Come on," she hissed at him. "Let us get away from them before they change their minds, or decide that it is improper for us to be roaming around the house alone."

George stopped. "Oh. Maybe it is improper."

"Fustian! As if we have not known each other for ever. We are like brother and sister. Besides, if Mama sees nothing wrong in it, then there cannot be the least objection."

"Lady Sara is in a good mood today," George said in surprised tones.

Grace shrugged. "Her last trip went well, I suppose. Where are the old lady's rooms? Let us begin there."

George led the way up the main stairs and along a series of corridors, then through a door into an older part of the house, with rough druggets on the floor and a damp chill in the air. Their footsteps raised a small cloud of dust.

"Phoo! Look at all these cobwebs," Grace said, waving her arms like a windmill to break a way through. "We shall look like ghosts before long. Are you sure this wing is habitable?"

"It was when great-grand-mama last stayed with us. Mind you, that was years ago. Here we are."

He threw open a door, and led the way into a spacious sitting room, with panelled walls painted a pale colour, and warm velvet curtains. The furniture was old-fashioned but expensive, and Grace guessed it must have been the height of fashion at one time.

"This is a pleasant room," Grace said. She ran a finger along a side table. "At least the housemaids get in here occasionally. Not a cobweb to be seen. What is through that door?"

Exploration revealed a small dining room and serving room, a smaller sitting room and a bedroom and dressing room.

"And everything is as it was?" Grace said. "The furniture is just the same as when your great-grandmother was here?"

"Exactly the same. Nothing has been touched at all, as far as I can tell," George said. "This will be easier to search than the attics. Look, all the cupboards and drawers are empty."

"That does not mean that the diamonds are not here. If they were hidden intentionally, and not simply lost, they could be in a secret drawer, or fixed to the underside of something.

23

We must check all the floorboards and wainscoting too, and on top of the wardrobes, and around the windows. It is astonishing where small hiding places may be found. Papà left money concealed in all sorts of odd places, you have no idea."

"Oh." George's eyes were round. "You really think...? Well, let us begin."

They worked methodically from room to room, starting with the dressing room and bedroom, which seemed the most likely places. Grace had rarely spent a happier afternoon than now, crawling about on the floor lifting rugs, pulling out drawers, examining every little space for hidden compartments, and even tapping the walls for possible secret spaces. George employed his greater height to good effect by stretching to see the tops of the wardrobes, peering behind the pictures on the walls. He drew the line at looking up the chimney, however.

"If ever great-grand-mama put her hand up the chimney, then I am a Chinaman," he said. "She was the most fastidious old stick I ever did meet, and her maid even had to spread honey on her bread for her, in case the slightest stickiness should attach itself to her. No, I draw the line at the chimney."

"Belle found a money box in the chimney of our book room," Grace said. "There was a special compartment made just for hiding valuables. That would be the perfect place for the necklace, and the maid could easily have put it there, if the old lady was too fussy to do the job herself. We must look, and if you will not do it, then I must."

"Grace, I do not think—" he began, but she had already pushed up one sleeve and stuck her hand up the bedroom chimney. A cloud of soot flew out, coating Grace, George and a fair amount of floor.

"Oh," Grace said. She looked at George, and then at herself, and burst out laughing. "We look like street urchins! To be sure, if I fail to secure a husband, I shall have no trouble finding employment as a chimney sweeper."

And then they both laughed until tears squeezed out of their eyes.

"Lord, but my sides ache!" Grace said, sliding across the floor to sit with her back against the wall. "I have not been so well entertained since that time Lady Harrison fell down the steps at the assembly and showed the world a great deal more than she intended."

"I remember! That was... very educational for a gently brought up young man. I always thought ladies wore drawers or some such."

"Well, some do..." Grace began, before realising the impropriety of discussing such an intimate matter with a man. "But never mind that. Do the bells work? We should get the servants up here to clean up this mess."

Just then a timid little tap on the door was followed by the angelic face of sixteen-year-old Alice Graham, her features surrounded by a halo of blonde curls fetchingly bound with a pink ribbon.

"Alice!" George boomed, beaming at his younger sister. "Finished your lessons already?"

"Lessons ended hours ago," she said in a tiny thread of a voice. "Mama sent me to tell you that the carriage is being brought round for Miss Allamont. Oh, what have you done!" She gazed at her brother and Grace, taking in for the first time the enormity of the devastation afflicting them. "Oh, Grace, you are so dirty! I am confined to the schoolroom for a week if I get so much as a mark on my gown. And is that... can it really be soot? Whatever have you been doing?"

"The chimney needs sweeping," George said.

"But you did not need to do it yourself," Alice whispered.

For some reason, this struck Grace as exquisitely funny, and started her laughing all over again.

"Oh, do not laugh!" Alice said distressfully. "Please come down, or I shall be in trouble for not fetching you."

Grace scrambled to her feet, and a loud ripping sound echoed round the room. She looked ruefully at the torn hem of her gown. "Oh dear."

"Oh Grace, you will be in so much trouble," Alice said mournfully.

Grace could not disagree.

3: Chimneys

"Lady Hardy," the butler intoned.

An elegantly attired young woman stood on the threshold of the Allamont Hall drawing room.

"Mary!" Grace shrieked from her seat near the window. "Do come and sit by me. I want to hear all about London!"

"Please moderate your tone, Grace," her mother said gently.

Grace jumped up, setting a small table wobbling, and bobbed a curtsy. "I beg your pardon, Mama."

She hoped her tone was demure enough. Mama had been more amused than censorious at her appearance after what she had come to think of as the Incident with the Chimney, but still, it would not do to incur her displeasure. Even though Grace was three and twenty, her mother still had the power to forbid her from visits or — horrid thought! — from attending the next ball. She might not be looking for a husband, but Grace enjoyed dancing as much as anyone, and the loss would be keenly felt.

Mary smiled at Grace's outburst, but she was too polite to neglect Lady Sara or the other callers clustered around her. She made a slow circuit of the room. Lady Sara, first. Then Sir Matthew and Lady Graham. The older Mrs Wills. Mr Torrington, the physician. Mr and Miss Endercott, and here she stuck, for Miss Endercott, old maid and village busybody, grabbed Mary's hand and practically forced her to sit down. Grace sighed. It would be some time now before Mary could make good her escape. No doubt Miss Endercott wanted all the details of Sir Osborne's illness.

Grace still could not get used to the idea that her cousin Mary had married Sir Osborne Hardy. Such an odd match! He was very eligible, of course, with the baronetcy and a great fortune, it was said, but his mama was formidable, and he had two elderly unmarried sisters living with him, as well as Mr Merton, his friend. An unusual household. And Sir Osborne had such a strange way of dressing, with those violently coloured waistcoats! He was always so concerned about his health, and the least spot of mud on a coat would send him into a paroxysm of fear. It was lucky he had married the tidy Mary, and not someone like Grace, who would have driven him to distraction with her torn hems and odd stains on her gowns that seemed to appear out of nowhere.

Marriage certainly seemed to suit Mary, and Grace was conscious of a twinge of envy of her cousin's fashionable pelisse and positively ravishing bonnet. So elegant! Mary was a fine-looking woman, but she had always dressed quite plainly. Now a little town polish set her off to perfection. She appeared contented with her lot, too. It had seemed she was quite on the shelf until Sir Osborne had taken the notion to marry her a year ago. Quite a sudden whim, after they had known each other for years.

Eventually Mary managed to satisfy Miss Endercott, and made her way to the window seat where Grace was ensconced.

"Well, Grace," Mary said, settling herself down. "It is dispiriting to repeat the same news over and over, so let us suppose that you have asked me how Sir Osborne does, and I have told you that he is tolerably well today, a little improved since yesterday, and then we may talk of something else. But I need not enquire if *you* are in spirits, for I have already heard all about your escapade with the chimney."

"Oh dear. Did Lady Graham tell you of it? For I cannot believe Mama would mention it."

"Indeed not. It was neither of the two. I stopped in the village on my way here to collect one or two things from the haberdasher's, and Mrs Wiseman told us of it. Your adventures have quite delighted everyone, I assure you. But there is no sign of this fabulous necklace, I collect?" Grace shook her head. "Ah well, that is a pity, but I daresay the maid secreted it away years ago and it will never be found now."

That was a possibility which had not occurred to Grace. Her spirits sank at once.

"But that puts me in mind of something else," Mary went on. "I hear that your mama has a new lady's maid, is that so?"

"It is. She brought Rushton back with her from London on this most recent visit, and Ellesmere is gone."

"Would it be presumptuous in me to ask why? For I am sure she was not caught pilfering the silverware."

Grace laughed. "Nothing of the sort. Mama just said she wanted a change, someone more up to date with London styles. Ellesmere was not very pleased about it, but she got her year's salary and a very good reference."

"Has she gone far? Because she would do very well for Susan. You remember Susan, the wife of Sir Osborne's heir? The present maid has not answered at all — Susan will not stand up to her, so the maid bullies her dreadfully."

"Ellesmere has gone to Newcastle, I believe. Mama found her a position."

"Oh. Well, that is disappointing. We shall have to look elsewhere. I should have asked in London, I suppose, but we had such a busy time of it that I never thought."

"Was it lovely in London?" Grace said wistfully.

"Oh — I suppose so. We were only there for two weeks, just the three of us — Mama, Susan and me — for I could not leave Sir Osborne for longer. Just shopping, you know, but Mama enjoyed herself so greatly that I was quite in charity with her for once. At home, we just do not get along, but London is her natural habitat, I declare. We seldom ventured beyond the shops and warehouses, although we did go to the opera twice." She lowered her voice conspiratorially. "You will never guess who we saw there."

"Oh, do tell!"

"Your aunt, the Lady Matilda."

"What, Mama's sister?"

"Indeed. I thought it was Lady Sara at first, but when we enquired, we discovered it was Lady Matilda, with some very distinguished names. Very distinguished indeed. I wonder we have not heard more of her in the Gazette if she mixes in such society."

Grace was silent, not sure what to say about Aunt Tilly, who was so disreputable that her own family had disowned her. Yet Mama went to stay with her sometimes, she knew that much.

"I will not tease you about her," Mary said. "I know something of the story, so perhaps the less said the better."

"Shall you go back to London for the season?" Grace said.

"I doubt Sir Osborne's health will permit it. His mama plans to go, however, and introduce Rupert and Susan to society. Poor Susan is terrified! Such a timid soul, she will hate it, I am sure."

"How sad, to be amongst such wonders and excitement, and yet not enjoy them," Grace said. "How sorry you must be to miss it all."

Mary smiled. "Not sorry in the least. Sir Osborne would certainly agree to let me go if I wished it, but I love the country in the spring, when I can ride for mile after mile through fields and verdant woods. Who would exchange that for dusty streets and smoky air and the smell of horse-dung everywhere?"

"But the balls and routs and parties!" Grace cried. "The fashions! The shops! The acquaintance you would make! You could be presented at court!" She could imagine no greater felicity.

But Mary shook her head. "Those hold no appeal for me, and as a married woman, I make my own decisions about what pleases me, and what I shall be happy to ignore. You cannot imagine, Grace dear, the freedom that comes from a few words spoken in front of the parson, and a plain gold ring."

"And a tolerant husband," Grace said.

Mary laughed. "That too."

~~~~~

It was not long before George resumed the search for the necklace. He poked around the other rooms in his great-grandmother's apartment, but his heart was not in it. What had seemed like the most tremendous fun when he and Grace had crawled about together was decidedly boring on his own.

He had examined the chimneys again, however. This time he had had the forethought to summon one of the gardeners, in his oldest clothes, to scrabble around in the chimneys. The housekeeper, displeased at the length of time it had taken her housemaids to scrub the room clean after the previous attempt, had insisted on laying dust sheets over the floor while this operation was underway. The result was much less sooty, but in one other respect the outcome was unchanged: the diamonds were still missing.

After that, he found himself quite bereft of ideas. There was only one thing to be done — he must go at once to

Allamont Hall and engage Grace's interest in the project once more.

"What are we to do next?" he said to her, having found her trying to mend a bonnet in the morning room.

"We?" she said, smiling archly at him.

"Very well, what am *I* to do next?" he said crossly. "Come on, Grace, do not be coy about it. You enjoyed the search as much as I, you know you did. Tell me what to do."

"The walls," she said with a sigh. "If you have checked all the furniture, the floors *and* the chimneys, then there remain only the walls. After that, you might look at any other rooms that the old lady might have used. Did she go into the saloons, for instance? Was there a sitting room other than her own that she was accustomed to use? What about the long gallery?"

"Excellent," he said, grinning. "Will you come and help?"

"I am not sure. My efforts last time gave your servants a great deal of extra work, and my own maid would not speak to me for a week after she saw the state of my gown. Besides, I am not sure I have got all the soot out of my hair yet."

He gave a bark of laughter. "When has that ever mattered to you? Do come! It is much more enjoyable with company, and I cannot get any of the girls to take an interest, and they would be the principal beneficiaries, after all, should the necklace be found. It is of no use to me."

"I will ask Mama."

George knew Lady Sara's ways, so he placed no dependence on that lady's compliance with the scheme. His own mother, on the other hand, was more malleable when approached in the right way. Besides, she was naturally very fond of her only son, and must wish him to be happy. Even so, he chose his moment carefully, after a family dinner when good food and wine had made her mellow.

"Mama, I have been considering Alice's situation," he began.

"Really, dear?"

"Indeed. I know you want her to go off in style next year and make a splendid match, and I am certain she will, of course. But perhaps what she needs just now is a more experienced friend to encourage her."

Sir Matthew lowered the book he had been reading. "This benevolence towards your sister is most touching, George."

"Oh... thank you, sir."

"I presume you have a more experienced friend in mind for Alice?"

"Why, I do," he said eagerly. "Grace would be just the thing, and I thought—"

"Grace Allamont!" his mother screeched. "You must be mad! Alice is a good, well-behaved child, and I do *not* want her learning to tear her gown and race around like a hoyden and shout loud enough to be heard in the servants' hall."

Sir Matthew lowered the book still further. "Grace is an enthusiastic dancer, my dear. Alice is still very hesitant, as you have remarked yourself. She could benefit from learning to execute her steps with a little more spirit."

"And have her tread on her partner's feet every third step? No, no. I thank you for the thought, George, but no."

"Oh. Are you sure? I believe if Grace came to stay for a while..." Seeing his mother's face, he gave it up.

"George, you have not developed a *tendre* for Miss Allamont, have you?" his father said, smiling gently.

"Good heavens, no! Nothing of the sort. Grace Allamont? I should think not! Indeed, she is just a friend, a good friend who has been out for some years and could perhaps give Alice a little more confidence, that is all."

"Do you know, I think you may be right," his father said.

"Sir Matthew, I really must object—" Lady Graham began, but her husband waved his hand with a sweet smile.

"Invite her to stay for a few days, Julia. Alice can hardly pick up any bad habits in such a short time, but it will do her good to have a female friend to talk to about fashions and… well, whatever young ladies talk about."

"She has her sisters to talk to," Lady Graham protested.

"With whom she quarrels constantly."

"If we must have one of the Allamont girls here, let it be Hope, who at least will not knock over the vases or trail mud through the house."

"Hope is as timid as Alice. No, let it be Grace. Just a few days, Lady Graham. That is not so much to ask, is it?"

And with that, he picked up his book again and composedly began to read.

4: An Assembly

Before Grace's visit to Graham House could be contemplated, there was a ball at the assembly rooms to enjoy. Brinchester was the county town, and boasted of its premier position by holding an assembly once a month for the enjoyment of anyone able to find the cost of the subscription. For the Allamont sisters, deprived of the possibility of a London season, it was the only opportunity to mingle with a wider society than their own neighbourhood. It was unfortunate that the county boasted few eligible men. Had Grace wished to marry the son of a wealthy farmer or the better sort of merchant or shopkeeper or banker, she might have chosen from a score or more. Gentlemen, sadly, were scarcer. Nevertheless, it was an evening of dancing, with a good supper and a chance to meet up with far-flung relatives.

Of these, Grace was most pleased to see her sister Belle, now happily married to the former curate of Lower Brinford. Once Mr Burford had been head over ears in love with Hope, but he and Belle had discovered a mutual love of books and now they spent their days contentedly buried in their library at Willowbye. It was not a life that would have appealed to Grace, and she scarcely thought it would have suited Hope, either, although Hope herself could never be convinced of it. Poor Hope! She had never quite got over the loss of her first and most ardent admirer, and every suitor now was held up to the example of Mr Burford, and found wanting.

The other Willowbye family were of less interest. Cousin Henry, who was really Papa's cousin, was friendly enough, but his second wife, Cousin Vivienne, had not a good word to say about anyone. She was never happier than when others were in trouble. Of Cousin Henry's four children, only Mary was tolerable company. The three boys had been wild as children, and the memory of the tricks they had played on the Allamont sisters still rankled. Still, they had improved somewhat as they grew into adulthood. James was quite settled with his young wife, and Mark had taken up a life preaching the word of the Lord, which could hardly be faulted. Even Hugo, always in a scrape at school, had found a useful role managing the Allamont estate.

Grace was fully occupied for the first few dances, but seeing Belle sitting alone at the side of the room, fanning herself, she declined the next and went to sit beside her sister.

"What, no doting husband in attendance?" Grace said.

"He has gone to fetch me some lemonade. I am a little hot." She blushed.

Grace guessed the reason — another baby on the way. "Ah! I wondered why you did not dance, for I know how much you delight in it."

"I do, but I am so tired tonight that I have not the energy to stand up, even for the country dances. But how are you, sister dear?" Belle rushed on. "I do not see a certain person at your heels, so I must assume he has given up the chase."

"If you mean the person I think you mean, I sent him back to his splendid but much encumbered estate in Wiltshire."

"Was he very much disappointed?"

"Not so much disappointed as astonished that I could fail to be dazzled by the prospect of becoming mistress of... what was it called? Darrowhall. And such a privilege for me to settle all his debts and see him able to take his rightful place in the world. How could I possibly refuse the honour?"

Belle smiled a little, but said, "Ah, you are becoming cynical, Grace. A man may like to have your dowry and also have a genuine affection for you."

"Perhaps, but I have seen little of genuine affection this last year and a half. Seventeen offers, sister, since Dulcie married and my dowry was released. And how many before that? Not one."

"True, but you could not consider marrying earlier, Papa's will was very clear on that point. It is an odd arrangement, and I have no idea why Papa chose to order things in quite that way, but you would not have wished to marry before your turn. If you had, then all of us would have lost our dowries, and you would never have done anything to harm your sisters' prospects."

"Of course, but a man who cared for me might attempt to fix his interest, even if we could not be married immediately."

"That would not be honourable, to attach a young lady without being in a position to marry her. I do believe, Grace, that a number of your disappointed suitors would have been very happy to offer for you sooner, and were delighted when Dulcie married and they could in good conscience make an approach to you. Look how they swarmed around you the winter before last!"

"And now they are all gone," Grace said with a sigh.

Belle laughed, and squeezed her hand. "You will find someone, never fear. Somewhere in the world is the perfect match for each one of us. You just have not met yours yet."

~~~~~

The supper room was hot and crowded, but Mr Burford, who had always been a solid man and had not grown any less so after two years of marriage, forced a way through for the ladies. He managed to find seats for Lady Sara and Belle, but Grace and Hope were left to stand, pushed into a corner by the press of people. While Mr Burford and one of Hope's swains went off to fetch something to eat, Hope fanned herself vigorously.

"This room is so stuffy! It is insupportable! Really another room should be opened up so that we need not be crushed to pieces like sheep at the fair."

"The assemblies are getting so popular," Grace said. "Half of Brinshire must be here, I swear it."

"They should raise the subscription," Hope said. "That would keep out the riff-raff. Every tradesman with a few coins can come here and pretend to be a gentleman."

"Oh, let them all come, I say. Who are we to keep them out, especially when their attempts to dance the quadrille are so entertaining they make even my feeble efforts look accomplished. At least they make the effort to dress in the latest fashions, unlike some others. Look at the Baron's mother over there. I dare say Queen Anne would have thought that a vastly stylish ensemble. Or the deacon's wife with the patches and rouge — I am sure I had a doll once that looked just so. Sometimes I wonder if the higher ranks exist merely to provide amusement for the lower. They amuse *me*, that much is certain."

Hope looked up at her sister. "You are fortunate in seeing the amusing side to everything, sister. I wish I could see the world that way, and not notice all the unpleasantness around us."

"Oh, I notice it, but it does not do to dwell on it. So long as I am busy and have entertainment enough, I can ignore it. But do you not find it boring, this life of ours? Nothing but visits to the same small round of neighbours, and an assembly once a month, and a few card parties or dinner engagements. A private ball once or twice a year, if we are very lucky. It is not enough, sister. It is nowhere near enough."

"Then you should have married one of your *many* suitors," Hope said, pursing her mouth. "You have had some excellent offers, and as a married woman, you would have your own establishment to keep you occupied. Why, you could even go to London or tour the continent or… or anything you wanted."

"I could not do anything of the sort, for I should be kept at home by babies. Look at our sisters — a baby apiece already, and Amy has two. And now Belle is increasing again, and is too exhausted to dance, which she loves above all things. That is what happens when one marries, and I do *not* want to give up every pleasure and spend all my time thinking about nursery maids and wind and teething and… well, all those sorts of things. How I wish I had *real* work to do, something exciting and dangerous. A pirate, perhaps. Ernest and Frank were always talking about going to sea. I wonder if they truly did, when they ran away? No wonder we have had no word of them all these years."

Whatever answer Hope might have made was interrupted by the sight of Cousin Mark, his smiling face visible above the sea of chattering heads filling the supper room. He ploughed into the throng and the crowds parted for him as the Red Sea had for Moses.

"Cousin Grace! And Hope, too!" he boomed at them when he was still some distance away. "How are you?" Finally he made his way to their side. "I am delighted to see you both, for there is someone I wish you to meet. Where are you, Ralph? Ah, there you are. Cousins, may I present to you my very good friend and mentor, Mr Wright of Gravesby Hall in Grimsby."

Mark's former tutor from Oxford was not at all what Grace had expected. She had formed an image in her mind of an older man, kindly and gentle, his Bible always to hand, and perhaps elderly enough to need his cane for support. This man was not much older than Mark, handsome in a roguish way, his garments plain, as befitted his occupation, but well-cut and expensive. He was powerfully built, with the broad shoulders and muscular upper legs that betokened an active life. Mark had done some boxing at Oxford, and she could imagine Mr Wright, too, being handy in a fight.

"Oh, you are the preacher!" Grace said, so diverted that she forgot to curtsy. "I have so wanted to meet you, for we are all dying of curiosity to meet the man who could turn Mark into a holy man, you know. For he was the wildest creature imaginable when he was a boy, I must tell you. And now he is quite reformed, and all because of you."

"My cousins Miss Allamont and Miss Hope Allamont," Mark murmured, but Grace thought he looked quite cross.

Mr Wright, to the contrary, smiled benignly, and bowed in acknowledgement. "It is my life's work to spread God's word to the unheeding masses, and I was so fortunate as to find a receptive ear in your cousin, that is all. I do not reform anyone, Miss Allamont, I merely encourage those who hear me to find the goodness that is within every one of us, imparted by God at the instant of our birth."

"That is a novel view, Mr Wright," Grace said. "You do not hold, then, to the idea of original sin?"

"Indeed I must, for to do otherwise would be to set myself contrary to the teachings of the church, and how should any man have the presumption so to do?" he said sweetly, not at all discomfited by the question. "We are all born into sin, but there is, I believe, a kernel of goodness deep within each of us, as the sweetness of the nut is hidden by the hard, rough exterior shell. But we can, if we choose, draw out that kernel of goodness, and rise above our sinful natures, with God's aid."

Grace forbore to argue the point, but she felt there must be some deep flaw in the argument, although she could not quite tease it out.

"But why has no one procured a chair for you?" Mr Wright said, looking about him. "One moment..." He moved towards a nearby table, where several gentlemen sat, drinking wine and engrossed in some story that one of their number was telling. Mr Wright tapped one of them on the shoulder. "God's blessings on you, brothers, but may I make so bold as to solicit a chair for a young lady who must otherwise be forced to stand?"

His tone was so soft and gentle yet respectful that two men sprang to their feet immediately. Mr Wright waved Grace over, but then, instead of offering the other chair to Hope, he took it himself. "Your sister is talking to her beau, and it would be a shame to separate them, would it not?"

It was true that Hope was deep in conversation with the young man who had led her into supper, so Grace let it be.

"I cannot tell you how pleased I am to meet you at last, Miss Allamont," Mr Wright said, smiling in a way that made his eyes crinkle most attractively at the corners. "Mark has told me so much of his many charming cousins, and I find he has not exaggerated in the slightest. Indeed, all the Allamont ladies enhance the evening with their charms. As I look around these rooms, what do I observe? That Mrs Henry Allamont is the most elegantly attired lady here tonight, Lady Sara Allamont the most striking and Mrs James Allamont the most enthusiastic dancer. But I can see that you and your sister are the shining jewels of the evening, far and away the brightest diamonds of Brinchester."

Grace inclined her head graciously at the compliment, having heard many such sentiments before, and most of them less felicitously expressed. She was not, however, in the mood for idle flirtation. "What brings you to this part of the world, Mr Wright? The last we heard of Mark, he was away up in Northumberland."

"I like to move around, you know. Never outstay my welcome, that is the principle I follow. Having exhausted the possibilities of Northumberland, I felt that Brinshire would be welcoming to my particular area of expertise. I plan to preach to the devoted in all parts of the county within a day or so's ride of Brinchester. Mr and Mrs Burford have been so kind as to offer me accommodation. Mr Burford being a man of God himself is naturally delighted to oblige a fellow in the same profession as himself. At present I am concerned with the eastern reaches of the county. There are numerous little villages around the periphery of Brinwater Heath, quite isolated, some of whose inhabitants, I flatter myself, have benefited greatly from my words."

"Brinwater Heath?" Grace said in some alarm. "You must take the greatest care, Mr Wright. There have been reports lately of highwaymen preying on helpless travellers on those roads."

To her surprise, Mr Wright only laughed. "How kind in you to be so concerned for my safety, gentle lady. But you need not fear for me. A poor clergyman is of no interest to highwaymen, I assure you." He leaned forwards to whisper confidentially in her ear. "Besides, I do believe it would be quite exciting to be attacked by gun-wielding ruffians, would you not agree? A little flutter of alarm and the loss of a purse would be a small price to pay for such a tale to relate to one's acquaintance. And as for the highwayman himself, consider how thrilling it must be to derive a living from such nefarious methods."

"Not if one were to be shot," Grace said at once. "That, I believe, would remove some of the enjoyment from such a profession."

But he only smiled at this sally, tilting his head to one side to gaze at her with frank interest. "Ah, Miss Grace, I applaud your attitude. Not for you the screeching and quaking that most ladies would resort to at the very thought of such a dire situation. How brave you are! I cannot but admire so stout-hearted a lady."

His eyes were sparkling with a light that Grace, experienced in the ways of admirers, could not mistake. For an instant, her breath caught in her throat. His smile, his sudden intensity, and the intimate way he had leaned close to whisper in her ear, all engendered an unexpected warmth in her. It was fortunate, perhaps, that Mark interrupted them, dragging over a chair to sit between them.

"Why did you run away with my cousin, Ralph? You must not monopolise her, for I am sure she has many admirers awaiting their chance with her."

"I do not doubt that Miss Grace adds to the number of her admirers every day," Mr Wright said, his eyes fixed on Grace.

Mark made a huffing noise. "Take no notice of him, cousin. It is—"

Grace was suddenly struck by the sight of Cousin Vivienne near the door. Her usual sardonic smile was quite gone, her face waxy and pale. She leaned on Cousin Henry's arm so heavily that she might have fallen over without his support.

"Mark, what ails your mama?" Grace said urgently. "She must be feeling the heat in here, and who can wonder at it? Do bring her over here. She may have my seat with pleasure. Perhaps some lemonade would cool her."

At her words, Mark jumped up with alarm, and made his way towards the door. Grace followed in his wake, ready with her fan to apply cooling air to the stricken lady. It was too late. Even as Mark reached out to take her free arm, Cousin Vivienne slipped from her husband's grasp and slumped insensible to the floor.

5: French And Latin

The crowd gasped and swirled around the fallen lady.

"Stand back!" cried Mark in stentorian tones, but no notice was taken. It was Mr Wright, with a quiet word here and a touch on a shoulder there, who persuaded the horrified onlookers into a wider circle.

In the centre of it, a pool of green silk sprawled, two dainty slippers peeking out at one end. At the other, a face as white as a sheet. Cousin Henry knelt beside his unconscious wife, chafing her hand. "A physician!" he cried, his voice cracking. "She must have a physician! Vivienne, speak to me!"

From the crowd, the stately form of Lady Sara materialised, and knelt beside Vivienne, feeling for her pulse. "Her heart is beating strongly," she said, as calmly as if talking about the weather. "It is no more than a faint." Her eyes scanned the circle of onlookers. "Mark, pray carry your mama out of this heat. Henry, do you find a cooler room for her to rest and recover herself."

An elderly lady proffered a small vial. "Smelling salts, my lady. That is what dear Mrs Allamont needs."

"Thank you, just the thing," Lady Sara said, taking the vial.

Mark scooped up his mother without effort, and strode out of the room, with his father and Lady Sara in his wake. Grace and Hope scuttled along behind. Cousin Henry took them to one of the card rooms, almost empty now that everyone was at supper, and chased out the last remaining group of whist players.

"Here, lay her on that sofa, Mark. Vivienne! Wake up, *ma cherie*, wake up!" He patted her cheek ineffectually.

"Move aside, Henry," Lady Sara said. She waved the smelling salts under Vivienne's nose and she gasped, then moaned a little. Her eyes fluttered open.

"Henri? Que s'est-il passé?"

"Dieu merci! Je pensais que tu etais morte ou que quelque chose n'allait pas avec le petit."

"Le petit?" Grace said. "Oh, Cousin Vivienne, are you increasing too? How famous!"

Her mother clucked. "Really, Vivienne! At your age, too! I should have thought you would know better. There are perfectly reliable ways to take care of such things."

"I know, I know," Vivienne moaned. "But Henry made a mistake and—"

Cousin Henry coughed. "Sara, Vivienne, the girls! Perhaps this is not an appropriate discussion for their ears?"

Lady Sara turned, and stared vaguely at Grace and Hope. "Of course. I forgot. Grace, Hope, go back to the supper room. Reassure everyone that Vivienne is quite recovered and was merely overcome by the heat. Mr… erm… Wright, I do not remember inviting you to accompany us, but now you may be useful. Would you be so good as to see Grace and Hope back to the supper room? Mark, stand outside, if you please, and make sure no one else enters the room to disturb us."

Grace had not noticed Mr Wright, but he must have followed the group into the card room. Now, quite unabashed by Lady Sara's set down, he shepherded the sisters outside. In the passageway, they found Hope's admirer, wringing his hands in anguish, and several dowagers, too curious to stay away but too afraid of Lady Sara's displeasure to venture further.

"Mrs Allamont will be quite better directly," Grace said. "She is resting quietly, and must not be disturbed."

The dowagers seemed disinclined to take this hint and go away, but just then the first notes of music wafted up from the ballroom on the floor below, and this seemed to settle the matter. The supper room was now half empty. Grace flopped gratefully into a chair, found her discarded plate and resumed her interrupted meal, while Mr Wright went off to fetch them lemonade.

Hope clutched her fan, her face anxious. "Will she be all right, do you think?"

"Of course! It is just a little faint. She will be perfectly well again before long."

"No, I mean..." She lowered her voice, although no one was near enough to overhear. "The *baby*! She is so old, sister, and it cannot be safe at such an advanced age."

"How old is she?" Grace said.

"I do not know exactly, but James is twenty four, and I believe she said once that she was not yet twenty when he was born. So..."

"Forty three or four," Grace said. "There is nothing in that. Mrs Lorne was about that age when she had her youngest, and I am sure that old Mrs Garmin had one at almost fifty. Besides, Cousin Vivienne has had three children already, and it is the first that is the most dangerous. So Mr Ambleside said when Amy was expecting the second time."

"But he is a *man*. What does he know about it?" Hope said.

The point was unanswerable, so Grace ate and drank lemonade while Hope fretted, and when Cousin Henry came to tell them that a carriage had been brought round and they were all leaving, they followed him in sombre silence.

~~~~~

Grace's visit to Graham House began not long after. As visits went, it was not the most novel or exciting that could be devised. The journey there was no more than ten minutes in the carriage, and the usual dread of travel, that of leaving one's hairbrush or some other vital item behind, did not apply, since a footman could be dispatched to procure the offending article within the hour. So began her role as instructress and confidante to Miss Alice Graham.

Alice having left the schoolroom behind, her days were now filled with the preparations for her debut the following winter. Teachers of dancing, Italian, the harp and violoncello, singing, painting in watercolours and deportment came and went at their appointed hours. Alice spent one morning a week with her father, perusing the London newspapers and learning to discourse knowledgeably on the events of the day. Each afternoon when the weather permitted, she rode out with two grooms to improve her confidence ready for the day when she would join the cream of society in Hyde Park. For Alice was to have the benefit of a London season, under the wing of her sister Lizzie, now Viscountess Helsby.

Grace soon discovered that she was not needed for much of this. She knew no Italian, could play no instrument except the pianoforte, and that not expertly, and had never learned to ride. The dancing was the most tremendous fun, however, and she found that six years of even such paltry entertainments as the monthly assemblies made her more than experienced enough to demonstrate the steps.

The dancing master was a dapper little Frenchman, who flirted outrageously with Alice and also with her younger sisters, for they were learning ready for the far-off day when they, too, would emerge like butterflies from the chrysalis of the schoolroom. Monsieur smiled and twirled and joked and winked, speaking half in French and half in heavily-accented English, although occasionally his accent slipped into something more recognisable — Welsh, perhaps. The thought made Grace smile whenever Lady Graham came to view her daughters' progress and spoke to Monsieur in painstaking and ill-pronounced French.

Monsieur also flirted with Grace, but she had been out for long enough to know how to deal amusingly with such a man without encouraging too much licence. Once or twice she caught Alice listening, wide-eyed, to their banter and realised that this, too, was a useful skill for the girl to learn.

The dancing master and Italian instructress, a stout lady permanently dressed in deepest mourning for relatives back in Italy, stayed to dine on their respective days, for correct behaviour at the dinner table was another skill being imparted to Alice. While she struggled to hold a conversation in the language of the day, her mother issued a stream of edicts.

"Sit up straight, Alice, do. Not that knife. Cover the glass with your fingers if you want no wine. Do not attempt to speak while chewing. Let the footman pour it, dear. Do not slouch so!"

Grace found herself automatically responding to these commands, straightening her back, holding her head a little higher, and setting her silverware down gently and not all aclatter as she usually did. Once or twice she caught Sir Matthew smiling knowingly at her, and then she laughed at herself and allowed her back to adopt a less rigid pose.

When Alice was otherwise engaged and Grace's attendance was not required, she aided George in his continuing search for the Durmaston Diamonds. In fact, she discovered that he had done nothing further, apart from the chimneys.

"I wanted to wait for you," he said, when she remonstrated with him over the lost time. "You have all the good ideas, Grace. Besides, I did not want you to miss the fun."

"That is thoughtful, George." They had moved on to examining the walls of the old lady's apartment, tapping panels for hollow spots. "This is far more entertaining than watching Alice walk around with a book balanced on her head."

"Really? Is that what she does?"

"It is supposed to give her the proper degree of uprightness in her carriage as she walks."

"Good grief! Did you have to do that, too?"

"We never needed such methods, for we had Papa's ruler." When he looked puzzled, she added, "He rapped us over the knuckles if we slouched. It was very effective, I assure you."

George pulled a face. "You will forgive me for saying so, Grace, but your father was a bit of a tyrant."

"Indeed he was. No one would disagree there. Well, there is nothing on this wall. Shall we try the other side?" They crossed the room and began tapping again. "Still, whatever one may say about Papa, he ensured we were well educated. Why, when the Signora was here yesterday, I found I could understand a great deal of what she said, and if I addressed her in Latin, she could understand me, too. I never thought a study of Latin would prove useful, except for reading inscriptions in churches, and that has limited application, I feel."

George blinked. "I cannot say I have ever felt an urge to understand Latin inscriptions in churches," he said faintly. "And if I did, I should apply to my father. There was quite enough of that sort of thing at school and Oxford. It was the greatest relief to leave it all behind."

Grace laughed. "Yes, indeed! I was never so happy as when Papa died— No, no, that is wrong and not what I intended to say! I was very sorry he died, of course, but it meant that we could stop our lessons at last, because we should have been long out of the schoolroom by then. But even though I have not looked at a Latin book in three years or more, it is still stuck in my head, somehow, and there it is whenever I want it. Do you not find that?"

"Not Latin, no. Maps, now — I always enjoyed maps and globes and learning the names of the rivers. The Eden, the Lune, the Ribble, the Mersey, the Dee... that is how the English ones start. The Wye, the Severn, the Avon... I can do the kings, too. William the Conqueror, William Rufus, Henry the First, Stephen of Blois, Henry the Second, Richard the Lionheart—"

"You missed out Empress Matilda—"

"A woman? She does not count!"

"—and *all* the Saxon kings."

"Oh, well, I was always hazy about the Dark Ages. Such silly names they had, too."

"That was hardly their fault. They were given their names by other people, just as we were. It is not *my* fault that Papa named us all alphabetically, and after virtues. Amy, Belle, Constance, Dulcie, Ernest, Frank, Grace, Hope. Cousin Henry once said that Papa only had eight children because he could not think of a virtue beginning with I."

"Idiot," George said at once. "Idle. Ignorant. Imbecile. Icy. Improvident. Inferior."

"*Virtues!* And those are not even names. *You* are the idiot, George." But she was laughing too hard to be cross with him.

"Well, I had a great-aunt once who was— Wait! Did you hear that?" George said excitedly. "There is no wall behind this panel."

Grace was beside him in a moment. She tapped gently, and then more strongly. "You are right! This is it, a secret door!

And look, now that I observe it properly, I can see that it is a little different. And just here is where the handle would have fitted. It has been painted over, but there is still an indentation. George, this is so exciting! Just think, we may be the very first to uncover this in centuries!"

"I hope not, for then there would be no necklace inside, would there? But it has all been painted so that the gap no longer shows. I shall have to get a knife and see if we can get it open."

He was gone for a few minutes, while Grace checked all the remaining panels, but only one had the tell-tale hollow sound that suggested there was a space behind it.

"Ten to one it will just be an unused cupboard, or something of the sort," George said, as he worked with the knife to cut through the paint and open up the gap around the door. For that was what it was, that much was evident. By the time he had chopped his way around all four sides, leaving little flakes of paint on the floor, the gap was large enough to show the clear outline of an opening.

"Now all we have to do is open it," Grace said cheerfully.

"And how do we do that without a handle to turn?" George said. "And it may be locked."

"I see no sign of a keyhole. Cut away the paint where the handle must have been, and let us see if there is still a latch or... or whatever doors have."

Obediently, George chopped at the paint again, revealing a round hole. "Now what?"

"Stand aside." As he moved out of the way, Grace put her finger into the hole. "It goes all the way through. I can smell fusty air, can you? So I think we just need to pull." She pushed her finger as far in as it would go, curled it around the far side and heaved as hard as she could.

Nothing happened.

A second attempt produced a few more flakes of paint, but still the door would not budge. "Phooey. You try it, George."

Cautiously, he poked his finger in and pulled. No movement. He pulled harder, and more paint fell.

"It moved!" Grace cried. "Pull again, harder!"

George pulled with all his might.

The door flew open, and George, with an 'Oof!' of surprise, fell backwards, a cloud of paint and dust and cobwebs following, and coating both of them liberally. A dank smell assaulted their nostrils.

"Well, that was easier than I expected," Grace said. "How exciting!" She peered through the door. "And it is *not* a cupboard — there are stairs here. Quick, a candle, George! Let us explore."

6: *Secret Passages*

George insisted on leading the way, carrying the candle. Grace crept along in his wake, one hand on the wall, the other holding up her skirts. It would not do to fall down these mysterious stairs, for who knew how far down they went into the darkness? She could break her neck, and if she fell on top of George, he might fall and break *his* neck, and then where would they be?

"I wish I wore breeches," she said as they inched their way downwards. "So much easier for creeping about in dark tunnels."

George let out a bark of laughter. "It is to be hoped that you will not have more than one such to creep about in. As secret passages go, this one is not unpleasant. These walls are plastered, I think, and the steps are quite even. Are you looking out for diamonds? Or anywhere to hide them?"

"It is hard to see anything when the light is so far in front of me."

"Oh. Do you want to go first? Or carry the candle?"

"Let me go in front. I am terrified of falling on top of you."

He stopped, and there was a long silence. "Are you truly terrified?" he said at last. "We can go back if you really want to."

"Great heavens, George, there is no power on earth that could persuade me to give up our little adventure, but my skirts are such a nuisance. If only I had been a boy, just think what fun we could have had, with nothing to stop us doing just as we please."

"Nobody can do just as they please, not even boys," George said firmly. "Which is a great piece of mismanagement in the ordering of the world, if you ask me. The more money one has and the more one rises up society's ladder, the more one *ought* to do exactly as one pleases. And yet, somehow, one is even more hedged about by restrictions than a chimney sweep. I should like to have been a chimney sweep," he added wistfully. "Then I could be as dirty as I pleased, and no one could object, for it would be my profession, you know. Bathing every day takes up an intolerable amount of time that could be spent much more enjoyably. That and tying one's cravat. Such a performance, Grace. Think yourself lucky you have escaped the rigours of gentlemen's dress."

"If you have finished philosophising, might we get on?" Grace said. "For I have no idea what time it is, but I do not want to be late for dinner."

"Lord, no! Mama gets so cross."

"I do not regard that! It is only that your cook is roasting a goose today, and I am very fond of goose. I should hate it to be spoiled because I was stuck on these stairs for hours with a foolish boy who only wants to stand about and set the world to rights."

"Sorry," he said, his grin eerie in the candlelight. "You squeeze past me and go on ahead. Here, take the candle."

Somehow, Grace managed to accomplish all this without tripping, or knocking over George or the candle, or setting fire to anything. After that, candlestick in one hand and her skirts bunched up in the other, she made good progress.

"Ah, the stairs end here," she said gleefully. "How far down have we come, do you suppose? Are we in the cellars?"

"I am not sure. Wait — is that a light further on?"

"Shh!" Grace hissed. "I can hear voices."

Silently they crept along the passage, and the voices grew louder. Two women, one older, one younger, chattering away. "Tuppence a pair, they are, and good quality, too. So Tilly said, anyway, but it's hard to believe when I ain't never paid less than fourpence before. No, four of they ones — best bring four. And two of they glass ones. Aye, those. That'll be enough. Anyway, I'm going to have a look..."

The voices faded, and a door clicked shut.

George sighed. "That was old Rona and Lilian, and it sounds like they were in one of the storage rooms. And this is the end of the passage, right here. We can go no further."

Examination revealed another door, firmly locked, between the passage and the storage room, with a grill-covered window high up, through which the maids' lamp had been visible.

"Why would there be a secret passage from great-grandma's rooms to a storage room?" George asked. "That is very peculiar. No wonder it was closed off and painted over, for there cannot have been much use for it."

"I imagine that storage room was something more important once," Grace said. "It would have been very useful then, but perhaps the house was redesigned, and it was no longer needed. Well, that is disappointing. We have found a secret passage, but it leads nowhere."

"And no diamond necklace, either," George said gloomily. "I begin to suspect that it is not in the house at all."

~~~~~

The following day, a letter arrived for Grace from Allamont Hall. Cousin Vivienne was unwell, and Mama was to go to Willowbye to look after her. Hope was sent to stay with Amy, and Grace was to go there too.

But this announcement was greeted with alarm by Lady Graham. "Indeed, you must not go yet, I insist upon it. I cannot at all spare you just now, for I have had the most appalling news, it could not be worse."

Sir Matthew looked at her over the top of his newspaper. "Really? What catastrophe has now befallen us?"

"Anne is coming!" she said, in tones of the deepest despair.

George gave a yelp, and Alice set down the tapestry she had been painstakingly working on and burst into tears.

Sir Matthew laid his newspaper down altogether, and removed his spectacles. "You astonish me. Is it Christmas already? I had not suspected."

"It is *not* Christmas, but nevertheless she is coming. Oh, whatever does she want?"

"I imagine you might guess," her husband said calmly. "She has heard that the Durmaston Diamonds are missing, possibly in this house, and she intends to search for them."

"She will not find them!"

"I daresay she will not, any more than George will, despite all this crawling around in secret passageways, but she will be looking for them, you may be sure. You had better tell Cranford to lock up the spoons."

Grace listened to this exchange with the liveliest interest. She had not heard of this particular relative before, but one who might take the spoons with her when she left was something new in her experience.

"Is she really so bad?" she whispered to George, as Sir Matthew and Lady Graham discussed plans to protect the household from the ravages of the impending visit.

"Dreadful," he said. "Cousin Anne cheats at cards, every single game, and Papa lets her, because it would hardly be the thing to object when she is the only daughter of Mama's only sister. And she steals anything she can find. Do not leave any money where she may find it."

"Goodness!" Grace said, shocked. "But I should be safe enough, for I have very little money, and it is tucked away in a drawer in my room."

"She goes into the bedrooms," George said. "You need to find somewhere with a lock, and keep the key with you. And any jewellery you have, too. *Nothing* is safe with her."

"That is appalling!"

"It is, but the worst of it is, I believe Papa is right and she is coming to look for the necklace. And if she finds it, then she will be gone with it in her pocket and nothing we can do about it."

"Then we shall just have to find it before she does," Grace said firmly.

~~~~~

Cousin Anne was a bony woman of more than forty years, with little, dark eyes like currants and a nose as pointed as the prow of a ship. She arrived by private post-chaise, which Sir Matthew was obliged to pay for, since the lady had not enough money about her, or so she said. She brought three enormous boxes, as if she planned to stay for a month at least, and a maid as sour-faced as she was herself.

George had disliked her heartily for as long as he could remember, and since she made no effort to engage his good opinion, had never had any reason to change his earliest impressions. She was, he thought, rude, selfish and avaricious, but he found even this low opinion declining still further when she was introduced to Grace.

She looked her up and down with a sniff. "What is *she* here for? I thought you wanted the Chilborough girl for George?"

"Grace is helping Alice prepare for her come-out," said Lady Graham coldly. "Teaching her society ways, you understand."

"Is that so? Which society ways are you hoping Alice will copy — the rats' nest of a hair arrangement, or the smudge on one cheek, or the torn sleeve?"

"You will not criticise a guest under my roof, Anne," Sir Matthew said sternly. "Grace is a good-humoured young lady who never has an unkind word for anyone, and I shall always value that above a perfect appearance."

"Well..." She sniffed again. "I speak my opinions honestly, Uncle Matthew, and I trust no one could fault me there. You will not find me the sort of mealy-mouthed milksop who speaks in platitudes."

"That is the very last thing anyone would say of you," George burst out, unable to hold his tongue any longer. His mother frowned at him, and whisked Cousin Anne upstairs to her room, but his father smiled genially, although he shook his head, too.

"Water off a duck's back, my boy. Water off a duck's back."

The first dinner with Cousin Anne was an uncomfortable business. Even Grace, usually the sunniest of guests, was reduced to silence more often than not. Alice, made of less resilient material, shivered and ate little and said less, and retired to bed with the headache at the earliest opportunity.

When the ladies had withdrawn, and the gentlemen stretched out thankfully to enjoy their port, Sir Matthew said to his son, "Are you making any progress in your search for the diamonds?"

George sighed, and told his father all about the secret passage they had discovered, which was not so secret now that the door had been exposed.

"If I recall correctly, those store rooms are where the kitchen was at one time," Sir Matthew said. "I have seen the plans from the earliest days. So those stairs would have been no more than the back stairs for the servants to use. Nothing terribly mysterious about them."

"Plans?" George said eagerly. "You have plans of the house? Do they show these stairs then? Or perhaps some other long-forgotten hiding places?"

"Well, I have not looked at the plans in years, not since we first moved into the house, but I will retrieve them from their box in the library if they are of interest to you. I have to say, though, George, that your mission may be a fruitless one. I should not wish you and Grace to waste too much time on an enterprise which is doomed from the start."

"But the diamonds must be *somewhere*, sir. They are not at Uncle Jasper's house, which surely has been very thoroughly searched by Aunt Lilian, and great-grand-mama never went anywhere else apart from here. So they *must* be here, do you not agree?"

"As to that, I could not say," his father said slowly. "I do feel, however, that it is rather unlikely that they were simply left in a drawer or dropped or forgotten about. They are far too valuable for that. Besides, they would have been in the care of the lady's maid, and she would have been in the most terrible trouble if they had disappeared under her guardianship."

"But great-grand-mama was so forgetful latterly, and the maid might have stolen them—"

"I think that is unlikely, although one cannot discount the possibility of theft. Wherever they are, I do not believe that a casual search will uncover them. You have had some sport with the hunt, but it might be for the best to abandon it now."

"That would be the greatest pity," George said. "I should so hate to give up now, and even if the diamonds never turn up, I have learned a great deal about the house that I never knew before. There must be other secret ways and hidey-holes, and think how exciting it would be to find them after they have been hidden for years and years! If you do not object, I should very much like to examine the plans."

"Far be it from me to interfere with your pleasure, my boy. Enjoy yourself."

~~~~~

Grace could not make head or tail of the plans, which were, to her eyes, a jumble of dots and lines and spidery writing. The oldest ones were faded and crumbling, and the newer ones were a mass of tiny marks that meant nothing to her. None of them seemed to show the whole house.

Yet George read them as easily as the pages of a book. "Look, here are the stairs we found," he said delightedly. "They start here, on this floor, do you see? And come out over here, into the room labelled as a... I cannot make it out. Can you read it?"

"Buttery," she said. "The words at least mean something, but all this... muddle here. How can you make anything of it? It is worse than Greek."

He grinned at her. "What a perfect team we make! You read the words and I... I *love* maps! And these are wonderful! Except they *will* curl up at the edges. Can you fetch that snuff jar from the shelf? And the figurine? We can weight down the corners."

Thus arranged, with the whole array spread out on the library table, George settled down to examine them in detail. Grace, bored, wandered around the room examining Sir

Matthew's extensive collection of books, and idly pulling one out here or there.

"This would be a good place to hide the necklace," she said. George looked up with interest. "You could tuck it away behind a book on a high shelf, or even *inside* a book. That is a clever trick that I have heard of — cutting out the middle of a book to hide something valuable. No one would ever find it. Or rather, one would have to examine every single book, and that would take months."

George got up and came across to where she stood, gazing up at the shelves reaching to the ceiling, and every one of them filled with books.

"I am not sure." He chewed his lip thoughtfully. "I cannot imagine great-grand-mama climbing the ladder or cutting middles out of books. It would have to be a very large book, you know, for the thing is by no means a delicate little piece. It is huge. Now if *Papa* were to hide it, I can well imagine he might do such a thing. Some of these cases are locked, too, where the most valuable books are kept, and only Papa has the key. That would be a very safe hiding place. But great-grand-mama? I do not think so."

"Her maid, perhaps?"

"She was almost as decrepit as the old lady. No, it is a good thought, but I am afraid it will not help us. But come and look at the plans, for I believe I have found another secret passage."

"Ooh, truly? Where? Near the other one?"

"Not at all. It is in quite another part of the house. Here, see? Definitely a corridor leading off this room, but that is Mama's winter parlour and I know perfectly well there is no sign of a door or corridor at all."

"The writing says *'Dining Room'*," Grace said, her voice quivering with excitement. "If that was its intended function, it is a very likely place for a concealed service entrance. How thrilling! But is it likely your great-grandmother would have known about it? It is a long way from her apartment."

"She used to sit in there with Mama. I remember being brought there to see her sometimes when I was quite little, so she knew the room well."

"In that case, we must examine the room at once," Grace said.

"But we must be very careful not to let Cousin Anne know what we are about," George said. "I shall put these plans away again so that she gets no inkling of our ideas. It would be the most infamous thing if she finds the necklace before we do."

7: *Identity*

Their scheme was thwarted almost at once. No sooner had the plans been safely returned to their box and stowed in a cupboard than Cousin Anne came into the library.

"What are you doing?" she said suspiciously, making Grace glad that she had not entered a minute or two earlier, when the plans had been spread out all over the table.

"I have been reading the newspaper," Grace said hastily. "I like to be up-to-date with the current news before discussing it with Sir Matthew and Alice."

"Hmph. At least you look respectable today, Grace. Not a tear anywhere. A great improvement."

"Thank you, Anne."

"Miss Durmaston to you, if you please."

"Oh, but you called me Grace, so I assumed we were intimate friends," Grace said in innocent tones. Behind her, George sniggered.

Cousin Anne's eyes narrowed. "I suppose you are a close friend of the *family*, at least, so you may call me Cousin Anne. However, I do not think you should be alone in here with George, quite unchaperoned. I shall stay with you, to protect your reputation."

"You are all consideration, Cousin Anne," Grace murmured. "How should I go on without you to advise me?"

George sniggered again, but Cousin Anne's lips curled in what might have been intended as a smile. "It gives me the greatest pleasure to correct such errors. Young ladies these days are allowed a great deal too much latitude, in my opinion. It was not so when *I* was a girl, you may be sure of that. Correct behaviour was paramount, and any hint of wildness was positively fatal to a girl's prospects. It astonishes me that your mama has not seen fit to stamp out such tendencies in her daughters. That was most remiss of her, and so I shall tell her if ever I have the opportunity. If I had been so fortunate as to have daughters, I should have been a great deal stricter, you may be sure."

"What a pity you never married, then," Grace said demurely. "Such a loss to society."

This time George actually snorted with laughter, and Cousin Anne was not sufficiently satisfied with the conversation to continue it.

~~~~~

From then onwards, Cousin Anne became a constant thorn in Grace's side. She found herself followed everywhere, and on the rare occasions when her shadow disappeared, she could be discovered disrupting the servants by poking about in the kitchens and pantries, annoying Sir Matthew by loitering in the library or upsetting the horses by banging about in the stables. Grace even found her rifling through drawers in her bedroom one day.

"Are you looking for something, Cousin Anne?" she said sweetly, thankful that she had locked her valuables away in the writing desk.

"Oh — I left some stockings here last time I had this room. But I cannot find them. I daresay the maids have taken them. I have always said that the servants here are a nasty, grasping sort, but Aunt Julia never listens to me."

"Oh, I am sure she listens to every word most attentively," Grace said. "You make your points so... so *eloquently*, it would be impossible to do otherwise."

"Ah, it is true that I can be eloquent when I feel strongly about a subject. You can be most perceptive, sometimes, Grace. I would not have suspected it in you. Perhaps my fears are groundless, and you will be an influence for good with Alice after all."

If Grace's hopes of looking for a second secret passage had been thwarted temporarily, there was compensation in spending more time sitting with Lady Graham and her visitors. Lady Graham held the usual at home mornings every week, but she was a sociable soul who welcomed callers at any time. Since she provided generous refreshments and delighted in the presence of small children and dogs, her saloon enjoyed a near-riot every day between noon and five, Sundays only excepted.

One of the most frequent visitors, to Grace's surprise, was Mr Wright. Sometimes he brought Mark with him, but mostly he came alone. When Grace wondered aloud at his presence in the neighbourhood, so far from his present residence at Willowbye and his preaching activities at Brinwater Heath, Mr Wright had a ready explanation.

"I always like to think ahead, Miss Grace. When I have completed my planned activities around the Heath, I believe Higher and Lower Brinford would be very suitable locations to which I might profitably turn my attention next. I have already approached Mr Endercott, and he is amenable to allowing me to speak to his flock, with the permission of the bishop, naturally. You have a most charming church in Lower Brinford, Miss Grace."

"Yet most students of ecclesiastical architecture consider the church at Higher Brinford to have the greater merit," she said. "It has a very fine medieval rood screen, and the bell tower is much admired."

"I believe the neighbourhood is blessed with many enchanting sights worthy of the greatest admiration," he said, leaning forward and speaking in an altered tone that made her blush. "I look forward to spending much more time here."

Grace was very conscious of his nearness, and the effect it had on the beating of her heart. Such a fine looking man, tall and well-proportioned, and he dressed with a certain flair, although never ostentatiously. His present profession was a wandering one, but she supposed he would settle down eventually. And then... But how foolish, to begin weaving a future around a peripatetic preacher. No, she must not think of him, however much she enjoyed his company.

Still, the image of him disturbed her thoughts whenever she had a quiet moment, and it was odd how often his name managed to insert itself into her conversations.

"You like him, I think?" Lady Graham said archly one day as they waited for the dinner announcement. "He is a splendid fellow, to be sure. Grimsby, I understand? He has a property there?"

"Gravesby Hall."

"There now, that sounds just the thing," Lady Graham said. "A snug little property, no doubt, and I understand he has two or three thousand a year... I am certain I heard that somewhere. Mrs Donborough, perhaps."

"I do not like him," George announced loudly.

"Why ever not?" his mother said.

"There is something underhand about him. I do not like him crawling around Grace. He is only after her money, you may depend upon it."

"Nonsense," his mother said. "Anyone can see that he is a perfectly respectable gentleman. His manners cannot be faulted. I feel quite comfortable in his presence, and I should not, you know, if there were the least hint of anything disreputable about him."

"That is just the thing, Mama, we see only the clothes and the creeping way he behaves. We know nothing at all about him except what he chooses to tell us."

"*I* know that he is a friend of Mark's of long standing," Grace said heatedly. "He was Mark's tutor at Oxford, which is a perfectly respectable profession, and now he is a holy man, travelling around in poverty to preach God's word. No one can have the least objection to that!"

"He is so impoverished that he has his own chaise and pair, *and* a riding horse, and more clothes than I have, and all of the first style. And no one has ever seen his house or met his family or his neighbours or remembers him from Oxford."

"What nonsense! They must do," Grace said. "He met Mark there."

"Well, *I* do not remember him, nor do any of my friends," George said.

"Oh, you have asked them all, have you?"

"Those I have written to lately, yes. No one knows of Mr Wright."

"You cannot know everyone! Oxford is a large town. It is perfectly possible he was at a different college."

Sir Matthew raised a hand. "For myself, I have no objection to the young man, but it is true that we have no acquaintance in common with him. I am not your father, Grace, but if you wish to set your mind at rest regarding Mr Wright, I will myself undertake to make enquiries. I still have some acquaintance at Oxford who might, with discretion, ask around amongst their colleagues."

"I thank you most kindly for your offer, sir, but I am not in danger of losing my heart to a man so little known to me. I find him of interest as a friend of my cousin, but no more than that."

"Then we will speak no more of the matter. Ah, here is Cranford now. Excellent. I am sure we are all ready for our dinner."

~~~~~

There was no escaping the watchful eye of Cousin Anne, and Grace grew heartily sick of her shadow, creeping along a pace or two behind her wherever she went, and offering the benefit of her accumulated wisdom whenever the opportunity presented itself. Anne had never had children herself, but she was confident that the world must feel the loss keenly. Therefore, she had taken it upon herself to instill her own precepts into her numerous nieces. As a result, she felt wholly qualified to instruct young ladies, in or out of the schoolroom, on the correct behaviour required of them, not excluding Grace and even George, if he crossed her path. The little patter of homilies never seemed to end. Grace would have given a great deal for a few hours of freedom.

Sir Matthew came to her rescue, either accidentally or by design, she could not be sure.

"Should you like an outing, Grace?" he said as they sat at breakfast. "I am bound for Lower Brinford this morning, as I am pledged to spend an hour or two at the school reading to the children."

"That is a kindness, sir. Miss Firth is an excellent teacher, and manages very well, but it is always helpful to have a little change now and then. I go there when I can, but it is not as often as I should like."

"Margaret Firth is a very good sort of girl," Lady Graham said. "Have I not always said that she would do well, if given the opportunity? Her potential was obvious to me many years ago when she read so beautifully in church. Her father is one of Mr Ambleside's grooms or footmen or some such, Anne."

"A footman's daughter teaching in a school?" Cousin Anne said. "That is very singular!"

"Mr Ambleside paid for her schooling," Lady Graham said.

"Why would he do that?" Cousin Anne said.

"That is because he is a benefactor to the whole village, Anne," Sir Matthew said. "He established the school here in Higher Brinford, and paid for several of the most promising pupils to receive further teaching in Brinchester. Miss Firth was one such beneficiary, and repaid the debt by assisting at the school. I believe that she intended to become a governess, but her background was against her for that. However, she is very well suited to run a small school like that at Lower Brinford. Better suited, I believe than the previous occupant of the role. Mr Drummond was too much of a gentleman to adapt well to the constraints of such a small school, but Miss Firth manages very well."

"She has an aunt and uncle living with her to help out," Grace said. "The aunt takes in sewing, and the uncle contrives to sell some of his surplus vegetables, so they manage splendidly. Poor Mr Drummond had such trouble with the vegetables. And as for the pig! He panicked whenever it grunted, poor man."

Sir Matthew smiled. "Indeed, it has all worked out for the best. Should you like to visit the school with me, Grace? Or perhaps you have errands at Allamont Hall? I can drop you there and pick you up later if you wish."

"Oh, the Hall, if you please. I should like that of all things! Thank you so much! I can collect some music for Alice, for there are several pieces which would suit her. And I could fetch one or two different gowns, too."

"I shall come with you," Cousin Anne said. "You should not be unchaperoned."

"Grace hardly needs a chaperon in her own home," Sir Matthew said.

"Miss Bellows will be there," Grace added.

"So she will," Sir Matthew said. "That is settled then. I shall have the carriage brought round directly."

Grace enjoyed the short drive to Allamont Hall enormously, and the freedom from Cousin Anne was not the least of it. The weather was so benign that they could let down the windows and enjoy the late spring greenery and the scent of blossom to the fullest. The road was dry, the hedgerows were brimming with dainty flowers of yellow and white, and in the fields the first bent heads of poppies swayed above the growing wheat.

Sir Matthew was, as always, an amiable companion, asking about the latest news of poor Cousin Vivienne and her sisters in his comfortable way. He always made her feel as though nothing was quite so bad as it might at first appear, but without making her feel foolish for worrying.

How pleasant it would have been to have had such a man as her father! So gentlemanly, so well-read and thoughtful, and he never judged one. Not like Papa! With him there was only ever one way to do a thing, and that was his way and no other could be contemplated. Poor Amy had been so terrified of making a mistake! No wonder she was so contented with Mr Ambleside, who told her exactly how to behave. Belle had been clever enough to earn Papa's approbation, and Connie, Dulcie and Hope had had the good sense not to cross him.

But Grace had never learned to mind her tongue. How many times had she missed an outing because she had had to learn an extra passage of Greek off by heart, or write out a hundred times *'I must not argue with my betters'*?

"I am pleased to see George so settled," Sir Matthew said, drawing her out of her reverie. "Usually he flounces off to stay with one of his disreputable friends whenever Anne descends on us. You are a very good influence on him, my dear."

"I?" she said, astonished. "Even when I explode soot everywhere?"

He laughed and said, "I do not regard a little dirt here and there. George has given us cause for alarm in the past with some of his escapades, but he has been very well-behaved of late, and he has finally learned to tie his cravat. Ah, I see you smile, but it is no small matter to have a son who looks like a jumped-up shopkeeper, I assure you. He is finally beginning to be a credit to his tailor and valet — and to me — and for that I am profoundly grateful. Ah, the Hall gates are open. That saves us from waiting for someone from the lodge."

The reason for the gates standing open was soon apparent, for a post chaise was stopped at the end of the drive, with boxes strapped on the back.

"Is your mama home, then?" Sir Matthew said.

"She would not travel post, not from Willowbye," Grace said. "Besides, that lady arguing with Young is certainly not Mama."

The visitor was a tall, spindly woman, dressed from head to toe in black. She could be seen waving a cane menacingly at the butler, who was shaking his head firmly. Behind him, the footman looked on with great interest, and the housekeeper waited in dignified silence until the matter should be resolved. A couple of grooms and a gardener loitered on the drive, pretending not to be watching avidly.

As soon as the carriage door was opened and the steps let down, Grace hurtled to the ground, and tore up the steps. "Whatever is happening, Young? Who is this?"

"Oh, Miss Grace!" he said in relief. "Pray tell this lady that Lady Sara is not at home. No one is at home today, madam. No one is receiving and you cannot stay here."

"Are you Grace?" the visitor said, turning to her with surprise on her face, and the glimmering of a smile. "Well now, how grown up you are! And is this your husband?" she added, as Sir Matthew came up the steps at a more sedate pace.

Grace giggled. "No, indeed. This is Sir Matthew Graham of Graham House in Higher Brinford. A kind neighbour, no more than that."

The stranger looked Sir Matthew up and down. "My apologies, sir. An easy mistake to make when I have never been in the neighbourhood before."

"Is that so?" he said in his quiet way. "I wonder, then, that you should expect to be admitted to this house."

"I expect it, sir, because I am family!" she said, drawing herself up to her full height, so that she almost looked directly into Sir Matthew's eyes.

"Yet a daughter of the house does not know you, nor the butler. Had you sent notice of your intent to—"

Her eyes flashed in anger. "I need not justify myself to *you*, sir. I am indeed family, although you would scarcely know it, from the dreadful treatment I have received from some members of it, nor have I travelled all the way from Liverpool to be turned away like a beggar."

"Liverpool?" Grace whispered. "Can it be...? Is it really...? Are you... Aunt Lucy?"

The anger was instantly replaced by a beaming smile. "I am, child, that I am. Come and give your aunt a hug."

"You may be who you say you are," Sir Matthew said calmly. "On the other hand, for all any of us can tell, you may be a fraud and an impostor. You will forgive me, I am sure, if I ask you to prove your words."

8: Seed Cake And Madeira

For a moment there was an icy silence. Then Aunt Lucy smiled, and it was as if the sun had peeked out from behind a cloud, and a dull winter's day had become summer all at once.

"There is justice in what you say," she said. "I am not certain what proofs will convince you, but you shall see all I can produce. But I have had a long and miserable journey, I am chilled to the bone and should be glad to finish this conversation beside a fire."

"Of course!" Grace said. "Do come inside, Aunt Lucy. Young, light the fire in the book room, and bring some tea and cake. Or would you prefer something more fortifying than tea, Aunt?"

"A drop of Madeira would be just the thing to help me recover. Oh, and perhaps you could pay off the chaise? We were set upon by highwaymen in some wild country, and all my money was taken."

"Of course it was," murmured Sir Matthew. "I shall see to the chaise, Grace. Take your visitor inside. Yes, yes, you may unload the boxes, my good fellow. You there — you had better unhitch my horses and take them to the stables. I can see I shall be here for a while. And I shall need someone to take a message to Miss Firth at the school."

The fire was lit, the Madeira was poured, tea and cakes were set out and, divested of her coat, hat and gloves, Aunt

Lucy settled herself in Papa's wing chair beside the hearth, her feet near the flames. With a glass of Madeira in her hand, she sighed, and leaned back in satisfaction. In her black gown, her thin arms stretched out to either side, she looked like a giant spider.

"Well, this is delightful, niece. All these years I have wondered what you looked like, and now that I see you, it is quite clear that you are your father's daughter. There is nothing of Sara in you at all. Mind you, dark hair is more fashionable, is it not so? Sara was always accounted a great beauty, but I never saw it myself. Too pale by half. But where is everyone? I expected to find a house full, and there is only you, and the *very* kind neighbour." She looked archly at Sir Matthew, and laughed loudly. "Oh, and who is this, creeping round the door like a servant, yet *not* a servant, I surmise?"

"That is Miss Bellows, our former governess and now companion and friend," Grace said.

"Oh, Grace, dear, I do not aspire to friendship," Miss Bellows said. "But how very kind to say such a thing — so flattering."

"Lavinia, this is Mrs Roger Langdon of Liverpool."

"Oh. How do you do, Mrs Langdon." She bobbed a curtsy, looking mystified.

"It is Aunt Lucy, Lavinia," Grace added. "Papa's sister."

"Oh, I see! Oh my goodness! And Lady Sara not here to meet you. How very unfortunate. Are you staying long, Mrs Langdon?"

"We move on a little too fast," Sir Matthew said quietly. "I remain to be convinced that this is indeed Mrs Langdon."

Aunt Lucy smirked, and rummaged in her reticule. "Here, sir. My card."

"How fortunate that your cards were not taken by the highwaymen." He scanned it carefully. "It looks well enough, but anyone may have cards printed. Is there no one hereabouts who would recognise you and vouch for your identity, madam?"

"Amy would," Grace said. "Belle, too. Aunt Lucy saw them through their London season."

"So I did," that lady said cheerfully. "It was more than ten years ago now, but I daresay I have not changed so very much. Are they still here?"

"They are both married, but still live nearby," Grace said. "Amy lives barely five miles from here."

"Then this matter may be resolved speedily," Sir Matthew said. "I shall have my carriage brought round again, and I shall myself drive you to Staynlaw House, madam. If Mrs Ambleside recognises you, then I will be satisfied. If not, I will drive you to the coach station and pay your ticket home on the mail coach. So enjoy your Madeira while you may."

"You are very sure I am deceiving you, Sir Matthew."

"I am tolerably sure, that is true, for I ask myself a simple question: why should a widow who has seen nothing of her family for years suddenly arrive with so little advance warning that her hostess is not even here to greet her? It is, if you will forgive me saying so, a very *odd* thing to do."

"I am not a widow," Aunt Lucy said, sitting upright. "My husband is perfectly hale, or was when I left home. No, I wear black in mourning for my *brother*."

"Your... brother?" Grace said, bewildered. "But Uncle Thomas has been dead these twenty years or more."

"Not *that* brother!" she hissed. "My brother William — Mr William Allamont of Allamont Hall, your father, who died these three years or more ago — and *no one bothered to tell me!*"

Grace was too shocked to utter a sound, but Miss Bellows gasped, and even Sir Matthew murmured, "No!" under his breath.

"But that is quite dreadful!" Grace burst out. "Your own brother died and you were not informed? How could that be?"

"I ask myself the same question," Aunt Lucy said. "How is it possible that no one saw fit to inform a man's only living sister of his death? I know Sara and I have had our differences, but a line or two on the occasion — is it so much to ask? Even something impersonal from the solicitor would have been better than nothing. A notice in the newspaper, even. But no, not a word."

"You were not in communication with any of the Miss Allamonts?" Sir Matthew said.

"Dear me, no! If my own brother and sister-in-law refused to write to me, it would be astonishing indeed if the girls had been allowed to do so. I had one letter from Amy and Belle thanking me for bringing them out in London, and explaining that they would not be able to write again. There is no blame attached to *them*, you know. They could not disobey their parents. So it was that I knew nothing until a week ago, when I met a man in Liverpool who originated from around here. Naturally that attracted my interest, and I engaged him in conversation. He was very ready to talk about himself, and his kin remaining in this county. He was, he told me, related to Mr William Allamont of Allamont Hall — the *late* Mr William Allamont. I cannot tell you what a shock it was to hear those words. We were playing whist at the time, and it was as much as I could do to keep my composure. The *late* Mr William Allamont."

"That is indeed a dreadful way to find out such news," Sir Matthew said. "Yet I am intrigued by this relative of Mr Allamont's. I cannot imagine who that might be, for Mr Allamont had no relatives in the county beyond his own wife and children and his cousin's family, all of which leads me once again to wonder about the veracity of your story, madam."

"I know who it is," Grace said in subdued tones. "It must be Jack Barnett, and he is indeed a relative, although not of any kind which might be mentioned in polite society. Connie's husband chased him away from here."

Aunt Lucy perked up. "Connie? Constance? She is married, too?"

"Yes, and Dulcie," Grace said absently. "How fortuitous that the Marquess sent him to Liverpool, where he meets *you*, of all people, Aunt."

"Constance married a marquess? My, how grand!"

Sir Matthew tutted in annoyance. "That is hardly to the point. You have told a tragic story, madam, but the question remains — why have you come here at all?"

"What a suspicious nature you have! Why, I have come to examine the will, naturally. My, that seed cake looks delicious. May I? And you must tell me all about your sisters, Grace. I want to know everything."

While the carriage was being brought round, Aunt Lucy consumed four slices of seed cake and three glasses of Madeira, having no compunction in asking for her glass to be refilled whenever there was the least danger of it running dry. She asked so many questions about the four eldest sisters, their husbands, houses, carriages and children, that Grace had no opportunity to ask Aunt Lucy why she had an interest in the will. Sir Matthew looked serious, and she thought she understood his concern — was Aunt Lucy planning to contest the will? To claim something for herself, perhaps? She appeared — and it pained Grace to admit the thought — to be a greedy person, and not just for seed cake.

Aunt Lucy's boxes were strapped to the Graham House carriage, in case it should be necessary to convey her to the coach station, and the two ladies took their seats. Sir Matthew was about to step in when Grace noticed Miss Bellows standing forlornly before the front door with the servants.

"Poor Miss Bellows!" she said impulsively. "We descend on her for an hour and now we are leaving her all alone again."

"Then let her come with us, by all means," Sir Matthew said cordially. "She will like to see Mrs Ambleside again, and observe how well-grown the new baby is."

So, with only a brief delay for a delighted Miss Bellows to fetch hat and pelisse, the carriage rumbled down the drive and made the short journey back to Higher Brinford. Their arrival being unexpected, there was a wait in the drawing room before Mr and Mrs Ambleside could be found and fetched. Mr Ambleside arrived first, and looked solemn when the situation was explained to him. But then Amy arrived, and her squeal of delight and the many hugs she bestowed on the visitor set all doubts to rest. This was indeed Aunt Lucy. Grace had never doubted it, for any deception seemed to her too audacious and uncertain to have any likelihood of success. Still, she understood Sir Matthew's caution. She had herself once been taken in by a plausible rogue, and he had stolen a quantity of money as a result. How humiliating it would have been to be deceived a second time. She hoped she was not so gullible now.

Hope came rushing into the room, and there were more hugs, and exclamations of delight from Aunt Lucy.

"Do come to the nursery and see the children!" Hope said. "They may, Amy, may they not? Such sweet little boys! They are both awake just now, so you will see them at their best."

Aunt Lucy clapped her hands with glee, but Grace clucked in impatience. "We did not come all this way to coo over babies. What are we to do with you, since Mama is from home? We cannot take her away from poor Cousin Vivienne, who is not at all well, and deserves every comfort we can offer her. Sir Matthew, will Lady Graham be terribly offended if I abandon her to return to the Hall? I know she was depending on me for her card party tonight."

"And so am I," he said at once. "I must have at least one competent whist player to call upon. If circumstances were otherwise, I should have invited Mrs Langdon to join you at Graham House. However, Lady Graham has arranged for the house to be full to overflowing, and I do not feel able to overset her careful plans."

"Oh, but Aunt Lucy must stay with us!" Amy cried. "Of course she must. Mr Ambleside, you will not have any objection, I am sure."

"Mrs Langdon is more than welcome here." He glanced at Sir Matthew as he spoke, who gave an almost imperceptible nod, as if some signal had passed between the two men. Perhaps they were still suspicious of Aunt Lucy, and Mr Ambleside was offering to keep a watchful eye on her as well as hospitality.

"If we are settling accommodation arrangements, perhaps Miss Bellows would care to join us at Graham House?" Sir Matthew said. "If you do not mind sharing your room, that is, Grace. The Hall must be very dull for a lady used to a busy life."

"Oh, Sir Matthew...!" Miss Bellows exclaimed, almost too overcome to speak. "How kind! How exceptionally kind, but I cannot think that... It would hardly be... No, I must protest that—"

"Nonsense, Lavinia," Grace said. "What a splendid idea! And I daresay Miss Bellows' skills at the whist table had nothing to do with it."

Sir Matthew laughed and acknowledged the hit. "Since my brother will be visiting, I shall be guaranteed an evening of perfect happiness, at least so far as whist is concerned. And now, Mrs Langdon, you may go and coo over the babies."

Hope and Amy led Aunt Lucy away, with much girlish laughter. Grace, sat in the corner of the drawing room beside Miss Bellows hoping to escape notice as the gentlemen talked. She was curious to know Sir Matthew's real opinion of their visitor and what she might be about.

"I hope your cook has plenty of seed cake on hand, Ambleside," Sir Matthew said. "As for your cellar, Mrs Langdon is partial to a drop of Madeira."

"You have discovered that already?" Mr Ambleside laughed. "Well, if that is all, I shall bear the depredations with fortitude. But you believe there is more to this, I take it?"

"Our unexpected visitor has expressed an interest in the will, and that does concern me. His sister might have a claim."

Ambleside shook his head. "I should be surprised if that were so. The will was very explicitly worded, with a number of bequests to servants and so forth, but no mention of any sister. Nor his cousin, either, which surprised me. One might have thought... however, that is nothing to the purpose."

"Except as evidence that he had no intention of making bequests beyond his immediate family and household."

"True. The family solicitor may know something of this — a fellow by the name of Plumphett in Brinchester. I believe I shall suggest a visit to that gentleman to Mrs Langdon to clarify the situation."

"But you will go with her?" Sir Matthew said. Ambleside nodded. "Then I am satisfied. I can leave all in your capable hands, unless Grace perhaps wishes to make some alternative suggestion? For I am aware that you are still here, my dear."

"I am content to leave everything to Mr Ambleside," she said.

"Good. Then we are all agreed."

"I cannot thank you both enough for your good offices in this matter," Grace said. "I do not know how matters would have turned out without you. Even if I had thought of putting Aunt Lucy to the test in this way, I should never have dared to do it! If a person presents themselves with conviction, it seems mean-spirited to question what they say. I am relieved that she is who she claims to be, but it is unsettling to realise that I could not have determined it for myself. In all probability I should have fed her seed cake and Madeira until Mama came home."

"A lady should not be troubled with such questions," Mr Ambleside said. "You have no man at the head of your family now to take care of these worldly matters. It is the greatest pity that your brothers have not been found, but you are by no means alone. Your cousin, Mr Henry Allamont, would, I am certain, offer you his aid and advice whenever you should feel the need. And you now have four brothers-in-law who are very much part of the family. Mr Drummond is, perhaps, too distant in Scotland to offer much practical help, but I am very close at hand, and Mr Burford not so far away. And in Lord Carrbridge you have a powerful ally indeed."

"It is also true that you are not without friends from beyond your own family circle," Sir Matthew said. "Lady Graham and I would, I trust, be accounted in their number. You are very capable, Grace, and can manage your life perfectly well without interference, but you should know that you have many, many well-wishers who would be happy to offer you whatever aid you might need. If ever you have a difficult question to answer, you may seek counsel from without your family as well as within."

Grace was so much overcome by this declaration that it was as much as she could do to murmur, "Thank you, sir."

9: *Lady Graham Entertains*

A card party at Graham House was no trivial matter. Lady Graham had a love of company, and her greatest fear was that one of her entertainments should fall short in numbers. This fear drove her to invite everyone of consequence in the neighbourhood, and to offer so much food and good company and merriment that only the most churlish or reclusive could possibly refuse. To guard against the dreadful possibility of rain, a moonless night or other weather catastrophe, everyone who lived at a distance was invited to stay the night, thus guaranteeing an enjoyable evening even if it should snow in May.

The addition of Miss Bellows to the list of guests caused her ladyship not a moment's alarm. If dear Grace did not mind sharing her room with her governess, then another cover could certainly be squeezed onto the dining table without any trouble to anybody, she declared airily. Only the slightest lifting of an eyebrow suggested that the butler might disagree with this assessment. Yet somehow, an extra cover was laid, the chairs were moved a little closer together and the guests seated themselves around the huge table without too much crowding.

With the need to help Miss Bellows unpack, Grace was late to the drawing room, and had no chance to meet any of her acquaintance before they were summoned to dinner. Grace waited until Cousin Anne had sat down before choosing a seat as far from her as possible. That done, she had no particular preference for dining companions. It amused her to leave such matters to chance and see who sought her out, for sometimes such unexpected arrangements were the most interesting, so she made no move to attract anyone to her side.

She saw George with a group of his Oxford friends, laughing and joking, as usual, although it was a smaller group than on previous occasions, as one by one his cronies fell into matrimony. They moved further down the table, surrounding Alice, whose terrified face lightened as they settled either side of her. The Brinford Manor party was there, Cousin Mary in close attendance on her husband, Sir Osborne Hardy, who was as thin and pale as death, although he talked composedly to Lady Graham. None of Grace's sisters were there. Belle was too occupied, no doubt, with Cousin Vivienne's illness, and Amy was not yet inclined to leave the baby for a whole evening.

Unfortunately, that meant that Aunt Lucy could not attend, either. Grace was rather disappointed about that. It would have been pleasant to spend an evening with her aunt, and hear more of her life in Liverpool, of which so little was known. What a strange family she had! Her parents seemed to have quarrelled with almost all their kin. Hardly a word exchanged with Mama's family, and as for Aunt Lucy, it seemed that all ties had been broken, with not a visit nor a letter for years. How cruel to find out that one's brother had died years before, and yet know nothing about it.

The most surprising guest was Mr Wright. Why had Lady Graham invited him? More to the point, why had he come? As he entered the dining room, he caught her eye across the room and smiled, an intimate smile that made her blush. Then she was annoyed with her lack of composure. After that, when he strode purposefully round the table and settled beside her, it was not so astonishing. She was secretly rather pleased, although she was not entirely sure why she should be. He was handsome, of course, and excellent company, but was that all that warmed her heart and made her lower her eyes demurely when he smiled at her?

On her other side, she had Mr Sidderfin, the clergyman from the Higher Brinford parish. He, at least, was a known quantity. He would enquire politely after her mother, and then each of her sisters in turn. After that he would apply himself to his plate, and she need not concern herself with keeping up a conversation with him, and would be free to talk to Mr Wright. That gave her a little thrill of pleasure. Immediately she berated herself. He was, she reminded herself, an unknown quantity. She must not lose her heart to him, or at least not until she had some better idea of his prospects. No, that was jumping too far ahead. She needed to know more about his background.

So when she had answered all Mr Sidderfin's enquiries, she turned to Mr Wright, and said, "Do tell me something of Grimsby, Mr Wright. I have never been there, and know nothing of it except that it is a great port. Is it a pleasant place to live?"

"As pleasant as any other coastal town," he said, with his ready smile. "There is nothing special about it, I believe."

"But surely every town has its points of interest, to differentiate it from the general run of towns. Is there a cathedral? Or a castle? I have a fondness for a castle, I confess."

"No castle, I regret to say. And no cathedral, either, although the town boasts a minster dating from... I am not sure. Henry the First, possibly. History is not my strongest suit."

"A minster! That is almost as good as a cathedral, is it not? Except without a bishop."

He leaned towards her to speak in lowered tones. "There are those who say that it is no more than a parish church, but for myself I am inclined to agree with you, Miss Grace."

She smiled, but for a moment her confidence in him wavered. It was such a small point, and in a man who had known her for many years she would let it pass. But Mr Wright was a stranger, who had been introduced to her just days before. To call her *'Miss Grace'* in that intimate way was jarring, somehow. With all her older sisters married, she was *the* Miss Allamont now, and civility called for the correct title. Did Mr Wright mean to imply a certain degree of closeness with her? Or did he, perhaps, not fully appreciate the proper form?

"How far from Grimsby is your family home?" she asked to cover her confusion.

Oddly, he did not answer with his usual smoothness. "Ah — you speak of Gravesby Hall, I collect? It is a few miles away from Grimsby town. Yes, no more than a few miles."

Was there a reticence in his answer? That was curious. Why would a man not want to talk about his home? When she was younger, Grace would have asked the question directly, but experience had taught her greater discretion. "That must be convenient. We are but a few miles from Brinchester, and although it is but a modestly sized town, it furnishes almost all our needs. We have every kind of shop, and several mantua makers and milliners and haberdashers and cobblers. We have a circulating library, too. I dare say you must read a great deal in your profession, Mr Wright."

Was that relief in his eyes. "Indeed, yes, although I do not feel able to justify the expense of a subscription to a library. I have been fortunate in my host while in Brinshire, for Mr Burford has an extensive library, from which I am generously invited to borrow whatever catches my interest. As you may imagine, Miss Grace…"

He rattled on in this vein for some time, leaving Grace with nothing to do but wonder why a man so expensively dressed could not afford the subscription to a library. Mr Wright was a great puzzle to her, and although she enjoyed his company, and found herself greatly drawn towards him, yet there was a little knot of unease within her.

~~~~~

After all the guests had eaten their fill, they made their way through to the drawing room and saloons for the important business of cards. Sir Matthew claimed Grace and Miss Bellows, and introduced them to his younger brother, a clergyman. A greater contrast could hardly be imagined, for where Sir Matthew was tall and handsome, with a rangy physique, his brother was short, tending already to stoutness. He beamed at them genially.

"How delightful to make your acquaintance after all these years, Miss Allamont, Miss Bellows. So much has been heard of the ladies of Allamont Hall, and here you are before me at last!"

"Yet we have heard almost nothing of you, Mr Graham," Grace said. "Where have you been hiding all this time? Have you been abroad?"

He laughed heartily at that. "That would have been a fine diversion, and had I been the eldest son, undoubtedly I should have taken myself off to the continent and squandered the estate in traditional style. Sadly, being only a younger son, I am obliged to earn my bread, and the only living I could obtain saw me sequestered in the depths of Yorkshire these several years, which is not a fate I would wish on my worst enemy, let me tell you, Miss Allamont. But now fortune — and the good offices of my brother here, who is the best of fellows — finally sees me installed in the living long intended for me, not ten miles from here."

Sir Matthew looked amused. "Yorkshire is not so bad as all that. I have heard that the natives hardly ever daub themselves in woad these days. And you would not have had me turn poor Thompson out to make way for you?"

"Not in the least, but who would ever have expected such a frail old man to live so long? I hope the living has as virtuous an effect on me. Now, Matthew, let us break the cards, shall we?" He rubbed his hands together in glee.

Grace was glad to find herself partnering Sir Matthew, for he was a superior player, and could generally be depended upon to end the evening ahead. Tonight, however, she discovered that the pairing of Mr Bertram Graham and Miss Bellows was even more superior, and Sir Matthew's smiles soon changed to frowns of silent consternation. Grace found herself fully stretched, and even with the deepest concentration found herself losing more tricks than she won. The two gainers, meanwhile, chatted amiably as if only half attending to the play.

"Well, Sir Matthew, I have let you down," Grace said, as they rose from the table for supper. "You will want to find another partner for the rest of the evening, I make no doubt."

"Grace, if you condemn me to another game with Mrs Wills I shall never forgive you," he said sternly. "Oh, the irritation of a partner who asks constantly what suit is trumps! It is more than a man can bear. It is certainly more than her husband can bear, and he is but an indifferent player himself. Besides, you have played very well, at least as well as I, but sadly it has not answered. I knew Miss Bellows to be a most accomplished player, but I now discover how my brother has been engaged during his desperate years in Yorkshire. For you were not so able when last I played against you, Bertram."

"The winter evenings are very long," he murmured, "and the wind howls round every corner. One must pass the time somehow."

"Well, you may pass the time in this manner whenever convenient," Sir Matthew said. "I shall try not to mind you thrashing me soundly on every occasion."

"Ah, the pleasure of besting my older brother in something — anything! You know what it is like, Miss Allamont, to be one of the youngest in the family. Whatever one does, it has all been done before, at an earlier age or to greater proficiency. Did you not find it so?"

"No, for Papa found fault with all of us equally, and Miss Bellows was far too kind to make comparisons," Grace said at once. "Besides, the world is a vast place full of possibilities, and there is always some activity one might find which none of one's older siblings has thought of. It needs only a little imagination, or a book, perhaps. The ladies in books have so many exciting adventures."

"Exciting to read about, no doubt, Grace, but uncomfortable to experience," Sir Matthew said in serious tones. "And somehow the heroines in novels manage to conquer adversity so that all ends happily, whereas real life is not always so obliging. Now, shall we follow the others to the supper room? Lady Graham has prepared her usual enticing spread for us."

"Ah, excellent, excellent!" his brother said, clapping his hands in delight. "I need something to fortify myself before setting about thrashing you again." And he chuckled amiably all the way through supper.

~~~~~

It was a long-standing tradition that all Lady Graham's overnight guests partake of a walk around the gardens of Graham House before breakfast on the morning after a party. Grace had never participated before, but she rose and dressed eagerly. She told herself her enthusiasm was due to the benign weather, or the chance to stretch her legs after several days without a walk anywhere. She told her maid that she was looking forward to seeing Lady Graham's famous reflecting pool again. But she knew in her heart the real reason, even though something inside her urged caution.

Yet when the group gathered on the terrace, it was not Mr Wright who sought her side. Instead George Graham leapt forward as soon as she appeared.

"May I offer you my arm, Grace? I should not like you to tire." He spoke with force, and his expression was so fierce that she drew back in alarm, wondering why after so many years of amiable disinterest he should suddenly choose to squire her about.

But then it occurred to her that he might want to talk privately to her about the diamond necklace. A frisson of excitement rushed through her — perhaps he had found it, and it was even now locked away safely in his room! That would be famous, indeed. So she smiled and accepted the proffered arm, and allowed him to guide her down the steps to the path through the rose garden.

The group proceeded on the allotted route. Lady Graham herself never rose from her bed so early, but Sir Matthew led the way with his brother, and Alice was still surrounded by a gaggle of George's friends. Then Cousin Anne and a few distant relatives, with Grace and George behind. At the rear, side by side but silent, Miss Bellows and Mr Wright.

They had not gone far when Mr Bertram Graham came striding back. "There you are, Miss Bellows! Do pray join us, for Matthew is telling the most dreadful tall tales about our victory last night, and I need you to help me put him in his place." Miss Bellows protested at the very idea of putting Sir Matthew in his place, but went willingly enough. They had not gone two paces, however, when Mr Bertram turned again. "Mr Wright! You must not walk by yourself, you know. Do join us at the front, and help me remonstrate with my brother. The words of a fellow clergyman must carry some weight with him, I believe."

Mr Wright could not refuse, and within moments Grace and George were left at the rear of the procession, and dropping further behind with every step.

They left the rose garden behind, and entered the shrubbery, the plants towering over their heads like a forest, their leaves hanging silent and still. The others were quite out of sight, and Grace assumed that George would now take the opportunity to convey whatever of import he had to tell her.

Instead, he remained obstinately silent, his expression brooding and sullen.

"Did you want to talk to me about something, George?" she said at last, tiring of his gloomy countenance.

"I? No, whatever gave you that idea?"

"You chose me very particularly, and I cannot believe you are impelled by any desire to make love to me—"

"Good God, no!"

"— so naturally I supposed you had something you wished to say privately to me. Have you found the necklace?"

"The necklace? Oh, no such thing. I cannot move without Cousin Anne following me about. It is impossible. No, I merely wanted to ensure you were not monopolised by that oily Wright fellow."

"Not monopolised—?" She let go of his arm, and spun round to face him. "George Graham, what business is it of yours who I talk to? How *dare* you interfere! You are insufferable!"

"Now, now, Grace, I am just looking out for you. Like a brother would, you know."

"But you are *not* my brother, and you have no right, no right at all!"

"No, but—" He stopped, chewing his lip, and once caught his breath as if about to speak. But then he waved his arms in angry dismissal. "Have it your own way, then! You always do, it seems to me. Mama is right, you are wilful and foolish, and you may go to perdition for all I care!"

10: A Morning Walk

With these impassioned words, George strode away down the path, leaving Grace a view of his back vanishing into the distance. She was quite alone. From somewhere in the depths of the shrubbery ahead came the faintest echo of voices, and an occasional burst of manly laughter. If she were to run, she could catch up with the others, but she had the strongest wish not to meet George again until her anger had cooled. On the other hand, to return prematurely to the house might be taken as an insult to her kindly hostess, who would certainly enquire of her everything she had enjoyed about the walk.

As she stood indecisively, the foliage behind her rustled. "All alone, Miss Allamont?"

She jumped. "Oh! Mr Wright, you startled me!" Then, puzzled, she added, "I thought you had gone far ahead of me."

He laughed, his eyes sparkling. "Ah, but I am no Johnny raw, to be taken in by such clumsy tricks as that. Can't gull me with such a bag of moonshine. As soon as a chance offered itself, I slipped away into the bushes. I see what they are about, but it won't answer, I can tell you. And I was right, for here's young Master George run off and abandoned you."

"I have not the least notion what you may be talking about, Mr Wright."

"Why, these Grahams are making a play for your money, Miss Grace, that's what. They see you have a tidy sum as a dowry, and they are setting you up with the heir. Why else invite you to stay, and push the two of you together?"

Grace laughed out loud at the absurdity of it. "I assure you, Mr Wright, you are quite wrong about that. The Grahams have no need of my dowry, and would never encourage such a match. Lady Graham has far grander plans for George. The very idea is ridiculous! Why, George and I have known each other for… oh, a long time! Fifteen years, I dare say. We played together in these very gardens as children. We are almost like brother and sister."

His smile broadened. "How touching! Then I beg your pardon." He made her an ironic bow. "Shall we walk? There is a very pretty little shelter just through here where we may rest and enjoy the view." He pointed back the way he had come, where a narrow path led through the bushes.

Grace was tempted. Mr Wright was excellent company, and a pleasant half hour with him would sustain her through many a long, boring day in attendance on Lady Graham, or helping Alice learn the cotillion. The folly was rather secluded, well away from the route the rest of the party had taken, but what was there to fear from a man of God, as Mr Wright was?

He must have seen her hesitation, for he lifted her hand to his lips, and said, "Ah, but have pity on me! In a few hours I shall depart this house of delights, and return to my frugal life as a travelling preacher. Let me enjoy just a little more of your charming company before I go. How can I bear it if you send me away with a refusal on your lips? Such enticing lips…"

He leaned a little closer, and ran one finger down her cheek, his eyes fixing her with an expression so intense that for a moment she felt as if she were drowning. Her heart hammered furiously, and she was dizzy, as if she had drunk too much claret. He was so mesmerising, it would be all too easy to succumb to his charm. He was close enough that she could feel his breath on her cheek.

So close... "Grace," he murmured. "My sweet Grace..."

The world turned upside down. Anger boiled through her, dissipating the spell. How dared he call her by name, like a lover? For he was *not* a lover, not even a friend, yet. She barely knew him. This was no honourable courtship, played out in public, with gentle steps and the utmost courtesy. This was not how a man should treat his future wife, if he even had that intent.

She snatched her hand away, and stepped back. "You are too bold, sir."

For an instant his face shifted, the charm replaced by frowning calculation. Almost as swiftly, he smiled with sudden warmth. "Of course. My deepest apologies if I have been too forward. Your beauty is enough to make any man lose all reason. Come, let us walk on. We may yet catch up with the rest of the party."

Grace could hear no sound ahead of them. "They must be long gone by now," she said. "I believe I will return to the house."

"By all means," he said equably. "I shall take you directly there. Do take my arm, Miss Grace. You must be tired."

"I do not think that would be wise," she said slowly. "If the others have already returned, or if the rest of the household awaits us, it would look most particular for us to return together, and quite alone. I am sure you wish to avoid comment as much as I do, Mr Wright."

His face registered surprise, but he nodded. "As you prefer, Miss Grace. As you prefer."

She made him a small curtsy then, with as much composure as she could muster, she turned and set off back to the house. For some unfathomable reason, her feet wanted to run as fast as she could, but her knees were shaking, and it was as much as she could do to walk in a straight line.

By the time she had regained the house, she had recovered some of her equilibrium, at least outwardly. Her mind was still a disordered jumble of thoughts, but she hoped that she displayed nothing untoward in her manner. She saw no one, but when she came to the hall, she found Miss Endercott sitting quietly on a marble bench.

"Grace! How fortunate."

"Miss Endercott? Whatever are you doing here so early? Surely you have not walked all this way? Are the servants not attending to you?"

Miss Endercott laughed. "You were ever direct, my dear. To answer your questions — I came to see you, I obtained a lift from Mr Garmin's cart and the servants know I am here. Is there somewhere we may talk? In private?"

Grace's heart sank, wondering if her visitor brought bad news from home, but she said lightly, "This sounds serious! I wonder what dreadful misdemeanour I have been guilty of this time. Will you come up to my room while I remove my bonnet and pelisse?"

They made their way slowly up the stairs, for Miss Endercott was no longer sprightly, and even before they had gained the landing, chattering voices and laughter filled the hall below them. They escaped unseen, to Grace's relief.

In her room, Grace threw off her bonnet and gloves, and began unbuttoning her pelisse. She waved Miss Endercott to a chair. "Miss Bellows may come in, but she will not linger. Do please set my mind at rest, and tell me the worst."

Miss Endercott looked her in the eye, her head tipped to one side. "You will think me an interfering old busybody, I daresay, my dear, but with your Papa in his grave and your Mama away, it falls to your friends to watch over you. You may not like what I have to say, but I mean to say it anyway, and then it is for you to do with that information as you please."

"This is being serious indeed," Grace said, dragging another chair across the rug to sit facing Miss Endercott.

The old lady fished in her reticule and produced a letter. "I have an old school friend who happens to live in Grimsby."

"Ah."

"Indeed. I noticed, as anyone would, that Mr Wright seemed inclined to favour you in particular with his attention, and... forgive me for saying so, but it seemed to me that you showed a distinct partiality towards him, and who could blame you for that? Not I. Yet so little was known about him. He mentioned his home, Gravesby Hall, but no one had the least idea of his connections or income or anything of his situation. So I wrote to my friend. I should like you to read it."

Grace took the proffered paper with foreboding, but she had some inkling now of what she might learn. She unfolded the sheet and began to read.

'My dear Phyllis, Your letter surprised me, for we all thought the young man gone for good. Hanged or transported, possibly. Let me state the facts as briefly as I may. Gravesby Hall is the home of the Destain family, a very ancient lineage connected to some of the greatest families in the land. Sir Roger is a gentleman of impeccable probity, but his younger brother Rufus was very wild and died young. Some years after his death, a woman appeared with a child which she claimed to be Rufus's son. Without any proof of marriage or other arrangement there was no obligation on Sir Roger, but he generously chose to take them in, to provide employment for the woman and some education for the boy. However, the boy went to the bad and was eventually turned off with a modest sum to allow him to settle in some respectable employment elsewhere, should he choose to do so. Since a quantity of silverware disappeared at the same time, it was widely believed that he was irredeemable, and would, in time, fall foul of the law. This is a very bald rendering, for I will spare you the expense of a second sheet, but

believe me when I tell you that there are many sordid details of the young man's wickedness that could be supplied. You may apply to Sir Roger for confirmation of this. I am very sorry you must bear such evil tidings to your young friend. Yours, Selena.'

Grace lowered the letter, gazing thoughtfully at Miss Endercott.

"You are not surprised," Miss Endercott said.

"Not entirely. I have already suspected that he is not quite the gentleman he appears to be. His manners are... not what I would wish for, and now I understand why. This sets my mind at rest on some odd behaviour that puzzled me."

"I am glad your mind is eased," Miss Endercott said. "You need not answer me on this point, but I very much hope your heart is also at ease."

Grace smiled. "My heart has never been fully engaged. I... liked him very much, it is true, but there was always *something* about him that felt... not quite right. And yet it may be that he has now reformed and wishes to leave the past behind. He truly seems to be a man of God now, and he has converted Mark to the same cause, which is greatly in his favour. So perhaps we may leave him be. He will move on to some other county in time and trouble us no more."

"It may be so. The Lord teaches us that any man may repent of his sins at any time and be forgiven. Besides, I have no authority to reveal the contents of this letter to anyone but you, and that I have done, so I shall be silent on the subject from now on, and hope, in my turn, to be forgiven my interference."

"Forgiveness is quite unnecessary, for you have my gratitude," Grace said. "I had begun to wonder if I should ask Sir Matthew to make enquiries, as he has offered to do, but this settles the matter. But why did he favour me with his attentions? He has no settled home and no income beyond the coins offered in charity by those who hear him preach. He could never support a wife."

"Perhaps he feels that he could support a wife who brought twenty thousand pounds to the marriage?" Miss Endercott suggested gently.

"And could he?"

"Hmm. If both were frugal, perhaps, with careful management. But it would not be a comfortable life."

"That is as I thought." Grace sighed. "I confess that I do not understand men, Miss Endercott. Is there not even one who can see me as a person to be admired for what I am, and not merely the owner of a large dowry? I long for a man I may depend upon, who is wise and kind and gentle, a man like Sir Matthew, perhaps. Young men are so... so self-centred or avaricious or frivolous, and yet they always think they know best and tell one how to go on when they should leave well alone."

Miss Endercott smiled. "But how fierce you sound! Young men grow into wisdom over the years, as do young ladies. Yet you are not thinking of Mr Wright now, I presume?"

Grace had not considered her words with much care, but she now saw that Miss Endercott was quite right. She laughed ruefully. "I had a spat with George this morning. He was abominably overbearing, trying to keep me away from Mr Wright. And what is it to George who I talk to, I should like to know?"

"Perhaps he feels a little jealousy?"

"What on earth does he have to be jealous about? It is not as if he had ever had any designs on me. The very idea would be abhorrent to both of us. Good Lord, no, you are quite wrong about that! We are friends, when he is not behaving foolishly, but nothing more than that, I assure you. Today he said he was looking out for me as a brother might, but that was nothing but his high-handedness. I am quite out of charity with him."

Miss Endercott smiled again, and shortly after made her farewells. It was not until sometime later that Grace realised that Miss Bellows had not returned.

~~~~~

There were many visitors that day. Some came to thank their hostess for a pleasant evening, and others, who had stayed at home, came to hear all the delights that they had missed. Amongst the latter number were Amy and Mr Ambleside, with Hope and Aunt Lucy. Lady Graham fell upon Aunt Lucy with joy, for a new face to the neighbourhood promised the most enjoyable exchange of enquiries on both sides. Her ladyship could boast of her newly married daughter, the Viscountess, and at the same time discover all that she might about the newcomer.

Grace was happy to see her sisters, but the first news was gloomy, for Cousin Vivienne was still unwell and Mama could not leave her yet.

"We are to take Aunt Lucy to Willowbye tomorrow to meet Mama," Hope said. "Not Amy, for she will not leave little Henry for the whole day, but Mr Ambleside and I will go. Poor Mama, stuck out there! Willowbye is so remote."

"It is generous of her to devote herself to Cousin Vivienne," Mr Ambleside said reprovingly. "She could have left everything in Belle's capable hands."

"What of this new physician?" Grace said. "Has he alleviated the pains at all?"

Amy shook her head. "Nothing seems to help except laudanum, but as soon as that is left off, the pains return as bad as ever. Mama is very gloomy about the outcome. She does not say so, but in her last letter she is not near so cheerful."

Something prickled in Grace's mind, but she could not think what it might be and the conversation moved on to Aunt Lucy.

"I have written to Mr Plumphett to ask if he will see Mrs Langdon with a view to discussing your father's will," Mr Ambleside said.

"To ask?" Grace said. "Surely he will not refuse?"

"Plumphett is an odd sort of solicitor," he said. "There is no knowing what he may do."

"Have you found out what Aunt Lucy's interest is?" Grace said.

"We do not like to enquire," Amy said. "Mr Ambleside will find it out, for he will accompany her to see Mr Plumphett."

"You have not even asked?" Grace said. "I am not so cowardly."

As soon as Lady Graham turned to some new arrivals and Aunt Lucy was released, Grace waved her across.

"Do come and sit by me, Aunt Lucy, for I have had so little opportunity to talk to you. We are all dying to know why you are really here and what you hope to find out from Papa's will."

Amy gave a little squeak at this effrontery, and Mr Ambleside looked grave.

Aunt Lucy laughed, however. "There now, I like it when a person says what they mean! The will is of the greatest interest to me because I want to find out whether my brother kept a promise, that is all."

"If you expect a legacy, then I fear you will be disappointed," Mr Ambleside said. "There were no bequests beyond Lady Sara, the Miss Allamonts and the servants."

That made her shake her head, still smiling. "No, no, no! It is not for myself, or for anyone other than William's own family." She hesitated, her gaze moving from one to another, before resting on Grace. "Do you want me to tell you everything? The whole truth, even though you might not care to hear it?"

Hope's eyes were wide, and Amy shrank towards her husband, but Grace had no fears.

"The truth, Aunt Lucy, if you please. Let us have no more family secrets."

"As to that, I am not privy to every secret in the family, you understand, but my own share of them you will hear, with nothing spared. Shall we find somewhere more private?"

"The gallery will be deserted at this time of day," Grace said.

"Then let us go there," she said, rising to her feet with a swish of black bombazine.

Silently Grace led the way.

11: Of Sisters And Brothers

The gallery was, as Grace had predicted, empty. The pale eyes of Graham ancestors stared haughtily down at them from the inner wall, a long row of men in doublets and great ruffs, or ladies with enormous powdered wigs and skirts four feet wide. They crept past these disapproving gazes, their feet echoing hollowly on the wooden floor, and found a group of chairs at the furthest end.

"Now," said Aunt Lucy, rustling her skirts into smoothness as she sat down, "what do you know of the house in Market Clunbury?"

She was gazing at Grace as she spoke. "Papa inherited it some years ago from a relative," Grace said.

"Indeed he did, child. From his great-uncle Josiah, to be precise. He married a Shropshire lass, who brought the house as her dowry. He had no need of it, being away up in Liverpool and having a house of his own already, so when the occupant died and the house fell vacant, it was let to a gentleman who used it for... er, business purposes. Josiah had numerous businesses, most of them illegal, so the less said about that the better. He had no children, so when he died he left the Shropshire house to William, and I inherited the Liverpool house. Well, I was already living in it, to look after the old man."

She paused. "My goodness, but this is thirsty work. Ring the bell, Hope, do."

"There are no bells in this part of the house," Grace said, smiling. "Shall I go—?"

Before she could rise, Mr Ambleside said, "I shall find a servant, Miss Allamont. You must stay and hear what Mrs Langdon has to say." So saying, he strode off down the gallery, his footfalls reverberating.

"Do go on, Aunt Lucy," Grace said.

"Very well, child. I can manage a few more words before I am quite parched. Now, you must understand that my husband, who is a solicitor, had the legal management of the Shropshire house, so we knew all about it, and the less than savoury purposes to which it was put."

"What sort of purposes?" Grace said.

"Now, now, child, how inquisitive you are! Gambling and… other things. It hardly matters. We were aware through various connections that William was collecting the rent on quarter days, in person, but he was so regular in his habits, always arriving at the exact time he had specified, that it was easy for Mr Smith — the manager — to conceal the truth from him. We thought it best, since he was so respectable by this time."

Grace frowned. "You say that as if you were *not* respectable, Aunt Lucy. You make it sound almost as if you were working hand in glove with this Mr Smith."

There was a long, strained silence. Then Aunt Lucy gave a little titter. "Did I give that impression? Oh dear me!"

"You said you would tell us the whole truth, Aunt," Grace said firmly.

"Oh, Grace, surely we need not know every little detail," Amy said in some distress. "Not *unsavoury* detail. Should we not wait for Mr Ambleside to return? He will advise us."

"I shall certainly spare you the unsavoury details," Aunt Lucy said. "Even though you are a married woman, Amy, there are some things that no respectable lady should talk about, except perhaps in private, with her husband. As for your sisters, they should know nothing of such matters. But Grace is quite right. I did indeed promise you the truth, and I hold myself bound by that. I am… respectable enough, shall we say. I know everyone, am invited everywhere, am acknowledged as a person of some consequence, or at least of enough wealth to convey that impression. No one cuts me, but I have few close friends outside the family. The other side of the family, that is, for there was a split some years ago. Your papa stayed on the respectable side, whereas I… I chose to follow in Great-uncle Josiah's footsteps."

There was a long silence as the three sisters digested this information. Their thoughts were disrupted by the steady tread of feet announcing a procession of the butler and two footmen, bearing trays.

"Ah, excellent!" Aunt Lucy said. "Refreshments!"

Mr Ambleside knew enough of Aunt Lucy's habits to provide adequately for her requirements. A decanter of Madeira, several cakes and a bowl of fruit were disposed on small tables and set within easy reach of the lady. Mr Ambleside himself poured her first glass of Madeira, with a nod of dismissal to the butler. Only once the servants' footsteps had receded and silence reigned again did Aunt Lucy take up the tale.

"So things stayed for some years. I was on reasonable terms with William, and we corresponded from time to time — not regularly, but whenever anything of import occurred. He knew of my life, although he asked no questions, and he told me something of his life. A little, a very little. But then a crisis. Amy and Belle were to go to London for the season, something long promised. But at the last moment, your mama refused to go, and then your papa would not go either. I have no idea why. Who knows what goes on within a marriage, and theirs was an odder pairing than most. To salvage something, since the rooms were already taken, William asked me to take care of it. Well, Amy, I did my best, didn't I, child? It was not easy, and I could not broach the highest level of society as Sara might have done, but we managed to dabble in the shallows of society."

She took a long swallow of Madeira and held out her glass to be refilled. "Before I went to London, I wrote to William asking for his instructions regarding dowries. As chaperon, I knew I should be approached to speak for the two of you, and it was necessary to know how much your portion would be. He would say nothing to the point. If you had an offer, he told me, then he would see. You must use your charms to attract husbands, otherwise you would be surrounded by fortune-hunters. He could not commit to anything because of the difficulties with the estate. A thousand excuses. It was unconscionable. He had a good income, I knew that, and he should have set aside a sensible portion, at least for one of you. I was so cross with him. Hope, may I trouble you to cut me another slice of the cherry cake? Lady Graham has an excellent cook."

They sat in silence while she ate, and then drank another glass of Madeira. Grace watched in fascination. "How do you manage to eat so well, and yet stay so thin?" she exclaimed. "Anyone else would be too fat to rise from their chair."

"Grace!" said Amy in horror.

Aunt Lucy only laughed. "I am just lucky. I should be wracked with gout, the amount of port and claret and Madeira I drink, but no. I have never suffered a day's illness in my life. It is very odd. Well now, where was I? Ah yes, the dowries. So, I decided that William was going to make provision for you, whether he liked it or not. So the very next quarter day, I went to Market Clunbury and met William. I told him the truth about the house there, and the… um, unsavoury activities that went on there, and told him that he was going to establish an account at the local bank and the manager of the establishment would deposit a proportion of his profits every week for the benefit of you girls. I made William promise to pass that money on to you, and to write it into his will in case he died early, because otherwise, you know, you would have known nothing about it, and the whole scheme would have been wasted. I made him swear to it on the Bible, for I did not trust him at all. He was so peculiar by this point, so *angry* all the time. Nothing like the brother I grew up with."

She paused. "I was able to put pressure on Mr Smith to continue adding money to the bank, but I could not say how much went there and how much to his own pockets. Nor could I know whether William had done what I asked. And since he died, I believe, before any of you were married, I wanted to be sure that he did what he promised and wrote it into his will."

"He did," Grace said. "We got very good dowries."

"You did? So there was enough money in the account? For all of you?"

"There was. We got twenty thousand pounds apiece."

For a moment her jaw dropped. "*Twenty thousand pounds? Each?* Dear God! That was far more successful than I had ever dreamed."

"There was a condition, however."

Her eyes narrowed. "A condition? There was not supposed to be any condition."

"We only got our allotted portion if we married in the proper order, the eldest first."

"*What?*" And then she laughed. "Well, that is just like him, the sneaky, conniving little son of the Devil! Oh, I beg your pardon, my unruly tongue! But you managed it, eh? Amy married first, then Belle. Oh, but Constance and Dulcie!"

"They married in age order, too," Grace said.

Aunt Lucy smiled, looking archly at Grace. "So — your turn next, child."

"I am in no hurry, Aunt. If Hope wished to marry, it would be different."

"I believe I shall never marry," Hope said timidly. "I knew someone once... but since then, no one. So Grace may marry or not, as she chooses."

"I am not sure I shall ever marry either," Grace said quietly. "Men are so unreliable. Young men, that is. And grateful as I am to you for your efforts to ensure we had dowries, Aunt, I cannot say that it has attracted the sort of man I would wish to marry."

"A true gentleman would not be motivated by your money," Mr Ambleside said. "Besides, it is not necessary to be romantically attached to the man one chooses to marry. Many couples marry for practical reasons, and find an affection within marriage later."

"Oh, no!" Hope murmured. "I should not like to marry without love. How dreadful that would be!"

"Well, you need not," Grace said bracingly. "So now we know all, Aunt, and you have no need to talk to Mr Plumphett after all."

"Oh but that is *not* all," she said. "I must know every detail of the will, and how it affects Ernest and Frank."

"It does not affect them at all," Grace said crossly. "They ran away ten years ago and not a sign of them has been seen since that day, nor have any of our efforts to find them borne fruit. They must be quite beyond our reach by now, or even dead."

"Now that is where you are quite wrong," Aunt Lucy said.

Amy gasped. "Oh, Aunt! If you know anything of them, anything at all, you must tell us at once."

~~~~~

Grace's head was spinning. As if it was not enough to discover the true benefactor behind their dowries, now there was news of Ernest and Frank. After all this time! It was too much to take in at once. Even if Amy had not become fretful to return to the baby, Grace hardly felt equal to asking Aunt Lucy many more details than she had already provided.

She was in no mood to be sociable, so she returned to her room, where she could sit quietly and consider all that she had learned. She found Miss Bellows there, just removing her bonnet.

"Lavinia? Have you been out walking all this time? You have missed breakfast."

"Oh, so I have!" She tittered. "How silly of me. But the day is so fine, and the woods just at their best. I do so like the *colours* at this time of year — such vivid greens! And then the birds — so many birds. We stood and watched for hours, I believe. So many different kinds, some that I had never seen before, and I am, as a rule, rather an observant person—"

"Yes, yes, but no one cares about birds, Lavinia, not when I have such news to share with you. You will never guess what Aunt Lucy told us. Well, of course you will not, how should you indeed? So much that we did not know! Our dowries — that entire business with the money from the Market Clunbury house being set aside for us in a bank account — all of that was Aunt Lucy's doing."

"Oh, goodness! Your dowries? Mrs Langdon? My goodness!"

"And she forced Papa to agree to it, although he did not want to, I daresay, not a bit. And she is not at all respectable, it appears. Gambling and... other things. Unsavoury things."

"Dear me," Miss Bellows said faintly.

"And she knows where Ernest and Frank are, or at least she *did*, but then they quarrelled and disappeared again... Lavinia, are you even *listening* to me?"

"Oh, of course, dear. Quarrelled, yes. I heard every word."

"Your mind is still away with the birds, I believe, and you have a smudge on one cheek."

"Do I, dear?" But she did not sound the least bit concerned.

Grace was too cross with her to stay, but she badly needed someone — anyone — to talk to, to discuss the dramatic news. She stomped out of the room and was halfway down the stairs before remembering that she had no one else in the house who could be accounted a friend. Lady Graham was not a person she could confide in, Alice was too young and Grace was still too angry with George to speak to him at all. But perhaps Sir Matthew might be someone who would understand. Accordingly, she determined to go directly to the library to find him.

The drawing room and saloons were still full of visitors, both the overnight guests who had not yet departed and morning callers. She could hear Lady Graham's raucous laughter emanating from the nearest room. Grace had no wish to be drawn into frivolous conversation, not when her head was still full of Aunt Lucy's revelations, so she tiptoed across the hall, raising a finger to her lips to silence the ever-present footman. He gave no outward sign of acknowledgement, but she thought his eyes twinkled.

She had almost gained the library door when footsteps rat-tat-tatted across the tiled floor behind her, then stopped abruptly.

"Grace?"

Heart sinking, she turned. "Mr Wright," she said coldly, adding pointedly, "Are you leaving?"

"My horse is being brought round as we speak."

His expression was rueful, but he had still not learned a proper degree of humility. "Good. I trust I shall never see you again."

That brought a surprised lift of the eyebrows. "Are you still so angry with me, Grace?"

"I am, and shall continue so until you remember your manners, sir. I am not *'Grace'* to you, nor ever will be."

He nodded thoughtfully. "I beg your pardon, Miss Grace, but—"

"Still incorrect."

He gave a tut of impatience. "Very well. *Miss Allamont.* My, but you are high in the instep these days. You are all the same, you wealthy women, one minute flirting like a light-skirt, the next looking down your nose at anyone who presumes to look at you. Pah!"

"Belling!" Grace called to the footman.

"Madam?"

"Pray escort Mr Wright outside immediately."

"With pleasure, Madam."

Grace turned away in an angry swirl of skirts.

Behind her, Wright's voice echoed around the high-ceilinged hall. "Better watch out, Miss High-and-Mighty! If I ever catch you alone, your precious dowry won't protect you then! Ow, stop that, you ill-mannered oaf! You'll break my arm, twisting it like that!"

The front door creaked open, there was a splattering of gravel accompanied by a cry of pain. The door slammed and silence fell.

Smiling, Grace moved once more to the library doors. Then she hesitated. Years of living under her father's strict rules had left her with a terror of disturbing a man in his private domain. Even though she knew that Sir Matthew would always receive her courteously, yet she trembled and hesitated to knock. Almost she had decided to go away again when she heard a thud from inside the room, followed almost immediately by an exclamation of dismay. And the exclaimer was female.

Grace paused, waiting for the low tones of Sir Matthew to respond — perhaps to remonstrate with a housemaid, or might it be Alice? Surely not. She was too neat and delicate to go about dropping heavy objects. Nor was it Lady Graham, for she was still in the drawing room.

Another crash decided her. Whoever was in the library was not reading books. Without knocking, she threw open the door and marched into the room.

From the far corner, Cousin Anne glared at her. All around her feet, papers and ink bottles and pen wipes and sticks of sealing wax were strewn about, together with two upended drawers from Sir Matthew's desk.

"Whatever are you doing?" Grace said, shock making her raise her voice. "Looking for stockings again? Or shall we just call it common thievery?"

"How dare you—" Cousin Anne began, then froze, looking over Grace's shoulder at the door.

"Ah, here you two are." Sir Matthew's voice was perfectly unruffled. "I thought I heard voices."

"Now you are in trouble," Grace hissed. "Explain all this if you can."

12: A Warning

Cousin Anne lifted her chin defiantly. Then, with a quick glance at the disorder at her feet, she said quickly, "Sealing wax. I needed some sealing wax."

"How remiss of Lidwell not to replenish the supplies in the writing desk in your room," Sir Matthew murmured. "Or in the drawing room. Or in either of the saloons. Or in Lady Graham's sitting room. Or in—"

"Naturally one thinks of the library first," Anne said. "But the drawer was stiff."

"That was probably because it was locked." Sir Matthew's tone was as mild as milk.

"Was it? Ah. I shall just take what I need, shall I? Grace, ring the bell for someone to clear up here."

"No need," Sir Matthew said. "I should prefer to set all to rights myself. Housekeepers never quite know how everything should be arranged, I find. Especially in locked drawers."

Her face reddening, Anne grabbed several sticks of wax at random and scuttled out. Sir Matthew held the door open for her, then shut it behind her.

"Obnoxious woman!" he said with some heat.

Grace giggled, but she was still shocked and angry. "How can you talk so calmly to her, when she is stealing from you? I should have been screaming with rage! Indeed, I believe I was."

"It never answers with Anne. No matter what we do — and we have tried every possible recourse, apart from the constables, over the years — she will not stop her tricks. So now, we get through her visits as best we can. But she does not usually stay so long." He frowned, then sighed. "Nor does she normally remove drawers in their entirety. Looking for a secret compartment, I suppose. No, I am very much afraid that she will not leave at all until she finds what she is searching for."

"The diamond necklace, you mean?" Grace pulled a face. "But if she never finds it, she will be here for ever, and how can you bear it?"

"I have absolutely no idea. And now I had better get this mess tidied up before Lady Graham sees it. Thank you for your attempts to remonstrate with Anne, but I would not keep you from the company."

"May I help you? The work would go quicker with two pairs of hands. But if there are private papers here—"

"Oh no, nothing like that. The important papers are… elsewhere. Thank you, your assistance would be appreciated."

Grace happily got down on the floor and began scooping up the fallen items by the handful, and shovelling them back into one of the two drawers.

"At least she did not break the locks," Sir Matthew remarked, as he straightened and sorted and neatened.

That brought Grace rocking back on her heels. "So how did she get these drawers out?"

Sir Matthew reached into the mess and brought out a ring with metal sticks hanging from it. "With this, I imagine. Cousin

Anne possesses lock-picking equipment. Or did. She will be cross when she realises she has lost them."

Grace took them from him, fascinated. "That seems… very professional," she said slowly.

"Indeed it does. I believe we are going to have to bar Cousin Anne from the house. If we can ever get rid of her, that is. There, that looks better." He produced a small key from a waistcoat pocket and locked the drawers again. "Thank you for your help, Grace."

She scrambled to her feet, hearing the all-too-familiar ripping sound. "Oh dear. I am so clumsy. If only I could be more like Alice. *She* never tears her gown."

Sir Matthew smiled. "No, but she never says or does anything beyond the commonplace, either. You have ten times as much spirit as Alice, and you are worth a thousand of Cousin Anne, and never let anyone tell you otherwise."

She was so overcome by the compliment that she could only blush, and scamper out of the room in embarrassment. Only later did she realise that she still had the lock-picking tools in her hand. And she had not yet unburdened herself about Aunt Lucy.

~~~~~

George had been so angry with Grace he could barely see straight, still less think. He had no wish for company, for the very idea of making polite conversation with anyone was quite unthinkable. Knowing the prescribed walk for guests, he strode determinedly in the opposite direction, to the far side of the lake and the small area of woodland just beyond. There, high in an ancient oak tree, was his secret place, a retreat from his younger sisters, a tree house built for him when they had first moved to Graham House.

Larkwood was how the house had been called when his father, new to the baronetcy, had first settled there, but his mother had not liked the name. "It sounds like a peasant's cottage," she had sniffed. "You are a baronet now, Sir Matthew, and your establishment should reflect that in every way possible." His father had acceded to his lady's demands, as he so often did, but George had always liked the name, and when old Bamfield, the estate carpenter, had nailed the final plank of the tree house into place, George had found some paint and daubed the name over the door of his own small domain: *'Larkwood'*. And below it, in smaller letters but quite distinct: *'George's House'* and *'No admittance to girls'*. And in fourteen years, no girl had ever crossed the threshold.

There were steps cut into the trunk of the tree with a rope handrail, in place of a ladder, and George scampered up and threw open the door. There was but one room, with a small stove, a cast-off chaise longue of his mama's, four wooden chairs and a wobbly card table, and a cupboard, where resided the items that told of the uses to which the tree house had been put in recent years — several bottles of brandy, cards and dice, and a box of fish, for George had never quite seen the point of throwing away money when just as much fun could be had with a proxy. Here George had brought his school friends when they visited, and later his Oxford cronies. Another type of man would have brought his women there, and the blankets neatly folded on a shelf suggested just that, but George had never been that way inclined.

He hurled himself onto the chaise longue to brood over the insults he had received. Grace was the most ungrateful girl alive! After all his care for her, and his efforts to protect her from the grasping hands of Wright, to be abused in that way by her was more than a man could stand. In a moment he jumped up again, too agitated to sit, and paced up and down the small room, muttering under his breath and gesturing sharply with one hand and then the other, half-imagining Grace standing before him, head meekly bowed under his disapprobation.

Except that her head would *not* be bowed of course. Was there ever a girl with more courage than Grace? Of course she would have answered every point he made with an argument of her own, and perhaps she would have had the better of him, too. Infuriating girl! And yet... grudgingly he had to admit that he liked her. She was the very opposite of Alice — shy little Alice, terrified of her own shadow, and a perfect mouse in company. Grace was terrified of nothing and no one. Look at the way she had joined in the search for the diamonds, and not even hesitated to put her hand up the chimney. She was as fearless as a boy.

With such thoughts, George gradually began to come down from his great rage and achieve a calmer state. He was still not minded for company, but he had missed breakfast, so took himself to the kitchen door to beg for a slice or two of pork pie, and then to the stables to fuss over his horse until the visitors should have left and it was safe to emerge from hiding.

He found the grooms in high glee, his own groom amongst them.

"Whatever has happened, Loxton? Did you all have a shilling on the winner at Ludlow?"

"More entertaining than that, Mr George. You know that preacher fellow, what's his name now?"

"Wright."

"Aye, him. Sent for his horse, so Grant took him round to the door, all saddled and laden ready to go. There he is, waiting on the drive, when he hears raised voices from inside. Next thing, the door flies open and Bellings tosses that Wright fellow out on his ear. Drags him right down the steps and hurls him onto the drive, and him screeching all the way. *'Ow, ow, ow! You're hurting me! Ow! You'll break my arm!'* he added in a girlish voice. "Near as dammit did, too. And poor Grant! It was all he could do to keep a straight face. *'Are you all right, sir?'* he asks, all concerned, like. Well, I won't tell you what Wright said to *that*. But he was cussing up and down about Miss Allamont, sir, and Bellings told us after that the fellow insulted her good and proper, and she got Bellings to throw him out."

"Did she indeed," George said in delight. "Ha! What a girl, eh! I can imagine she would take no nonsense from a slimy fellow like that."

"Aye, she's got spirit, that one. She'll be a lively wife and a half for some man, one of these days. Give him a royal run-around."

"Better that than too tame," George said at once, rather annoyed by this slur on Grace. "Can you imagine the irritation of a docile wife? *'Yes dear. No dear. Anything you say dear.'* It would drive me positively mad." He had a momentary vision of the timid Miss Dilworthy, and shuddered. "At least Grace would speak up for herself, and not let anyone push her around. That is a *proper* sort of wife for a man. Whoever she marries will be a very lucky fellow."

"Yes, sir," Loxton said, but he gave George an odd look before turning back to the horse he was grooming.

George enjoyed the tale so much that he handed out coins to all the grooms and went back into the house before he remembered that he was still hiding from everyone. But all the talk of Grace had put him in mind of their long-interrupted search. Having ascertained from the footman that Cousin Anne was safely ensconced in the red saloon, he made his way through the back corridors to the winter parlour.

~~~~~

Grace drifted absent-mindedly through the morning. Alice was relieved of her usual round of activities by virtue of having been up so late the night before, which meant that Grace, too, was free of her duties to the girl. Having changed her gown and summoned the maid to mend the torn garment, Grace could think of no other occupation than to find Lady Graham and sit quietly in the company of whichever of the visitors remained. Normally she would have been able to think of a hundred different activities more enjoyable, but the news from Aunt Lucy and her spat with Mr Wright had lowered her spirits dreadfully. She did not think she could settle to read even the most exciting novel, nor had she the patience for acrostics or drawing. So she fetched her tapestry work and made her way to the drawing room.

As she was descending the stairs, Mr Ambleside emerged at speed from the library and strode towards the doors. The footman sprang to open them for him. On the drive, Mr Ambleside's horse waited, still steaming from the ride.

Grace's heart lurched. What could possibly draw him here again so soon, and in such haste that he would not even send his horse to the stables to be tended?

"Mr Ambleside! Whatever is it? Has anything happened?" She jumped the last few stairs, to land almost at his feet.

He started, then laughed. "No, no, nothing in the world to trouble you, Miss Allamont. I beg your pardon if my unexpected return caused you alarm. Be assured that we are all well. I have had news of the highwaymen operating on Brinwater Heath, that is all. You will remember that Mrs Langdon told us that she had been attacked?"

"Yes, but I did not believe it. Do not say it was true!"

"It was. She herself made nothing of it, saying she had not been injured and could well bear the loss of a few coins and some paltry jewellery, as she described it. I supposed she had invented the whole to escape payment for the chaise she hired. But just today a man came from the inn where she had last changed horses, bringing her empty jewellery box, which had been found in a ditch not far from the very place where she had told them the chaise had been attacked. The ostler had had the full story from the driver as he returned that way, and it is all true, every word. Two ruffians, armed with pistols, although they fired no shot, for Mrs Langdon gave them everything they asked for."

"How dreadful! I had heard rumours, especially of late, but one always hopes that the truth is less terrible."

"The ostler told us they know of five confirmed attacks, just in the past month, and all in daylight hours. I am come to urge Sir Matthew to warn Miss Durmaston, for I am aware that her quickest route home crosses the heath. I must go next to Brinford Manor to warn Sir Osborne, for the Manor is very close to the western end of the heath."

"They would not attack the house?" Grace said in horror. "I should not sleep if I thought poor Mary might be at risk."

"No, I think not, but I know she rides that way on occasion, as I do, too, when my horse wants to stretch his legs. There is some excellent riding to be had in the open country there. But she will be safe enough inside the Manor grounds. I must not delay any further. Do add your voice to Sir Matthew's in urging Miss Durmaston to take a different route. I cannot vouch for her safety if she does not."

And with that he was gone, leaving Grace even more heavy-hearted than before.

13: Secret Doors

George crept around the upper gallery, shoes in hand. This was much easier when he was a boy and could crawl along beneath the level of the balustrade, quite invisible, to gaze down upon the saloons below. Now he had to skulk behind pillars to keep himself hidden, and pop his head out from time to time to gaze at the rooms below. The drawing room, sadly, was out of sight, but he had sent Bellings through to scout for him. The poor man had incurred Mama's wrath in so doing, and had resumed his post in the hall with a rueful shake of his head.

"I'd willingly do anything you ask, Master George, but I daren't go against her ladyship's direct order. I'd be out on my ear without a character, and then what would become of me? I've been in this house for more than thirty years, and I don't want to leave it now."

"Indeed, I should not want you to leave, Bellings. You have always been kind to me, and I should hate to be the means of you losing your position. But did you see Grace?"

"Miss Allamont weren't in the drawing room, Master George."

So George had taken to the upper galleries, and still there was no sign of her. He had even gone stealthily to her room and knocked on the door, but there was no answer. Despondent, he gave it up, retreating to the silent upper reaches of the oldest part of the house. Downstairs, the saloons were still busy with callers, and on the bedroom floor, the maids were bustling about with sheets and holland covers, restoring the guest bedrooms to their habitual quietude, but the attics were as empty as always. He strode through the full length of the building, then down two floors by way of the disused spiral staircase and along the service corridor, then up the south stairs, without seeing a soul.

Finally, he gained his objective and flung open the door of the winter parlour. A squeak of surprise from inside caused him to groan loudly.

"Grace, I have been all over the house looking for you! And here you are, skulking in the last place I should have thought to look for you."

She was sitting on the window seat, resting her chin on her knees, her tapestry bag abandoned at her feet. "I am *not* skulking. I was looking for some green thread for my tapestry work, and your mama said there might be some in here. And if you would knock before entering a room, a person would not jump half out of her skin in shock."

"Well, why the devil should I knock, when the room is— Wait… have you been crying?"

She practically growled at him. "Of course I have not! What a *stupid* question!" But she turned her face away from him all the same.

He hesitated, not sure whether to pretend there was nothing wrong, as she seemed to want, or to pursue the matter. She was very pale, and so still, sitting all in a huddle. It was so unlike her, and curiously unsettling. And he had an uneasy feeling he was the cause of it.

"Look, I meant no harm in trying to keep you from Wright, but I should not have lost my temper and said things that… Well, upsetting you was the last thing I wanted, you must believe me."

She stared at him. "What, you think your foolishness upset me? You must have a high opinion of yourself if you think *that*, George Graham. As if I care what you say."

"Oh." That was unexpected. "Then...?"

"I have had a trying day." The anger dropped out of her voice abruptly. "My aunt told me things I could never have imagined, and Cousin Anne broke into your father's locked desk, and all the rumours of highwaymen are true. And as for Mr Wright!"

George could not help smiling. "Ah, I heard all about the way you had Bellings throw him out on his ear. Famous! I wish I had been there to see it. But whatever did he do that set your back up?"

"He was very forward, and called me by my name, as if we were *betrothed* or some such. And he wanted to take me off to the folly, where he would have talked a great deal of nonsense, I make no doubt. But I have learned that he is not who he claims to be at all. Or at least, he is no son of Gravesby Hall, but a child born out of wedlock to one of the family and of no standing in society at all."

"Good God!" George said. "That is appalling! So he has been lying all this time."

She lifted one shoulder. "Well... I suppose he never said *explicitly*. Only that it was his home, which is more or less true. He was certainly raised there from a young age. Oh, but I forgot! I should not have mentioned it to anyone. George, you must say nothing, for it was all told to me in the strictest confidence." She lifted one pale hand to her brow with a sigh. "My head is so full of worries at the moment, I cannot think straight."

"Poor Grace!" he said at once, crossing the room and folding himself down to sit cross-legged at her feet. "Would it help to talk about them? Maybe I can help?" He took one of her hands and squeezed it gently.

"I do not think anyone can help," she said sadly. "Unless you can make Cousin Vivienne better, and drive away the highwaymen so that Mary is safe, and bring Ernest and Frank home, and send Cousin Anne away, and make Mr Wright leave the county and never come back, and... oh, so many things!"

George was not easily deterred, even from difficult situations, but this catalogue of woes left him feeling entirely helpless. "I cannot do any of those things," he said softly. "I wish I could, for I hate to see you unhappy like this."

"I am not really unhappy," she said. "Pray do not think me quite so lily-livered as all that. But so much has happened today that I feel... weighed down with it all. I was going to talk to your father about it, because he is so calm and wise and... and reassuring. But I was distracted. Well, anyone would be, finding Cousin Anne raiding the desk in the library."

"Was she really?" he said indignantly. "That woman gets everywhere. What was she doing?"

He heard the full magnitude of Cousin Anne's calumny, and Grace then told him all about her aunt and the highwaymen and Mr Wright, and a great deal more besides, the words pouring out unstoppably. He listened and made what he hoped were reassuring noises, and was thankful that she said nothing at all about his own behaviour in the shrubbery that morning, for he was beginning to feel quite guilty about the way he had stormed away in a temper and left her prey to that dreadful man.

"No wonder you are upset!" he said. "Anyone would be. I must say, Cousin Anne is beyond anything! The sooner she leaves, the better for all of us. And your aunt sounds like a rum sort of a person. But I do not understand about Ernest and Frank. Does she know where they are or not?"

"She does not, and it is the most frustrating thing in the world! If only we could find them, this horrid threat of losing the Hall would disappear. I should not mind if it were to go to a relation, you know, for that would only be fair — Cousin Henry, for instance. Or even one of the boys. Hugo would love to have it, I know. But to leave it to the church! What was Papa thinking?"

George was about to let her have the benefit of his considered opinion of the late Mr William Allamont before it occurred to him that perhaps Grace might not quite like to hear her father denigrated so forcefully. So he contented himself with saying only, "It is an odd arrangement, no doubt about it. But if your aunt has seen the boys recently—"

"Not recently. Did I not explain that? They went to her when they first ran away, and stayed with her for two years or so, but then there was a quarrel — she was vague about the details — and they ran away again. Or perhaps Ernest ran away, and Frank went to some other relative." She frowned. "Hmm, I am not at all sure now." But then she laughed. "I am not surprised you are confused, for I do not at all understand it myself."

Watching her expressive face switch from sadness to anger to bewilderment to amusement, all in the space of a few minutes, he was struck by the contrast with Miss Dilworthy, whose expressions had ranged from blank to even more blank.

"Oh Grace, life is never dull with you around!" George said impulsively. "But you do have some strange relatives."

"So do you," she retorted. "Cousin Anne is at least as strange as Aunt Lucy."

He laughed out loud at that. "I cannot deny it!"

"Stranger, I think," she went on. "At least Aunt Lucy does not go round people's houses breaking into locked drawers in search of a diamond necklace that is not even hers."

He jumped to his feet in glee. "Oh, but I had quite forgotten until you put me in mind of it just now. Guess what I have found?"

Her face lit up, eyes and mouth opening in surprise. "Not the necklace?"

"Ah — no, not the necklace." Her face fell. "But something almost as good. Remember what room this is?"

"The winter parlour... Oh, you have found the secret passage!" She clapped her hands in excitement, all her megrims cast aside.

"I have. It should have been easy to find, because I knew from the plans exactly where it must be, but it was very cleverly hidden. It is so ingenious. Come and see." He took her hand and led her across the room, past the shrouded sofas and tables in their holland covers, to a section of wall just to the left of the fireplace. "There! Can you see it?"

Her eyes roved over the panel he pointed to and then to its neighbours. She shook her head. "I cannot see a gap at all. Is there really a door there?"

He laughed in delight. "There is! But so ingenious, no one would ever spot it. Wait, let me lock the door first. We do not want to be interrupted." He bounded across the room, then stopped abruptly. "Oh, but that will not work. Cousin Anne can open locked doors."

"Not any more," Grace said gleefully, producing a handful of jingling metal from her tapestry bag. "She dropped these when I startled her."

"Ha! You are up to every rig, Grace! Was there ever a girl like you?"

It amused him to see her blush at the compliment. He turned the key in the lock, although surely there was little chance of anyone wandering into the room. Still, Cousin Anne was always on the prowl, and one could not be too careful where she was concerned.

"Now watch," he said, rushing back to her side.

The wall panels were decorated with ornate vines, heavy with bunches of grapes. Taking firm hold of one of the bunches, George pulled as hard as he could. After the slightest resistance, the door came free and slowly opened with a long, low creak of hinges not oiled for many years.

Unlike the previous passage they had discovered, this was no dark, noisome hole. They stepped through into an unfurnished square room with tiled floor and several mullioned windows, thick with dirt but providing enough light to illuminate the thickly hanging spiders' webs festooning the ceiling, and a good inch of dust on the floor. The walls were decorated with raised plasterwork nymphs. To one side, a staircase rose to the upper floor.

"What is this place?" Grace breathed, her eyes round. "Oh, I know, it is one of the tower things on the sides of the house."

"It is. On the floor below us is the gun room and the door nearest to the stables and the woods. I suppose there must have been stairs connecting to this floor at one time, but it must have been before Papa bought the place. There are six towers altogether, but most of them are used to extend whatever room they attach to. The one nearest to the ballroom is the only other one to have stairs in it."

"Shall we explore?" Grace said, eyes shining. "What is on the floor above us?"

"Let me see, it must be somewhere near Mama's and Papa's bedroom."

"They share a bedroom?" Grace said in surprised tones. "How odd!"

George had never thought there was anything odd about it before, but now that the idea was in his head he could not disagree. "It is a bit peculiar, I suppose," he said. "But Papa has a bed in his dressing room too."

"Oh, that is all right then," Grace said.

"I am sure you told me that you share a bedroom with Hope," George said.

"That is completely different. Why would anyone want to sleep next to a *man* all night?"

George could think of some very good reasons, but he had no intention of getting into a discussion of them with a young lady, even one so easy-going as Grace. "Shall we try the stairs?" he said hastily.

"Race you!"

She whirled in a flurry of skirts, and grabbing the front of her gown in both hands took the stairs two at a time. Laughing, he chased after her, arriving on the upper landing at almost the same moment.

"I won!" she said, and, looking at her glowing face, eyes sparkling with mischief, he had no heart to disagree with her. For a moment, he was mesmerised, unable to look away. Then she spun away from him and the moment was lost, leaving him bemused by his own response. Grace was like a sister to him, he told himself, trying to catch his breath.

"Look, there are *two* doors here," she said.

Slowly, and with some reluctance, he turned his mind back to the task before them. There were no more stairs here, but there were indeed two doors visible, distinguishable by the fine cracks surrounding them in the plasterwork of the wall. The first door he tried, however, dented his confidence. No amount of pulling on the nymph in the centre of it, or heaving or leaning against the door could shift it.

"I daresay it has been painted over or sealed shut on the other side," George said.

"Or locked. Try the other," Grace said, giving him a little shove in the small of his back.

This time, pushing caused the door to swing open instantly on silent hinges. Beyond was darkness, with an overpowering smell of camphor, combined with something flowery. Lavender, possibly.

Grace wrinkled her nose. "The furs closet," she said.

As his eyes adjusted to the gloom, George could see that she was right. Fur capes and tippets and muffs dangled from pegs in the wall or sat on shelves. On the far side stood another pair of doors, with a wide gap between them admitting light. Beyond the doors could be heard the sounds of movement, and drawers opening and closing.

George was torn. At any moment, the occupant of the room could throw open the cupboard doors and discover the two of them. But before he could suggest a withdrawal, Grace had crept through the hanging furs, setting them gently swaying, to put her eye to the crack between the doors. Moments later she was back.

"Cousin Anne," she mouthed at George.

"We should go."

She nodded, but almost immediately a loud shriek pierced the air. George froze.

"What are you—?" a voice wailed. Then, more calmly, "Oh! Miss Durmaston. I beg your pardon, *madame*, I was not expecting anyone to be here. May I to assist you in any way?"

The French accent gave away the identity of the newcomer — Lady Graham's lady's maid.

Then heavy footsteps and a male voice. "What is it, Heloise? Ah, Anne. Lost again? Your room is in the other wing, you know." Sir Matthew's calm tones, followed by the sound of a door opening and closing. "Has she taken anything, do you think?"

"I do not know, *monsieur*. Milady's good jewels are safe enough, but sometimes there are brooches or ear drops left out, if milady changes her mind after I leave her."

The door sounded again.

"Ah, there you are, my dear. Anne has been—"

Lady Graham's outraged tones cut across his words. "I passed her on the stairs. Great God above, will she not leave us alone? Heloise, will you follow her and make sure she does not go off into any other bedrooms? Matt, this is too much! I will *not* have her in the house any longer. You will have to get rid of her somehow. I care not how you do it, but get her out of here!"

"I will see to it. Hush now, you must not cry over her. Even if she takes a brooch or two, we can bear the loss."

"As to that, I care nothing for such things. It is the sneaking about, and never knowing where she might appear next, or what secret places she might get into. I cannot bear the uncertainty, Matt. My nerves are all to pieces. Shall you really get rid of her? You will have to carry her out bodily, I fear."

A low rumble of laughter. "Perhaps that will not be necessary, if I can find a means to make her go away of her own volition. Hush now, my little rabbit, hush. There, there."

George could hardly stop himself laughing. *"My little rabbit?"* he mouthed to Grace, and saw her struggling with her own fit of giggles, her hands over her mouth as if to stop the merriment from bursting out.

As quietly as mice, they crept back from the furs and onto the landing, pulling the door silently shut behind them. Then they both collapsed into giggles.

"Quick! Race you down!" Grace hissed, and instantly was off.

George leapt down the stairs three at a time, but even so he barely came alongside before they reached the bottom. On the very last stair, she stumbled, grabbed at him and they both went tumbling to the floor. He fell half on top of her, and for a moment they lay there, laughing too hard even to move.

Something shifted in George's mind as he looked at her, face alight with mirth, her eyes shining, her lips... her lips...

"Oh, Grace, you are so much *fun*!" he said.

Then bent his head and kissed those entrancing lips.

14: A Family Dinner

Grace froze as soon as his mouth moved onto hers. She had never been kissed before, and the idea rather revolted her, although a lot of people seemed to like it. She had once come upon Connie and the Marquess shortly before their wedding, sitting very close on a chaise longue, arms around each other's waists, faces pressed together, so absorbed that they were quite unaware of their interested audience. They had seemed to enjoy their kisses very much. But perhaps one had to be in love for that to work, for Grace was not at all sure that she liked George Graham pressing down on her with warm, firm lips. Yet somehow there was an intimacy to it that thrilled her, and after the first shock she felt a ripple of pleasure in the experience. She was rather sorry when he stopped.

It would never do to admit to such a thing, however, so as soon as he pulled away, she thumped him on the shoulder. "What did you do that for? Get off me!"

"I thought you might like it," he said in hurt tones, rolling away from her. "*I* liked it, anyway. You are not going to get all hoity-toity with me, are you, Grace? It was just a bit of fun."

"It was not at all fun," she said, scrambling to her feet. "Goodness, look at the state of this gown! Annie will be so cross with me again."

"Your maid? It is hardly her place to be cross with you," he said, jumping up and brushing himself down.

"Oh, it is just a game we play. She pretends to be cross, and I tell her she is lucky to have work to keep her busy. Just teasing."

"Even so, that is very familiar for a servant."

Grace huffed a breath. "I suppose you are right. I wish…"

"What do you wish?" he said more gently.

"Oh, only that my sisters had not all gone off and got married. We were all so close, once, but now… four of them are scattered to the winds, and Hope can be so dismal sometimes, and Lavinia is not really a friend, even though I pretend she is sometimes. Oh Lord, is that the dressing bell? We shall have to run."

~~~~~

After the multitude of unsettling events that day, Grace was thankful that the house had emptied, and she did not have to face an evening of crowded, noisy rooms and insipid conversation with people she did not especially like. A ball, with a partner for every dance, was her preferred mode of entertainment, and although there was generally some impromptu dancing at Lady Graham's card parties, last night Grace had been chained to the card table.

The drawing room felt almost empty when she entered it. Apart from Sir Matthew and Lady Graham, George and Alice, fourteen-year-old Joan was also present. Mr Bertram Graham was staying on for a week or more; he was chatting quietly to Miss Bellows beside the fire. On the other side of the fire sat an elderly aunt of Sir Matthew's, who would have departed that morning, had her maid not twisted her ankle on the back stairs.

And of course Cousin Anne was there. There was no escaping *her*. She waved imperiously to Grace, and patted the seat beside her with a bland smile. Grace cast about desperately for a plausible reason to avoid the woman, but could think of nothing. Usually she could depend upon Lady Graham to require her attendance, but that lady was fully occupied in berating her daughters for some misdemeanour or other, and failed to notice Grace.

There was no avoiding it. Trying to smile, she had not taken two steps before George was before her. He bowed to her formally, which took her aback rather, then said, "Will you take my arm, Miss Allamont? I have something to show you over here."

Automatically she curtsied and rested her gloved hand on his arm. He led her straight past Cousin Anne — Grace dared not look at her face as they sailed by — and to a group of chairs at the far side of the room.

"Here, pretend to look at this," he said, thrusting a journal into her hand as soon as she had sat down.

"What? Oh, a ruse! What fun."

"But you must look at it, you know, because she is watching, and I do not want her following us over here."

Obediently Grace lowered her head and flipped through the pages, as George seated himself beside her. "I cannot tell you how sorry I am that I took advantage of you this afternoon," he said in a low voice. "You are so good-humoured that I was misled into thinking that you would take it as lightly as I did. I meant it only as a... a kind of joke between good friends. I see now that was quite wrong of me. I hope you will forgive me, for I should hate to lose your good opinion."

"What makes you believe my opinion of you is good?" she said mischievously, but when she looked up into his face and saw the contrition there, she was immediately sorry. "Oh, George, it is of no consequence. I am not offended."

His face lightened perceptibly, but not entirely. "You are too good. Truly, Grace, I have behaved abominably towards you, and I am quite cast down about it. I should not blame you if you never want to set eyes on me again, and that is exactly what I deserve."

"Nonsense," she said, but his intensity worried her. "You refine too much upon it. We are still friends, are we not?"

"Are we?"

"Of course we are. For my part, I hope that will never change."

He smiled then, and looked more his usual self. The butler came in at that moment to announce dinner, and as she rose, Grace noticed Sir Matthew's eyes on her. She wondered if something was amiss with her hair or her gown — there was usually some aspect of her attire that was not as it should be, but she had examined herself in the long mirror before she came down and had noticed nothing untoward. She dismissed it from her mind.

~~~~~

With only ten around the table, it was possible to hold conversations with almost anybody, or to listen to what others were discussing. Although Grace paid some attention to her immediate dinner companions — George, subdued and solicitous on her left, and Alice, making an effort to be ladylike on her right — she could also amuse herself by attending to the deep discussion of warblers and finches between Mr Bertram Graham and Miss Bellows, and Lady Graham's constant stream of instruction to Joan on the proper manner of eating, drinking and conversing with other dinner guests.

Grace noticed that Cousin Anne was watching her, and guessed that she would be obliged to sit with her after dinner, unless Sir Matthew rescued her by inviting her to the whist table again. She could not determine which fate was less enticing to her. She enjoyed whist, up to a point, but Sir Matthew was such a keen player, that his enthusiasm generally continued at a high level long after Grace's had waned and she longed to stretch her legs. Cousin Anne was not a pleasant companion, for she only talked to one when she wanted something, but Grace was rather curious as to what it might be in this instance.

She was mulling over the possibilities while helping Alice to some of the braised tongue when Sir Matthew said, "George, how are you getting along with your scheme to discover the Durmaston Diamonds somewhere about the house? Have you found your way into all the secret passages yet?"

Grace froze. She dared not look at Cousin Anne, but surely she was listening intently? George set his knife down carefully, but made no immediate answer. Grace dared not look at him, either, nor could she imagine what Sir Matthew was about, to discuss the matter so openly, and in front of Cousin Anne, too, whose visit was largely made in pursuit of the diamonds.

Sir Matthew did not wait for a response. He turned to Cousin Anne and said, in his most casual tones, "George has formed the notion that the necklace was left behind here, and may yet be found if only he looks hard enough into all the dark corners of the house. For myself, I suspect he is wasting his time. What do you think, Anne?"

"I hardly know what to think," she said gamely. "Is it likely that the necklace has been here all along?"

"Well, George believes it has, and who can disprove the idea? But since he has not yet returned from his searches triumphantly waving the necklace aloft, we must assume that he has not yet been successful. Is it not so, George?"

"It is, sir. Not a sign of a diamond anywhere."

"The house is very large," murmured Cousin Anne. "If it were well concealed—"

A clever answer, deftly turning the question back onto Sir Matthew.

"True, but Grandmother was a very old lady, and her maid even more so. There are limits to the number of locations where she might have concealed such an item, and George has already searched them all. She kept very much to her rooms, latterly, and even took her meals there. George has examined those rooms, and also the concealed stair from there, the stables, the drawing room — he has been very thorough. I have myself searched the library."

Grace began to get a glimmering of Sir Matthew's plan — if he could convince Cousin Anne that every likely hiding place had already been searched, she would give up and return home, to everyone's relief.

"The attics!" Grace cried. "George has searched the attics, too."

Sir Matthew's eyes twinkled. "Thank you, Miss Allamont. So you see, it is difficult to think of anywhere else to look."

No one mentioned the winter parlour, but nothing had been found there, so it hardly mattered.

"She was in no other room?" Cousin Anne said. "Not the dining room, or any of the saloons?"

Sir Matthew shook his head. "Not since the last time the necklace was seen here. Lady Graham made a note of the event in her diary, for it was such a rare occurrence."

"Oh, but there was that time..." Lady Graham began. "You must remember it, Sir Matthew. There was something amiss with the chimneys and no one could get the fires to draw properly in Grandmother's rooms. She moved into the Peacock Room for a week or so, until the sweep could be got."

There was a long silence. Grace's stomach turned over — another possible place to look, and now Cousin Anne knew of it too!

"Your memory is excellent, Lady Graham. There you are, George, now you have somewhere else to search tomorrow. Is there any more of the veal?"

The rest of the meal passed by in a haze. Grace could hardly sit still, and certainly could not attend to anything else that was said, for the desire to leap up and search the Peacock Room *at once* was so compelling she could barely breathe. Beside her, George fidgeted and shuffled about, too, and no doubt for the same reason. When Lady Graham rose from her chair to lead the ladies back to the drawing room, Grace jumped up at once. Then there was a restless half hour to be got through somehow, watching Cousin Anne with raptor-like intensity, before George reappeared and they could creep away to begin their new investigation. Never had gentlemen sat so long over their port!

But at length the three emerged, Sir Matthew to one side of George and Mr Bertram to the other. The two brothers made an interesting contrast, Sir Matthew tall and elegant, always so beautifully dressed and yet without ostentation, as befitted his rank, and Mr Bertram short and round, plainly attired, as befitted his station as a clergyman.

And George — when had George turned from the unkempt child or the wild young man into this immaculate gentleman? So much of his father in him that she had never noticed before, yet now she saw George for the first time as the baronet he was destined to be, in time. He was looking at his father, eye to eye, since the two were much of a height, and laughing at some joke, when his gaze scanned the room and fell on her. At once his expression changed, softening to something that, for some unfathomable reason, made her heart jump. Then she chided herself for her foolishness. Just because he had kissed her did not mean he cared for her in *that* way at all. That was just fun, had he not said so himself? Any affection he felt for her was no more than that of a friend. Or a brother, perhaps.

He came straight to her, whispering, "As soon as they settle to their cards, we will slip out."

But it was not to be. "Miss Allamont, may I call upon your services as whist partner again?"

"I, Sir Matthew? Surely you have had enough of my ineptitude? May I not tempt you to a superior partner? Miss Durmaston, I am sure, would be happy to oblige you."

"I must beg to be excused," Cousin Anne said promptly. "My head aches so much that I shall retire at once, if my dear Aunt will excuse me."

Lady Graham could not well object, and to Grace's intense annoyance, Cousin Anne left the room with alacrity. If only she were willing to lie with such ease herself, how many unpleasant duties could be avoided. But Grace was too honest to resort to falsehood.

"You are too modest, Miss Allamont," Sir Matthew said. "Come, we must be avenged for our defeat last night. Bertram and Miss Bellows must not be allowed to triumph again. And George, will you be so good as to play with your sisters and Lady Graham? Alice needs a great deal of practice before she can play comfortably in company."

"Alice will be dancing when she is out, not playing cards," Joan objected.

"It is a skill she needs to learn, nevertheless," Lady Graham said in a tone that brooked no argument.

Thus defeated, Grace and George took their places. Grace tried to concentrate, but her mind was all on the Peacock Room, wherever that might be. She envisioned Cousin Anne already there, opening drawers, lifting rugs, peering behind paintings, quite unhindered, and it distracted her so much that she could barely focus on the cards.

"I beg your pardon, Sir Matthew," she said eventually. "I am being particularly stupid tonight. I do not usually muddle the trumps like that."

"It is of no consequence, Miss Allamont," he said cheerfully. "Another rubber, everyone?"

By the time they all finally rose from the table, it was well after midnight and Grace was too tired to think of anything beyond her bed. She could tell from George's gloomy face that he, too, had given up all hope of a discovery in the Peacock Room. If anything had been concealed there, it must now surely be in Cousin Anne's hands.

"Be up early tomorrow," he whispered as they parted on the landing. "We must try, at least."

Grace nodded, but she felt sure it was too late. When she descended the stairs the next morning, all her worst fears were confirmed by the sight of Cousin Anne's boxes piled in the hall.

George was moodily kicking one or two of them. "Well, it is all over," he said.

"She is leaving today?" Grace said.

"Right now, this very hour. As soon as the horses can be hitched to her coach. She must have found the diamonds and now she is running off with them, and there is nothing at all we can do about it."

"Oh, do not be so lily-livered," Grace said. "Those diamonds belong to your mother, and we are going to make sure that she gets them. We are not going to let Cousin Anne get away with this! "

15: Departures

There was no time to consider a plan, for almost immediately Cousin Anne's coach was at the front door, the boxes were being loaded aboard and the lady herself appeared, clad in her travelling attire, with her maid scuttling in her wake carrying her mistress's jewel case.

Grace eyed the case sorrowfully, wondering if the Durmaston Diamonds were, even at that moment, resting inside it. Even if she had not had the thought, Cousin Anne's triumphant expression gave all away.

"Well, you two are up early. How kind in you to rise at this hour just to see me on my way. For I daresay everyone else is still abed."

"We thought we would make a start on the Peacock Room before breakfast," Grace said at once, curious to know how she would respond to a direct reference. "Although I daresay there is nothing at all to be found there."

Cousin Anne's smile widened. "I am sure you are right. After all, your searches have not been successful so far, have they? Ah, I see that all is ready for me. Goodbye, Grace. Goodbye, George. Pray give my regards to your mama and papa. I have left a little note for them in my room, but I am sure that they have long been wishing me elsewhere."

George said nothing, and stood chewing his lip, with his arms folded. The self-assured future baronet was gone, and in his place stood the scowling youth Grace remembered so well. Cousin Anne hesitated a moment, as if waiting for him to speak, but his sullen silence was impenetrable, and Grace did not feel it was her place, as a mere visitor herself, to make the usual solicitous farewells to the departing guest. So, without the smile dropping even for a moment, Cousin Anne proceeded through the front doors, down the steps and into her waiting travelling coach, her maid following two paces behind. The door was closed, the butler signalled to the coachman and the equipage lumbered into motion.

Only when the butler and footmen had closed the front door and withdrawn did George heave a great sigh. "If only we could have stopped her somehow."

"How could we have done that?" Grace said, laughing. "What should we say? *'Excuse me, Cousin Anne, but we believe you have stolen a valuable item of jewellery. We shall now search all your property and your person.'* Really, George, you could not do it, not under your father's roof. No, you must go after her."

His face broke into a huge grin. "Do you think—? Truly? I shall order my horse brought round at once."

"No, no, no! You do not want anyone to know what you are about, for just think of the surprise when we return! We must go directly to the stables and talk only to your own groom. What is his name?"

"Loxton."

"Tell only Loxton what you plan to do. Oh, how I wish I could ride, so that I might come with you!"

"You could, if we go in my curricle. We could take Loxton, then, so that it would be quite unexceptional, you know."

For a moment Grace could hardly breathe for delight. "May I? Oh, may I indeed come with you? For I should enjoy it of all things!"

"Then that is settled."

They raced round to the stables, almost deserted after the unexpected bustle of Cousin Anne's coach being summoned before breakfast. Loxton was dragged away from his morning ale and buttered bread with the other outdoor servants.

"Do you not get fed in the servants' hall?" George said indignantly.

"Aye, but two breakfasts is better than one," Loxton said with a grin. "I'll have Black Duke saddled in a flash, sir."

"No, we need the curricle, Loxton."

His eyebrows rose. "At this hour?" His gaze flicked to Grace and back again. "Very good, sir."

"Now, I want none of that tone of voice," George said. "I know my father trained you to try to keep me out of trouble, and although you have not always been successful, no one could fault your persistence. However, I am no longer a child, Loxton."

"No, sir. Even so, sir, I'd advise you to rethink this little caper."

"Your advice is duly noted," George said. "You can come with us, Loxton, so it will be all right and tight. But you must get a move on, my good fellow, for we are going after Miss Durmaston, and every moment we delay will put her further away."

Loxton grinned. "Ah, no need to worry about that, sir. Miss Durmaston won't pay to change horses. She'll be going so slow, you'll catch her in no time with those sweet steppers of yours. Cartwright — her coachman, that is — he says he has orders never to drive above a walking pace to spare the horses. You two go and get changed, and I'll have all ready for you when you get back here."

Grace ran up to her room, taking the stairs two at a time. She had quite forgotten that Miss Bellows would still be abed, for she had continued to share Grace's room even after the party guests had left.

Miss Bellows was already up, sitting in a window seat reading a letter, and laughing gently to herself.

"Oh, Lavinia!" Grace stopped, nonplussed.

Seeing her thus unobserved momentarily, Grace was struck by how much younger she looked. Miss Bellows had always seemed to be a woman of middle years, but she could not be more than forty, at most. The same age as Cousin Vivienne, so sick from the coming baby. Grace shivered. At least Miss Bellows had been spared that.

Miss Bellows looked up, her countenance assuming its familiar patterns. "Grace? You are up bright and early today. It is such a delightful morning today, that I thought I might go for a walk in the woods. To observe the birds and... and other creatures. Are you going for a walk too?" she added, seeing Grace dragging a walking dress from the wardrobe.

"What? Oh, no. Drive. George is taking me out in his curricle."

"Oh. Then the blue, I think, with the matching pelisse and bonnet."

"Goodness, that would be far too smart for Brinshire's muddy lanes. The green, I think, and this cloak. Where is the cap that goes with it? Ah, here it is. Will you give me a hand, Lavinia? I have no time to wait for Annie to be fetched from the bowels of the house."

"What is the great hurry?" Miss Bellows asked as she began unfastening Grace's gown.

Grace paused. Part of her wanted to maintain absolute secrecy over the plan, not because she thought there was anything amiss with it, but so that she and George could astonish everyone in the most satisfactory way when they returned waving the necklace aloft. But she was too honest to resort to deception.

"You must not tell a soul, Lavinia, but we are going to chase after Miss Durmaston, for she has the diamonds and we are going to force her to hand them back."

"Hmm? Well, just as long as you are not eloping to Scotland."

"Not in a curricle, Lavinia dear."

"As you say. There! Have an enjoyable time, Grace."

~~~~~

George was a splendid driver, Grace decided. The horses were frisky, but he kept them well in hand and she had not a moment's alarm. To the contrary, it was thrilling to be rattling along at such a rapid pace, brushing the leaves of the hedgerows on one side, and racing past a farm wagon with an inch to spare without so much as slowing down. She threw sideways glances at George, admiring the concentration on his face and the competent way he handled reins and whip.

They asked after the coach at the lodge and again in the village, which rather destroyed the delicious secrecy of the mission but was essential to be sure they were following correctly. Loxton's prediction was correct for as they bowled down the hill from Higher Brinford, there before them on the next rise was the unmistakable shape of Cousin Anne's travelling coach ponderously climbing the hill.

"There she is!" George cried gleefully. "Lord, how slow that coach is. So what do we do next, Grace? Force her off the road, or wait for her to stop at an inn? And what shall we say? She will likely just laugh in our faces, you know."

This aspect of the plan was beginning to gnaw at Grace, too. They could stop the coach easily enough, but no matter what they said or did, Cousin Anne would not allow them to search her boxes and they had no way to compel her. It had seemed easy enough when she stood in the stables at Graham House, but now her heart misgave her.

"Grace?" George said. "What shall we do?"

"You had better stop," she said in a small voice. "This will not work."

For a minute or two, George was fully occupied with the horses, but once he had brought the curricle to a halt at the side of the road, he turned to face her, his expression sympathetic.

"Thought not," he said sadly. "If only I had the courage to wave my pistols at her. She would be too terrified to do anything but hand over the necklace."

"You have your pistols with you?"

"Of course. One cannot be too careful with all these stories of highwaymen."

"Oh! Wait — what road is this? It must be the Brinwater Heath road, for that is Brinford Manor over there, is it not?" The house was tucked away behind high walls and woods, but the road was high enough at that point to reveal the roofs and smoking chimneys glowing in the early morning sunlight.

"It is. Grace, what devious plan is brewing in your mind?"

She giggled, hand over mouth. "Oh, the most famous scheme! We shall need a few things — have you a cloak about you? And... and masks, or something of the sort? To cover our faces, you know."

"To cover our—?"

"Oh, but... we shall need to get past the coach without being seen, so that we can get ahead of her, you see."

George chuckled. "Get ahead—? Masks? Grace! You are the wickedest girl alive, I swear it! Are you in earnest?"

"Perfectly. And it will give Cousin Anne such a fright, that is the best of it. Serve her right!"

The chuckles turned to a deep, rumbling laugh, and that set Grace off too, and they sat side by side, the curricle rocking as they laughed till tears ran down their faces.

"'Scuse me, sir, but I don't think this is a good idea," Loxton said from behind them. "I'm sure Sir Matthew would agree, if he were here now."

"Advice duly noted," George said between bursts of merriment. "How fortunate, then, that my father is *not* here at present. This is what we must do. We will turn off at the bottom of this hill into Lismoor Woods and stop at the village there for everything we need. That road loops back to this one at Dalbury Cross, and, if we are quick enough, we shall be onto the moors ahead of Cousin Anne."

"And then, sir?" said Loxton, in his most lugubrious tone.

"And then, Loxton, we will become highwaymen and hold up Cousin Anne's coach."

16: Brinwater Heath

Lismoor Bottom was a nondescript sort of village which at this hour of the day would habitually be half deserted, the men out in the fields and the women occupied with household duties, the streets given over to children, chickens and a few gaunt curs. Today, however, it was all abustle, the streets crowded with small carts and pens full of bleating sheep.

"Market day," George said gloomily.

"So much the better," Grace said stoutly. "Everyone is busy with their own affairs, so they will not remember passing strangers. Well, *I* have certainly never been here before."

"Nor I," George said. "Look, there is an inn over there which does not look too seedy. It has been painted this century, at least."

George drove past it and pulled up a hundred yards further on, hidden from view by some overgrown bushes.

"Loxton, you must go in and bespeak a couple of cloaks, and some scarves."

The groom rolled his eyes and sighed dramatically, but obediently he got down. "Two cloaks and two scarves," he muttered resignedly. "So I am to become a highwayman, too, am I? Thank God my poor mother's in her grave, and won't have to see me hanged."

"Oh no, we cannot expect Loxton to do it," Grace said. "That would hardly be right, not for a servant."

"It isn't right for anybody to do it, miss, and that's a fact," Loxton said.

"But she is a *thief!*" Grace said passionately. "We are only taking back what is ours. Or Lady Graham's, to be precise. But you must not be part of this, Loxton."

"I am not sure I want to do this alone," George said, chewing his lip. "Anne has a coachman and a groom, as well as that fusty-faced maid of hers, and any one of them might be armed."

"The coachman keeps a pistol under his seat," Loxton said, "but he won't be able to get it out in time. He'll be busy with the horses."

"Loxton, you are a wonderful help," Grace said. "So long as we are decisive, and wave your pistols around as if we mean it, Cousin Anne will be so terrified that she will do exactly as you say, never fear."

"We?" George said faintly.

"Of course, *we!*" she said impatiently. "If it is wrong to expect Loxton to be part of our little adventure, it is equally wrong of me to expect you to undertake it entirely alone. I shall be a highwayman too."

"You will *not!*" George said. "I shall not allow it. Besides, you can hardly look the part in skirts, you know."

"Who are you to forbid me?" she said hotly. "But you are right about the skirts. Loxton, you must obtain some breeches for me."

"Breeches," Loxton said, in resigned tones. "Anything else, miss?"

"Some food, for we never thought to bring anything with us, and who knows how long we shall have to wait."

Loxton sighed again, but without further argument, he set off back to the inn to obtain what was needed.

"Grace, you are the most astonishing girl!" George said, a broad grin wreathing his face. "This is the most famous sport, and if it comes off, you will be the toast of the county."

"I shall settle for being the toast of Graham House," she said, smiling back at him.

~~~~~

Grace could not remember when she had been so excited. Her very first assembly, perhaps. Or Connie's wedding, awash with Lord This or the Countess of That, not to mention a bishop or two, minor royalty and even a duke. Or — a secret thought, that she could never admit to — when Papa had died so suddenly, freeing the sisters from his repressive scrutiny, and it had seemed that the world would open up for them like a rose blooming. That had not quite happened as she had hoped. For a while it had been fun, but Mama was repressive, too, in her way, refusing to let any of them have a season in London, even at no expense or effort to herself. One by one her older sisters had married, and either moved far away or else had little time for their unmarried sisters any more. Their husbands and babies seemed to absorb their every thought. Then Grace thought of Cousin Vivienne, and shivered. Yet her sisters seemed happy enough with their lot, and even Cousin Mary had preferred Sir Osborne Hardy to spinsterhood. There was no accounting for it.

The curricle bounced over the uneven road through the woods.

"You'd better slow down, sir, or we'll be breaking something," Loxton said, shouting to make himself heard above the rattling.

George shook his head grimly, and urged the horses on. "Have to get back to the high road before Cousin Anne, otherwise all is lost. We can take it more slowly over the moors."

The horses were sweating by the time they reached Dalbury Cross, a bustling village with two inns and a number of shops and taverns, as well as a blacksmith, for this was the last safe harbour of civilisation before the ocean of Brinwater Heath. Here many coaches stopped to change horses or rest before heading out into open country.

In the very centre of the village, at the hub of the several roads that met at that point, a stone cross stood on a wide plinth, and here gathered all the old men of the village, too infirm to help in the fields yet too restless to sit by the fire all day. Loxton was dispatched to make enquiries, and discovered that no coach answering to the description of Cousin Anne's had been seen that day.

"Excellent!" George said, setting the horses in motion with a deft touch of the whip. "We are in time."

"Will you stop at the King's Arms or the Drovers' Inn?" Loxton said as they slowed to negotiate a farmer's wagon.

"Neither," George said, intent on his manoeuvre.

"We should rest the horses, sir," Loxton said. "I'm sure you could do with some coffee, too, since you missed breakfast."

Grace heartily agreed with that idea, and looked hopefully at George.

"Dare not stop here," George muttered. "I am known at the King's Arms, and although I have never used the Drovers, it is directly opposite the King's. Too many people might recognise me or the horses. Not that I come out this way often, but still, we cannot take the risk. We do not want them to remember us... later."

Grace could understand his concern, although she thought it misplaced. If they managed to play their highwayman trick on

Cousin Anne, she would no doubt screech about it all the way home, but she would not be passing through Dalbury Cross again, and even if she did, who would associate the respectable Mr George Graham, son of Sir Matthew Graham, with highwaymen?

But she said nothing, allowing George to concentrate on managing his horses, and they were soon leaving the village behind and heading into open country, the trees and hedges and neatly ploughed fields giving way to heather and gorse and dark, peaty pools. Birds twittered up in alarm as they passed by, and away in the distance, hares frolicked in the sunshine. It was very pleasant, but even though the day was benign, there were so few trees to shelter them from the cool breeze that Grace was glad of her thick cloak.

As soon as they were well clear of the village, George and Loxton got down to lead the horses, and after that they proceeded at walking pace. Once or twice a coach horn sounded behind them and came bowling past, its team of horses straining to maintain the tremendous pace. A few vehicles passed in the opposite direction. But of Cousin Anne's travelling coach there was no sign.

At length they came to a reed-fringed lake, where George pulled aside and stopped. "We will rest the horses for a while, and have something to eat," he said, hopping back into the curricle to sit beside Grace. "There is a clear view back down the road from here, so we will see at once if Anne's carriage comes into view."

But even though they sat for a long time, Cousin Anne did not appear.

~~~~~

"That copse up ahead," Grace said. "That is the perfect place. Loxton can hide with the curricle out of sight in the trees and we can lurk behind the gorse near the road until Cousin Anne comes along."

"If she does," George muttered.

"Of course she will," Grace said bracingly. "Where else can she go, after all? She will hardly go back to Graham House, and even though Sir Matthew warned her about the dangers of this road, she seemed determined to take it. She was heading directly towards the heath, after all."

"She could have taken the southern road from Dalbury Cross to miss the moor," said the ever-helpful Loxton.

"That is greatly out of her way," George said. "It would add another day to her journey at least, and she will not pay for an inn unless it is absolutely unavoidable. She could have gone through Brinchester if she had wanted to steer clear of Brinwater. No, she is travelling this way, but she is very, very slow, that is all. I expect she stopped at Dalbury Cross to rest the horses for an hour or two, for there is nowhere else until the Pheasant on the far side of the moors."

They waited until a coach had gone by, and then manoeuvred the curricle off the road. The copse was obviously a well-used spot, for there was a clear path with cart tracks leading off the road towards a clearing in the centre of the little stand of woods, just the right size to hide the curricle and horses.

Once she was satisfied that all was concealed behind bushes and trees, Grace scrambled as best she could into the breeches Loxton had obtained. They were far too large for her, but that was just as well, since she could not undress, and had to stuff the skirts of her gown into the breeches, to the great amusement of George.

"Oh, stop laughing, do, and show me how to fasten these things. What strange devices you men choose to wear! Ow! What are you doing? Let go, I can do it myself if you will just show me... ah, there! I am secure now."

Loxton offered his hat, and with the scarf across her face and her cloak drawn about her, she felt very mannish.

"Will I pass muster as a highwayman, do you suppose?"

"A highway*boy*, perhaps," George said, still giggling. "You are very small for a man, and your boots are too feminine, and as for the curls around your face…!" He went off into another paroxysm of mirth.

"Oh, if that is all!" Some deft work with the scarf managed to hide the curls. "I can do nothing about my boots, and I doubt anyone would recognise them. How fortunate that I brought my oldest cloak, for a velvet arrangement with ruffles would hardly do. Well, that is the best that can be contrived. We ought to hide ourselves. Cousin Anne could be along at any moment."

Cautiously Grace and George crept to the edge of the copse, looking up and down the road. With no vehicles in sight, they ran for the shelter of some stout gorse bushes a few hundred yards closer to Dalbury Cross. There they concealed themselves and settled down to wait for Cousin Anne.

It was a long, uncomfortable wait. Coaches and wagons passed by, a shepherd with a lamb passed by, three men on foot passed by and still they waited. The sun reached its zenith and began to dip down the sky, and still there was no sign of Cousin Anne. Grace began to be uncomfortably aware that they had dashed out of the house without a word. Perhaps Lady Graham would send for her, discover her missing and grow concerned. Only Miss Bellows knew their plans, and she might be too engrossed in watching birds to tell anyone.

"Do you think we have missed her after all?" she said.

George's face brightened. "Do you know, I have been thinking the exact same thing. Those old men must have been mistaken. Either that or Anne has taken a different road after all. We have been out since early morning, and I really do think we ought to start back. Loxton will be tired of walking the horses up and down that little clearing."

Within minutes they had raced back to the little copse, Grace had divested herself of her breeches and they were back on the road. They had not gone far, however, when an uncomfortable lurching suggested that something was amiss with the curricle. George and Loxton jumped down to examine the vehicle.

Moments later, George's head re-emerged from below. His gloomy expression told Grace all she needed to know.

"How bad is it?" she said, her heart sinking to her boots.

"As bad as it could be. It is the axle, as Loxton so annoyingly predicted. How I wish you were more often wrong, my good fellow. Loxton and I will walk the horses from here, but if the wretched thing breaks altogether, we shall all be walking."

The axle did not break, so Grace was able to ride, although in such fear of a collapse that would pitch her head-first onto the road that eventually she got down and walked, too. One or two carriages stopped to offer assistance, but since they were within sight of the Dalbury Cross by then, there seemed little point in accepting.

"Besides, the fewer people we talk to, the better," George said. "I am going to be in enough trouble as it is, keeping you out all day like this. I do not want complete strangers pointing out what a fool I am, and how I should not have gone so far, and what on earth was I thinking? It is bad enough when Mama says it."

"Does your father not say such things?"

"He is worse, for he looks sorrowful, and if I have done something even more spectacularly foolish than usual, he tells me how *disappointed* he is in me. Lord preserve me from my father's disappointments."

Grace giggled. "Mine was just the same. "*'Now, Grace,'* he would say, '*you know better than that. I have taught you the correct principles, all you need do is apply them.'* As if it were that easy," she added, with a deep sigh. "Sometimes a thing looks so simple and straightforward, and one thinks it cannot possibly go wrong, and yet it does, somehow."

"Like today," George said ruefully.

"As to that, *our* plan was sound enough, but Cousin Anne must have changed *her* plans, that is all. And then the axle breaking — that is the worst ill-luck. I daresay Loxton is right, and that back road through the woods damaged it. But once we get to the village — everything will be all right then, I daresay? Someone will be able to mend the axle?" She could not quite keep the anxiety out of her voice.

He pulled a face but took her hand reassuringly. "Probably not. These things are quite tricky to repair. However, we can hire a chaise or some such to get us home, never fear. You will not miss your dinner."

She smiled wanly, not quite liking to admit how the hunger pangs were beginning to gnaw at her. They had long since eaten the food Loxton had bought in Lismoor Bottom, and the prospect of sitting down to one of Lady Graham's splendid dinners was much on her mind.

Not half an hour later, they turned in to the yard at the Drover's Inn, and George went inside to bespeak help for the curricle and to hire a chaise. He emerged with a face so pale that Grace was suddenly terrified.

"What is it? Tell me the worst!"

"There is not a chaise or a gig or even a riding horse to be had in the whole village, it seems, for everyone is gone to the market at Lismoor Bottom and will not be back until midnight, if then."

"Can you ride one of your own horses?"

"They have never taken a saddle, and besides, they have done enough for today. Whatever we may do, they will have to stay here for tonight."

"Can we get to Brinford Manor from here? Mary would help us out."

"So she would, if we could walk some ten miles through fields and woods, or more by way of the road. It will be dark before we get there."

"Then whatever are we to do?"

He chewed his lip. "I am sorry, Grace, but there is no help for it. We are going to have to spend the night here."

"At an inn?" she whispered. "With no chaperon?"

Their luck that day had quite run out.

17: Dalbury Cross

Grace sat in apparent composure in the private parlour George had secured, while the maid got the fire going. The urge to pace up and down the room was strong, or even to scream in frustration, but she had to appear calm in front of the inn servants. Inside, her mind was in turmoil. Of all the evil fates to befall a young lady, an unchaperoned stay at an inn was amongst the worst. Only elopement to Scotland or something described as ravishment, whatever that might be, would be worse. Yet what had she done that was so wrong? She had been driven about the countryside in a curricle by a respectable young man, accompanied by his groom, all of which was quite unexceptional. Yet now, through no fault of her own, she was to be quite ruined.

When George came in, she could see at once from his face that he had no good news, but he, too, maintained silence until the maid was satisfied with her efforts and had withdrawn.

"I have sent Loxton across to the King's Arms," he said quietly. "He will see if he can secure a vehicle from there, or even a riding horse. If so, he can be back at Higher Brinford in an hour or not much more, and will return with Mama's carriage."

"But you are not hopeful," she said.

"Not really. I waved enough silver under the innkeeper's nose to make him understand the situation, and I am sure he would have obliged me if he could, but there truly is neither carriage nor horse to be had."

"Then we must stay here for tonight," she said with resignation.

"I believe we must. But so long as no one sees us or knows who you are, we will be safe. The curricle will be mended by the morning, and all we need to do is to call in at Brinford Manor and explain all to Lady Hardy. Then, when we return to Graham House, we can say that we were forced to stay overnight at the Manor."

"Oh yes! Mary will help us!" she cried, suddenly relieved.

"Exactly. But for tonight, we must stay here. I have ordered a good dinner for us, so at least we will not starve, and I have secured our accommodation under the name of Castle, for I cannot give my own name, you know."

"Castle? Why Castle?"

"Oh... there was a painting on the wall of Brinchester Castle. I had to think up something, you know. So we are Mr and Mrs Castle of—"

"*Mr and Mrs!*" she squeaked. "George!"

He sighed. "Well, I could hardly say you are unmarried, could I? That would attract the very attention we are trying to avoid. They will take me for a rake and you for a lightskirt."

"A lightskirt? Whatever is that?"

"Oh, erm... never mind! The innkeeper mistook us for husband and wife and it seemed better to me to go along with that, for a married couple staying at an inn causes no comment. There is a room up above for us — for you, I mean! Naturally, I shall find somewhere else to sleep. Loxton's room, no doubt. Actually, I am not sure whether grooms get a room to themselves, but anyway, you need not worry about it."

"Oh," she said in a small voice.

A knock on the door heralded the arrival of their dinner, and there was no further chance for conversation for quite some time.

Despite the awkwardness of her situation, Grace was hungry and between the two of them, they demolished every dish presented to them. They had barely finished when Loxton arrived.

"Ah! What news?"

Loxton looked doleful. "Not a carriage or chaise or gig or farmer's cart to be had, and no riding animal, either, except a half-blind mule of the ostler's, which we could've had for five guineas. I took leave to decline on your behalf, sir, seeing as it wouldn't get a mile down the road before collapsing, judging by the way it was wheezing."

"Quite right, Loxton. Tell me, do you have a room to sleep in?"

"A room? For tonight? I usually sleep above the stables, and save the cost of—" He glanced from George to Grace and back again. "Oh. I can take an attic room, I daresay. Anything more salubrious would... attract comment."

"Yes, do that, Loxton, if you please, and then go and have your dinner."

"Oh, I had a bite and some ale at the King's, in the back kitchen with the grooms. It's a good way of picking up information." His lips twitched with amusement.

"Come on, man, spill it out," George said.

Loxton laughed. "It might interest you to know, sir, that you're not the only one with carriage troubles today. There's a private coach turned back just a mile or so onto the moor with a wheel amiss. A middle aged spinster lady, with her maid. She's putting up at the King's as we speak."

"Cousin Anne!" cried Grace.

"Good God!" George cried. "How unlucky! No wonder we waited in vain."

"Unlucky in some ways, perhaps," Loxton said. "Very lucky in others. If you'd chosen to stay at the other inn, you'd have bumped into her or the maid on the stairs as sure as eggs is eggs, or I'd have met Cartwright in the stables, and then we'd have been in the soup."

"How true!" George said. "What a dreadful prospect. But so long as we are careful, we should be able to avoid her tomorrow and escape undetected."

~~~~~

The bedroom was not large, but comfortably furnished and the bed linen looked clean enough. There was room for a wardrobe, a small table, a chair and the usual wash stand.

"I have seen a great deal worse," George said. "Shall you be all right alone here, do you think? You must lock the door behind me, you know. Ah, there is a bar to go across it, as well. As soon as I have gone, slide that into place, and you will be quite safe. Do not open the door to anyone but me."

She nodded glumly, too dispirited to speak, tossing bonnet and gloves heedlessly onto the table.

"We will leave at first light," he went on. "That way we will be away before anyone else is on the road, and can avoid any unwelcome notice. I daresay Mary will give us breakfast, and we will be home before noon."

"Your mama will be worried about us," Grace said.

"I suppose so, but that cannot be helped. She will find out that the curricle has gone, and guess that we have had a problem and have been obliged to take shelter. She will not have the least suspicion of the rest of it, for no one would guess such a clever scheme."

"Perhaps not, but I gave Lavinia — Miss Bellows — a hint of what we were about. If she has told your mama, they may be imagining us lying in a ditch somewhere with our brains blown out by Cousin Anne's coachman."

George laughed at this vision. "Then she will be so relieved to see us that she will forget to scold us after all. That is always the way of it. If she thinks I am dead, and then finds me restored to her maternal bosom unharmed, she weeps all over me and that is an end to it. Although then Papa berates me for worrying Mama, so I suppose one can never win with them."

Grace smiled wanly. "I would be more than happy to be berated by either of them just now, if only I could be transported instantly to the sheltering arms of Graham House."

"Come now, where is that wonderful indomitable spirit? We shall be back there soon enough, and you can tell me then how well you enjoy being berated."

She managed a smile.

"That is much better. I shall leave you now to get some rest."

"George..."

He was half way to the door, but he turned round to face her.

"Thank you. For... for arranging everything. For taking care of me."

For answer he took one of her hands and stroked it softly. "I will always take care of you, Grace. Nothing bad will ever happen to you, not if I have breath in my body to prevent it."

He lifted her hand and kissed it, leaving her blushing in confusion. Then he was gone.

At first she could not move, but her legs were trembling so, she collapsed onto the edge of the bed, hugging herself with her arms and rocking gently back and forth. What did he mean by it? *'I will always take care of you…'* It was almost like a proposal, but surely that could not be his intention? No, he was being a friend, that was all, or an older brother — a protective older brother.

Yet the firm touch of his lips on her hand made her shiver, and she remembered that other kiss, when they had fallen in a heap at the foot of the stairs. There had been such a glow in his eyes, and then he had leaned down and pressed his lips onto hers. So warm! And the weight of his body against hers, the musky male scent of him, and the slight prickling of his chin against her skin. Was that what it was like, when a husband and wife were alone in their bed — the weight, the scent, the warmth?

It was a long time before she slept that night.

~~~~~

George could not honestly say that he slept at all. As soon as he had gained the tiny attic room that Loxton had obtained for him, and secured the door with a chair wedged firmly under the handle, he lay down on the bed, blew out his candle and closed his eyes. There were no sheets, only a couple of rough blankets atop a mattress stuffed with… he could not say. He thought longingly of his feather mattress at home, with its silk sheets and fine wool blankets, the chill of the interior removed by way of a warming pan. Here, he had a strong suspicion that some unpleasant creatures lurked beneath him, creatures small but indefatigable, with sharp teeth. Or pincers, he could not be sure. The anatomy of bed bugs was not, happily, a subject familiar to him. Whatever biting devices the little devils were equipped with, he had no wish to be exposed to them, so he made no effort to undress, apart from carefully removing his cravat, which would have to serve for a second day, and must therefore be kept as uncreased as possible.

If his eyes were closed, his mind was still racing along as fast as his curricle would, if only it had a functional axle. George had got himself into some scrapes before — in fact, his whole time at Oxford had been nothing but a succession of scrapes — but they had never involved more than himself. Well, himself and a few of his closest friends. Usually, his scrapes involved wagers placed on the most unlikely events, and sometimes he had been the one wagered upon, it had to be said. There had been midnight escapes or pre-dawn returns to his college, involving scrambling up trees or climbing walls. There were drunken revelries in the streets, in the quadrangle and once, memorably, in the gardens of one of the Masters, whose daughter was the object of desire by half the college. Once or twice, he recalled uncomfortably, there had been females involved of the less than respectable variety, of a nature that he had felt obliged to confess to his father, but most definitely not to his mother.

Yet never in his life had he found himself in quite such an awkward predicament with a young lady of good family whose reputation depended on the outcome. He could hear his father's sorrowful voice in his head.

'Did you not consider what might happen if you stayed out so long, dear boy? If you had only taken a short drive and then turned for home...'

"It is a bit late to think of that now," his head responded grumpily.

'Miss Allamont was under your protection, and you have let her down.'

"As if I am not fully aware of that, sir. Now do please be quiet."

But his father's voice would not be stilled. *'You know, of course, what happens to a respectable female who stays at an inn without benefit of the highest standard of chaperonage?'*

"I know, I know! Is it not just how it went for poor Marston? Everyone agreed that no blame could attach to him, or to the lady, for that matter, but her reputation was destroyed and he was obliged to offer for her, even though there was no real affection in the case."

'And is he happy, your friend?'

"Of course he is not!" George's mind responded instantly, but he was at once assailed by doubt. To be sure, Marston had written long, impassioned letters at first about his manifold grievances, and the awfulness of his situation. But latterly, there had been less complaint. Was he happy, or had he merely become resigned to his fate? George could not tell, but he wondered. He had invited Marston to stay at Graham House more than once in recent months, but there had always been some excuse or other. And the others of his circle who had fallen into the grasp of matrimony, protesting all the way, explaining that they were forced into it by their parents or were just doing their duty — yet somehow, when he considered the matter more carefully, he realised that their letters oozed contentment. Why had he never noticed it before?

George had never thought much about marriage, believing that sometime in the far-distant future there would come a day when he would be quite ready to give up his freedom and set up his nursery, but not yet. Please God, not yet, no matter how much his mother pleaded and his father pointed out the joys of the married state.

Now he wondered for the first time what it might be like to share his life with someone in that way, to wake beside a sweet face framed by unruly dark tresses, and have someone to talk to over breakfast, someone to come home to after a day's shooting, who would smile at him over dinner and then, later... Yes, he could see the attractions. Oddly, this pleasant vision was filled with a face that was all too familiar to him these days, a face with sparkling eyes and an expression of delightful mischief. Perhaps marriage would not be so bad. But not yet. Definitely not yet.

With such unsettled thoughts he lay on his uncomfortable bed and tried to sleep. Yet every time he began to feel that perhaps, at last, he might be drifting off, he would see his father's face in his mind, and hear his stern voice.

'And if the worst happens, will you do your duty by Miss Allamont?'

He could only hope the worst would not happen.

18: Highwaymen

Grace was woken by a farm wagon rumbling past with a great commotion, its oxen bellowing as if the world were about to end. She leapt off the bed and raced across to the window. It was not quite dawn, but the farmers were abroad already. Across the road, the King's Arms was silent, a single light burning over the entrance to the yard as the only sign that the inn was open for business. The yard itself was dark, with no movement.

Not long after, a gentle tap on the door heralded the arrival of George. She removed the wooden bar and opened the door to let him in.

"Goodness, you look very rumpled," she said, eyeing his disordered cravat and creased greatcoat in surprise.

He yawned. "Well, you look... oh. The same as always."

She gurgled with laughter. "You mean I always look rumpled, I suppose. I cannot deny it. It takes two maids to crimp me into shape for an evening engagement, and I cannot curl my own hair, you know. This is my natural state."

He smiled and said gallantly, "You look very well, Grace, for I cannot imagine you have slept a wink, any more than I have."

She did not disabuse him of the idea, saying quickly, "Never mind that! Come to the window and tell me what you see."

With another yawn, he did so. "The other inn?" he said tentatively.

"Yes, yes, but what else?"

"Nothing else."

"Exactly! They are all still abed, including Cousin Anne. But can you see, just under the arch, there is a coach?"

"I can, but— Oh! *Her* coach, I suppose you mean. What of it?"

"It was not there last night, so it must be mended."

"So?"

"Lord, you are slow this morning, George! You have feathers between your ears, I swear. Her coach is mended, so she will be leaving for home this morning, and *that* means she will be crossing the heath again."

"What does—?" A sudden grin broke out. "Grace! What a devilish scheming girl you are! You mean to try our plan again, is that it?"

"Why not? If your curricle is mended and the horses are rested, we can get onto the road ahead of Cousin Anne. It was a good plan yesterday, and it is still a good plan today. We can get the diamonds back and be at Mary's in time for breakfast, if we are lucky."

"If we are lucky…We were not so lucky yesterday, but then… one does not surrender the game after losing a single trick. Let us try again and see if we can do better."

"Exactly! What do we have to lose by it?"

Within an hour, the curricle had been retrieved, the horses hitched to it and the bill at the inn settled. They rolled out of the Drovers' Inn yard just as Cousin Anne's horses were being put to the coach. Their horses were fresh, so they made excellent progress to their chosen hiding place.

"Someone's been here," Loxton said, as they led the horses into the clearing in the little spinney. "Look, the remains of a fire, still smoking."

"I daresay someone was overtaken by nightfall, and made camp here," George said. "They have gone now, at all events, so we need not worry about them."

Grace put on her breeches again, and they took up their positions behind the gorse and settled down to wait. They had made such good time that it was rather a long wait, and Grace had more than enough time to regret rushing out without any breakfast again.

But at long last their patience was rewarded, and Cousin Anne's coach lumbered into view.

"You remember what you have to do?" George said, carefully placing the pistol in her hand. "Do not say a word, leave it all to me, and for the love of all that is good and holy, do not wave that about, or touch the trigger."

"I know. Point it at the driver and hold it steady. And say nothing."

They arranged their scarves one last time, and stood up ready to leap out from behind the bushes. Even at this late stage, the whole enterprise might have to be abandoned if another coach were in view, and Grace could not decide whether she wished for such an outcome or not. Her whole body thrilled with excitement now that the crucial moment was upon them, but she was also aware that there were any number of ways for disaster to overtake them. The horses could bolt, the coachman might have a loaded pistol in his pocket, Cousin Anne might carry a weapon herself, or some heroic young buck might appear to rescue the victims and mete out summary justice to the dastardly highwaymen. It had seemed so simple when the idea had first occurred to her. Now, standing amidst wind-blown gorse on the lonely heath, there was a degree of uncertainty that made her quake.

The coach came nearer and nearer, the low rumbling of the wheels getting louder. From behind the bush she could no longer see it, but she could hear the heavy breath of the horses, and the occasional word of encouragement from the coachman.

George looked across at her, his face alight with excitement, the grin stretching from ear to ear. "Ready?" he whispered.

She nodded, not trusting her voice.

"Right. *Now!*"

He leapt up and out through a gap in the gorse, and Grace could do nothing but take a deep breath and follow him. Too late now to turn back.

"Stand! Halt at once, or I shoot!"

Even had he not been holding a pistol, the coachman would have been forced to stop, for George stood in the middle of the road, barring the way. However, he had misjudged somewhat. The coach was travelling so slowly that it stopped within a few feet and George and Grace had to run down the road.

"Raise your hands above your head and do not move!" George called to the coachman, whose pale face and wide eyes intimated that heroically tackling his assailants was not at the forefront of his mind.

Grace stood directly below the coachman's seat, pistol pointed at his head, feet planted wide apart in what she hoped was a manly stance. He stared at her, hands lifted as far as he could raise them.

George ran round to the door of the coach, where Cousin Anne was already letting down the window. "Why have we stopped? What is—? Oh!" She gave a little scream as George waved the pistol under her nose. Then, plaintively, "No, no! Please! Do not hurt me. Here, take my money and go away!"

She thrust her reticule through the window. George snatched it from her hand. "Your jewels," he said gruffly. "*Now!*"

Another squeak of alarm. The coach rocked slightly, and muffled voices could be heard within. Then, "There! Now please go away!"

Necklaces, bracelets, earrings, bejewelled combs and fans were tossed through the window, landing in a little pool around George's feet. "And the rest," he said, in the same gruff voice. "*All* your jewels! Do not make me use this!" He moved the pistol closer.

A little moan, then more rocking and low voices. Two hands emerged from the window, holding a velvet bag. "Here! Now you have everything. May we go now? If it please you, sir?"

Taking the bag, George opened it and looked inside. Then, with a nod, he stepped back and shouted, "Drive on, Cartwright!"

Grace stepped aside, too, although without lowering her pistol. Eyeing her nervously, the coachman slowly lowered his arms, and with a crack of the whip and a "Get up there now!", the coach rolled into motion past them and away down the road.

"Do not stand still," George said urgently. "No point being a sitting duck if Cartwright decides to take a pop at us. Come and help me gather all these things."

"Did you get them? The diamonds?"

He nodded, his eyes gleaming. Quickly they scooped up all the fallen jewellery, stuffing it randomly into pockets, and dashed back behind the shelter of the gorse, and thence to the copse where Loxton waited. For a few moments the two could do nothing but laugh in delight at the success of their plan.

"That went off better than I had dared to hope," George said. "My God, but you should have seen her face! I daresay she will never travel this way again, at least not without an armed escort." Another burst of laughter. "What amazing fun that was! If ever I need to turn my hand to a career, I could do a lot worse than setting up as a highwayman."

"You could do a lot better, too," Loxton said in his lugubrious way. "Highwaymen have short lives. And look at the state of you! What were you doing, rolling in the ditch? I never saw you so muddy, sir, and that's a fact."

"Oh, pish, what does that matter! For we have got the diamonds, and that is the most important thing."

"Do show us!" Grace said, handing her pistol carefully to Loxton. "I cannot wait to see it."

George sat cross-legged on the ground, in a spot where a shaft of sunlight filtered through the green canopy above. Setting his pistol down beside him, he opened up the velvet bag and dipped his hand in. When he brought it out, it was entirely covered in diamonds, the necklace so encrusted that nothing could be seen of his hand inside. As he wiggled his fingers, the gems sparkled and dazzled as the sun caught them, so that Grace almost had to turn her head away.

She gasped at the sight. "Oh! How many diamonds were employed to make such a thing? There must be hundreds and hundreds."

"I have been told it is a thousand," George said, "but I do not know who has ever counted them. They are beautiful little things, are they not?"

"Yet such an ugly thing to wear," Grace said. "It would quite cover the neck and throat. How hideous!"

"Designed as a show of wealth, it is incomparable," George said. "Its aesthetic qualities are somewhat less than pleasing, however, even if the diamonds themselves cannot be faulted. If you have finished ogling it, I had better tuck it away safely before—"

A twig snapped.

"Oh, do put it somewhere safe," a male voice drawled from behind them. "My hands, for instance."

Grace froze, her stomach turning somersaults.

Beside her, George jumped up, pistol in hand and spun round to face the intruder.

"You can put that down, my son," the drawling voice said, with a hint of amusement. "Don't want you hurting yourself. These things have a nasty habit of going off when you least expect it. Well, mine does, and we don't want any accidents, do we?"

Grace turned her head to look at the stranger. He was tall, a mask covering most of his face, and clothed entirely in black from the hood of his cloak to his polished boots. His pistol was black too, twice the size of George's and pointed directly at Grace in a hand showing not the slightest hint of unsteadiness. Just their luck, on the day they chose to play at being highwaymen, to encounter the real thing.

It was clear that George recognised that they had been outmanoeuvred, for he lowered his own pistol at once. "Who are you? And what do you want?"

The stranger laughed, and it was not a pleasant sound. "As to who we are, there is no need for you to know, any more than I need to know who *you* are, my son. But as to the question of what I want, I shall think your wits have gone abegging if you cannot work it out, for it must be obvious enough. I want that pretty little collection of baubles you have in your hand there."

"But it is not yours!" George protested.

The stranger laughed so hard at this, that Grace thought he would surely break a rib. Even so, his hand never wavered, the pistol aimed directly at her heart.

"No, nor yours neither, my son."

"Stop calling me that! I am *not* your son, thank God. My father is worth a thousand of you!"

That brought more laughter.

"Oh, will you stop cackling like a washer-woman and go away!" George said.

Grace was shocked at his bravery, or perhaps it was foolhardiness, it was hard to tell. Poor Cousin Anne had been petrified of George in his pretend highwayman's costume, and had handed over every last valuable without a moment's hesitation, so long as she escaped with her life. Whereas George...

"Just give it to him," she cried. "It is not worth getting shot for."

"Now there's a sensible lad," the highwayman said. "Very good thinking, boy. Hand it over, *my son*, and I might let you live another day. And don't try any heroics, either, because the instant you even think about using that little toy of yours, my friend over there will spill your blood all over this little clearing. Which would be a shame, don't you think? And I'm sure the boy agrees with me."

Grace cautiously turned her head. There behind them was another tall figure clad much as the first, and he too bore a pistol, this time pointed directly at George. It seemed a straightforward enough decision. They had been outclassed in every way by the professionals, and there was now nothing to be done except hand over the necklace and hope these desperate men would keep their word and let them escape with their lives. Heart pounding, blood rushing in her ears, Grace lowered her head, and began to pray, but in the turmoil of her mind, only the old familiar words rose unbidden. *"Our father, Which art in heaven, Hallowed be Thy name…"*

Still George hesitated, looking from one black-clad man to the other, as if weighing the odds.

Then everything happened at once. The first man gave an exclamation and spun suddenly, lifting his gun and running towards the curricle.

Loxton! Grace had almost forgotten him. And he had a gun, too. Four men, four guns. Fear lanced through her.

"Get down, George!" she yelled.

A crack rang out, then another almost at once. From the far side of the spinney, the horses whinnied in alarm.

Grace suppressed the scream that was building inside her, looking desperately around to see if anyone was hit. But no, they were all still on their feet, no one falling.

Then another crack.

With an exclamation of annoyance, George raised his pistol and fired. He was so much closer that the sound reverberated in Grace's head, and she gave a little start of alarm.

It was drowned out by a much louder scream. The second highwayman rocked on his feet, then slowly toppled over backwards.

"Oh God, George, what have you done!" Grace cried, scrambling to her feet and running heedlessly across the rough ground to the stricken man.

He lay on his back, clutching his left arm and moaning. Somehow in the fall his mask had been dislodged, and as she knelt down and gazed into the face of their assailant, she froze in astonishment.

"Mark?"

19: *Blood And Bandages*

"Mark, what on earth are you doing here with a *highwayman*? Why have you left Mr Wright?" She pulled her scarf away from her face as she spoke.

"Grace?" He stared at her uncomprehendingly. "What are *you* doing here?"

"He has *not* left me," said a weary voice from behind her. "Really, Miss Allamont, you are getting very tiresome. Not content with turning down my very reasonable advances upon your dowry, now you have to interfere with my professional arrangements, too. You will forgive me if I do not find your presence here amusing. Perhaps I should have shot you and your friend when the opportunity presented itself."

"Mr Wright? But—"

Mark groaned again, putting an end to questions for the moment.

"Let me look at him," said Wright. "I have some experience with such wounds."

"I have no difficulty in believing it," George said dryly.

While Wright attended to Mark, George took Grace a little aside. "Are you all right? You have taken no hurt?"

"Not the least bit. And you? Loxton?"

George shook his head. "No one is hurt, except for your cousin. I sent Loxton to see to the horses. You were wonderfully brave, Grace. I felt sure you would scream your head off and start them shooting, which was exactly what I was hoping to avoid. But they took fright when they saw Loxton. Perhaps they thought he had a platoon of redcoats waiting in the bushes somewhere. But what the devil are we going to do with them?"

"Mark must be got to a surgeon at once, and Wright must go to the constables. Oh, but... how awkward."

"Exactly. We cannot accuse him without explaining our own role in the business, and Mark is in even more trouble. We might get away with a ticking off, but Mark could be deported, or even hanged."

"But surely Wright cannot be allowed to get away with all his wickedness. It is one thing to try to entrap me into marriage, for men do that all the time and I am up to all their rigs, but it is another thing altogether to steal from innocent travellers on the road." She stopped and they were both silent. "Which is exactly what we have just done, I suppose," she added in a small voice.

"Anne is not innocent," George said robustly. "We have just taken back property that she stole in the first place. It is not the same at all."

"Even so, we must have given her such a fright! It was very bad of us. And we have all her jewellery, as well as the necklace. You have it safe?"

He nodded.

Grace looked at Mark, still prone on the ground, but he seemed to have regained some colour, and was talking a little to Wright. "It seems you have not killed him, which is a mercy. That would have taken some explaining."

"So long as we can get him to a surgeon, then, if he is lucky and the wound does not fester, he will be as right as rain."

Wright finished tending the patient, and came across to them. "The ball passed straight through and the wound looks clean," he said. "I have bound it with my cravat, to the detriment of my appearance, so I hope he appreciates the gesture. A surgeon should look at it, but he will do, I think. You will forgive me if I leave him to your tender care, Miss Allamont. I can be of no further assistance to him, and there is nothing to be gained by my staying."

"No, that is exactly what I should have expected of you, to desert your friend at the moment of his greatest need," she said scornfully.

He flushed, but looked her straight in the eye. "Were we alone, and his life depending on me, then I should have offered him every succour. In this case, however, you are the person best placed to look after him. If you go to the inn, they will send for a doctor. I will leave Mark's saddle bags with you, but I will keep the horse, if you don't mind, for he's valuable and I paid for him in the first place. I'll take the pistol, too, for it's a pair with mine and I'm fond of them. Will you shake my hand, Miss Allamont, to show there's no hard feelings?"

He held out his hand, and for a moment Grace was tempted to rebuff him. Such an insolent man, as well as being a thief and a liar and an insinuating toad. But then she remembered that he still had a pistol in his pocket, and might yet decide to use it against her if she refused. Reluctantly she shook his hand.

"You will understand, I am sure, Mr Wright, when I say that I hope never to see you again as long as I may live."

He grinned. "Understood perfectly. I am quite delighted with Brinshire and its manifold attractions, but there are many more counties that might be just as charming, and welcoming to a stranger. And there is always Scotland or Ireland."

"Ireland is very pretty, I am told," she said, and he laughed and waved his farewell.

~~~~~

The curricle was designed for gentle afternoon drives, conveying two people and a tiger in perfect comfort. With Mark propped up between Grace and George, and the saddle bags stowed under the seat, it felt uncomfortably crowded. No one complained, however. They were all thankful to be alive and heading back to safety.

"Shall we stop at the Drovers' Inn again?" George said. "The King's Arms is more likely to have someone to send to Mr Torrington."

"We will not stop at the village at all," Grace said.

"We could all do with breakfast," he said mildly.

"I am aware of it, for I am famished too. But the proper place to take Mark is to his sister at Brinford Manor. Mary will send someone for the physician and tend to Mark, and we shall also be able to enjoy a better breakfast than any inn can supply."

George brightened perceptibly. "Excellent idea." Then the smile faded. "But whatever are we to tell her? How can we explain Mark?"

"He was shot by a highwayman, of course. Which is, in its way, no more than the truth. But we shall have to take Mary into our confidence, since we need her to convince the world that I spent the night at Brinford Manor and *not* at some backwater inn with you."

"Will she help us, do you think? A great deal depends on it."

"She will help us," Grace said, although with more confidence than she truly felt. At one time she would have trusted Mary implicitly in the matter, but Miss Mary Allamont was now Lady Hardy, the wife of a baronet and a person of some standing in society, and perhaps she would not want to jeopardise her own reputation to help out a foolish cousin.

And she *was* foolish, Grace conceded. The whole plan had been fraught with danger, and her present predicament was a direct consequence of her own recklessness. If only she had stopped to think! But then, she knew herself well enough to admit that it would not have made the slightest difference. She had enjoyed the excitement of it, that was undeniable, and she could not complain if the consequences were rather more disagreeable than she had anticipated. That was as it should be. She had done something very bad, and now perhaps she would be punished for it. She would bow her head and accept whatever fate decreed.

There was a delay of some minutes at the gates of the Manor before someone emerged at a run from the lodge to admit them. Then there was just the long drive to the house and the natural nervousness in arriving unheralded in the middle of the morning with a man who had been shot and two people who looked as if they had slept under a hedge the previous night. Which was not so very far from the truth, Grace thought wryly.

As they slowed under the entrance canopy, they were spared any difficult explanations by the appearance of three horses ridden at a brisk pace from the shrubbery beside the drive. Grace recognised Mary and Daniel Merton. The third rider was a groom. Mary gave an exclamation of dismay and swiftly dismounted.

"Mark! Oh, whatever ails him? Wait — this is blood! Has he been shot? A duel?"

"Highwaymen," Grace said.

"He is very pale. Mark, you are safe now. Can you walk? Mr Merton, help Mr Graham carry him into the house. Martin, ride with all speed to Mr Torrington. Tell him it is a shooting, and he must attend with the utmost urgency." The groom kicked his horse into motion, hooves crunching on the gravel drive. "Quickly, get him inside. There is a small parlour with a chaise longue where we can put him until Mr Torrington gets here. Oh, careful on the step! Do not joggle him."

By this time, the butler and a footman had appeared with concerned faces.

"Oh, Edgerton, Mr Mark has been shot. We shall need the fire lit in the little withdrawing room, and clean cloths and hot water. Oh yes, and brandy, too. And when Martin returns, he must ride over to Willowbye to let them know what has occurred. I will write a note for him to take. Ah, Mrs Lassiter, we shall need the blue bedroom prepared, and two extra places laid for breakfast in Sir Osborne's dining room."

Grace followed, watching in admiration the calm way Mary dispensed her orders, without a trace of panic, the servants silently disappearing to do her bidding, even as more appeared, waiting to be instructed. By this time, they had reached the parlour and the two men gently laid down their burden. Mark groaned a little, eyes closed. He did look very pale, much paler than he had done just after the shooting, and when the concealing cloak was removed, a great pool of blood was visible, seeping down his arm.

Mary showed no alarm, kneeling down beside her brother and beginning to unwind the makeshift bandage. "Cloths! I need cloths at once. Ah, thank you. Sally, you are a sensible girl and will not be dismayed by a little blood — will you hold this? Mr Merton, would you be so good as to attend Sir Osborne. Tell him what has occurred, but on no account let him come down here. It would distress him too greatly. Tell him I shall come as soon as I may, and he should not delay breakfast on my account. Pray take Grace and Mr Graham with you, for I am sure they need some sustenance."

"I think we are not fit to be in Sir Osborne's company," Grace said.

Mary looked up then, taking in the bedraggled hair and filthy gown and cloak. With a smile, she said, "Perhaps you are right. Mrs Lassiter, prepare two rooms for our guests and have baths taken up. Now Sally, press firmly here."

~~~~~

Grace had never enjoyed a bath so much in her life. She soaked for an age, as maids toiled laboriously up the stairs with ewers to replenish the water, and laid out a selection of clean clothes for her to choose from.

At length Mary came in, still in her riding habit, a streak of blood on the skirt, and shooed away the moon-faced chambermaids.

"Oh, how is he?" Grace cried. "Did Mr Torrington come? Mark will not die, will he? For he looked as white as a swan."

"He is fine," Mary said. "Torrington came and unwrapped my neat bandage, and poked about a bit, and declared all in order. He applied some salve and a much less elegant bandage and we shall receive his astronomical bill in due course, no doubt. Now," she said, flopping down beside the bath and rolling up her sleeves, "I will wash your hair and you can tell me what *really* happened today and why Mark was bandaged with a gentleman's cravat with the laundry mark *'RW'* on it."

And Grace did, the whole story pouring out, the words tumbling over each other like pebbles rolling downhill. Mary listened and soaped and rinsed and said nothing, merely nodding occasionally.

"So will you help me?" Grace said. "For I know I have done a wicked thing, and if I am to be punished for that and lose my reputation I shall accept my fate, and I do not at all want to get *you* into difficulties. But I should rather *not* be cast out of all good society if it can be helped."

Mary laughed. "And you shall not be, not if I have anything to say in the matter! Should you like to stay with me for a few days, if Lady Graham can spare you? Then it shall be so. Mr Graham will go there immediately after breakfast to tell them that you are safe, and Lady Graham will send over your things and your maid. There, you had better get yourself dry and dressed, for Sir Osborne will not touch his breakfast until you are there."

"Oh no!" Grace cried distressfully, leaping out of the bath and sloshing water everywhere. "I had no idea! Not for the world would I keep him waiting. Oh, why did you not say earlier?"

"It is quite all right," Mary said with a smile. "He eats very little before dinner anyway, only some toast to please me. It is Mr Graham, I think, who is feeling the hunger pangs most keenly. There is a young man who is not much accustomed to waiting for a meal, I think."

"That is very true," Grace said, selecting a gown at random from those laid out on the bed. "And I have twice now dragged him out without so much as a piece of bread to ward off starvation and he has said not a word of complaint. He is very good-natured, I think, and he was quite splendid when there were pistols popping all around. Except for the matter of shooting Mark, of course."

"I think there was a great deal of provocation in the case," Mary said solemnly. "I would have shot Mark myself, in such circumstances, for I am quite adept with a gun. So you will not hear a word said against Mr Graham by me, I assure you." She eyed Grace speculatively. "You like him, I think?"

"Who, George? Oh, of course, who could not? He is very amiable, not at all stiff or pompous."

"And I can see that he likes you. He has been talking non-stop about your bravery and calmness under fire, and a great deal more besides."

"Has he? I expect he is just glad that we scraped through it without a disaster. Well, apart from Mark's being shot."

"Yes, apart from that!" Mary said, laughing. "Here, let me do your hair for you. Sit on the stool there, and I will have it fixed in no time."

"You will not be able to do much with it," Grace said gloomily. "It is as straight as a rod without curling papers."

"My hair is just the same, so I know how to deal with it. But Grace, I do wonder if the question of your reputation might be resolved very easily. If you and George—"

"Oh, no! No, no, no, that would not do at all. He has told me many times that he has no intention of marrying until he is thirty at least, and I certainly do not want to marry yet. Or maybe at all," she added in a small voice.

"But under the circumstances, he might feel obliged—"

"Which would be far worse, do you not see? To marry from duty, without love... what a dreadful fate."

Mary was silent for a moment, wrestling with a recalcitrant lock of hair, not looking at Grace. Then she said carefully, "Marriage without romantic love may still be very rewarding, Grace. So long as you have respect for each other and each behaves with consideration for the other's feelings, it can bring great happiness. One may *love* a person without being head over ears *in love* with him."

Spinning round on the stool, Grace said impulsively, "Are *you* happy?"

"Very happy." Her smile was confirmation of the truth of her words. "I married Sir Osborne for the worst of reasons, to escape from my step-mother. He married me because he felt sorry for me. Yet we have discovered that we are perfectly suited, and could not be happier with our situation. So you see, a pragmatic marriage can be every bit as fulfilling as one founded on romantic love."

Grace said nothing, but she was not convinced. She had four older sisters who had married for love, and in her heart she envied them the experience of a great passion that swept them off to a new and wonderful married life. All the difficulties and perils of marriage and motherhood would be nothing if one was truly in love. Mary might be contented enough with Sir Osborne, but perhaps if she had ever known the thrill of true love she would not feel the same way at all. Grace longed for a man to sweep her off her feet, to thrill her to her core and be so magnificent that she would find him quite irresistible. George was a great friend, and fun to be with, but never in her most fevered imaginings would she describe him as magnificent. She determined that she would never marry George, even if he was pushed into offering for her.

20: Graham House

With a decent breakfast inside him, George felt quite renewed. One of Sir Osborne's valets, a pained expression on his face, had brushed down his clothes. George hoped the fellow would not feel obliged to hand in his notice at being expected to minister to mud-bespattered country bumpkins who turned up unannounced before breakfast. Sir Osborne was too polite to comment on his bedraggled appearance, and since the baronet ate almost nothing himself, there was enough for George to enjoy second and even third helpings of several dishes without feeling guilty.

Grace ate well, too, but then nothing disturbed her appetite, any more than it disturbed George's. They were alike in that respect. Seeing her eating with gusto relieved his mind of one, at least, of his worries. She had not, as he had feared, been so shocked by all that had occurred as to cause her to fall into an outbreak of hysteria or faint clean away.

He had always had the utmost admiration for her spirit — was there ever a pluckier girl? — but facing a highwayman's pistol and then finding oneself in the midst of wild shooting was not something any gently-bred young lady could be expected to endure with equanimity. But she had gone straight to Mark, heedless of her own safety, and even his gushing blood had not upset her, and when all was resolved, she had settled down to eat devilled kidneys as if the day was nothing out of the ordinary way. What a splendid girl!

It was no more than an hour from Brinford Manor to Graham House, and the curricle bowled along the country lanes at good speed, the horses still fresh. In Higher Brinford, several passers-by recognised the curricle and bowed or curtsied to George as he passed by. The Grahams were not the principal family of the neighbourhood, but they were well-regarded and, indeed, well-liked. Such respect added to George's mellow frame of mind, for he had in his pocket that which would delight his mama beyond measure, and engender such goodwill towards him that his parents would surely overlook the small detail of his disappearing without a word, taking a young lady with him, and returning the next day alone.

As soon as the curricle halted, George handed the reins to Loxton and bounded to the ground, taking the entrance steps two at a time. The front doors were flung open before he reached them and a small figure rushed out.

"Where have you been! Mama has been so worried!"

"There was a problem with the curricle. The axle."

"Now, that is just what Papa said, but Mama would have it that you were lying in a ditch somewhere with your head broke in. Oh George, you are in so much trouble! And where is Grace?"

By this time, they had gained the entrance hall. Awaiting him to one side was a long line of bowing servants. On the other, his parents. There was nothing about them to suggest overt hostility, but there was a certain frigidity in the air.

"Ah, George, how good of you to return," his father said in his blandest tones. "We had all but given you up."

"Had a bit of trouble with the curricle," he muttered, his high spirits evaporating in a rush.

"The axle broke," Alice said. "Which bit is that?"

"An important bit," George said. "Look, may we—"

"Have you breakfasted, my boy?" Sir Matthew said.

"Indeed I have, sir, but—"

"Excellent! And Miss Allamont? She was well when you left her, I take it."

"Of course she was," George snapped, tiring of this inquisition. "What do you take me for?"

"Well now, that is a very interesting question," his father said. "One could discuss such a topic for many hours, without reaching a firm conclusion."

George had seen his father in this sort of mood many times, but not recently. Usually it was a prelude to one of his little speeches about disappointment, George would apologise, feeling like a nine-year-old who had broken a pane in the hothouse again, after which they fell into their usual habits and rubbed along tolerably well. But this was different. Never before had his father started up in this vein in so public a place, with half the household's servants in attendance.

"I am perfectly happy to discuss any topic of interest to you, sir, for as many hours as please you, but it seems to me that my travel-stained driving attire is less than suitable for such an activity. You will not object if I change into something more appropriate to my mother's drawing room?"

"Oh, that is very good, George. By all means. The library, as soon as you are ready." He spun on his heel and strode away, Lady Graham scuttling after him, towing Alice by the hand. George was left to make his way slowly to his room, wondering what on earth he was about to face.

His valet had already laid out a change of raiment, and would have rushed him through the business so as not to keep his parents waiting, but George was not inclined to rush. The more he thought about it, the more incensed he became that his father thought to speak to him in such terms, and in public, too. He could deal with anger or silent disapprobation or even the dreaded disappointment, but a public attack was intolerable. So he took his time, and only when he was sure that every aspect of his person was faultless did he make his way slowly to the library. He carried the Durmaston Diamonds with him in their velvet bag, depositing them behind an urn on a table just inside the door, to be produced with triumph at a suitable moment.

His parents were standing by the window, heads together, deep in whispered conversation when he entered. They sprang apart and his mother immediately crossed the room, her face red with anger.

"And not before time! You are insolent, George, to keep us waiting at such a time, when we have been so concerned about you."

That raised his eyebrows. "Concerned? Were you really? Because I have to be honest, Mother, your worries on my account have not been obvious so far."

"Not on *your* account, or at least… Well, never mind. But Grace is another matter. What were you thinking of, to go hurtling off without a word to anyone, and then to stay away overnight? Grace was under your protection, and you have served her ill, dragging her into some hare-brained scheme of yours. Really, George, just when I begin to imagine that you are growing up at last, you have another outbreak of this wildness. Grace was left in my care by her mama, and how I am to face her if you have done anything unforgivable or hurt her—"

"*Enough!*" George bellowed. "*More* than enough, Mother. If you imagine for even one second that I would harm a single hair of Grace's head, or allow anyone else to do so, you are entirely mistaken. It appals me that such a thought would even cross your mind. I would lay down my life to defend her, as you should be perfectly well aware if you knew anything about me."

His tone was so fierce that she backed away from him, eyes wide.

"Furthermore," he went on relentlessly, "I am tired of you — of *both* of you — treating me with so little respect that you find it acceptable to admonish me in front of the servants. I am not perfect, God knows, and I have made a great many mistakes in my life, and no doubt will continue to make them, but I will not be treated like a schoolboy. Say what you will to me in private, but Father, you will never again talk to me in that manner before the servants. You will treat me with the courtesy due to a future baronet. Have some respect for the title, even if you have none for your son."

"I did not admonish you," his father said coldly.

"Not in words, but your tone was unwelcoming."

"As your father, it is my right to speak to you in whatever manner seems appropriate to me."

"Certainly, but you demean yourself as a gentleman when you do so in public."

Sir Matthew's eyebrows snapped together, and there was a long, frosty silence, as the two glared at each other. In the end, it was Sir Matthew who looked away first.

"Brandy, George?" he said, and his tone was so placid that a stranger would not have believed he was the same man who had spoken with such icy contempt.

"Thank you, sir."

Sir Matthew poured two generous measures and handed one to George. "You will understand, I am sure, that anxiety regarding your welfare — and Miss Allamont's — makes us less than usually concerned with the niceties of convention."

It was as close as his father would ever come to an apology. For an instant George was triumphant — he had made his point, and forced his father to back down! Instead of crawling and being made to feel like a snail about to be crushed under his father's immaculate Hessians, he had succeeded in fighting back. As he took the brandy, he realised with astonishment that he and his father stood on equal terms at last. It might not last, it might only be a fleeting victory in a long succession of failures, but for now he could savour the moment, accept the proffered olive branch and offer up a little conciliation of his own.

So he swallowed his anger, and said mildly, "When you have heard all that I have to tell, you will understand that I have had a trying time of it, all things considered. But first, let me assure you that Miss Allamont is safe and well with Sir Osborne and Lady Hardy at Brinford Manor."

Lady Graham clapped her hands in delight. "Then she was not stranded somewhere overnight with you. For that would have been such a disaster, you know. She spent the night at the manor, which is quite unexceptional."

George was not quite ready to address that point yet. There were aspects of the adventure which he was rather nervous about revealing, and this was most definitely the worst of them. On the other hand, there were moments which he knew would arouse his parents' sympathy, such as the encounter with the highwaymen and the shooting. And there was also his great success, the retrieval of the diamonds, which would make them so happy and proud that perhaps the darker moments might pass with less comment.

"Shall we sit?" he said. "It is a long story, and we may as well be comfortable."

He told his tale as honestly as he was able, and if he made any alteration to the truth, it was only to lay less of the blame for the escapade onto Grace and more on himself, for guilt was pressing on him rather hard at this point. He started with seeing Cousin Anne leaving Graham House and realising that she must have found the diamonds, and had them in her possession at that very moment. He then described how he and Grace had formulated the idea of following, and how, when they realised the direction Cousin Anne was taking, they agreed to attempt a pretend hold-up of her coach.

"George, you did not!" his mother exclaimed in horror. "Such foolishness!"

"And did you achieve your objective?" his father said, with just a hint of amusement in his voice.

"Well... things did not quite go according to plan," George said, and his father chuckled. George relaxed a little. His father, at least, was taking this very well, and that was by far the greatest hurdle to jump.

He described in some detail their actions that day — the buying of scarves and a cloak, the race over the rutted and stony back road to reach the main road before Cousin Anne, the slow progress across the heath, walking the horses to rest them, and then the long futile wait in the heather.

His mother smiled. "So you did not get it from her after all?"

It was curious that she seemed so pleased about that, but he could not consider the point properly, for he had come to the crux of the matter. If he were to tell the tale in sequence, he must now relate the episode of the broken axle and the overnight stay at the inn. He did not feel himself quite strong enough to tackle a subject which, he knew, would distress his parents greatly. Instead, it was time to produce his great triumph.

Jumping up, he retrieved the velvet bag from its hiding place and set it on a table before his mother.

"Actually, I did get it from her. There you are, Mama, the Durmaston Diamonds."

With a flourish, he tipped out the contents of the bag, which shimmered and sparkled in the afternoon light in the most satisfactory way.

The response was not what he had expected, however.

His father looked grim, and his mother screamed. "Oh, George, you silly, *silly* boy! What have you done? Oh, now it is all ruined, and I thought we were safe at last. Oh, George, why oh why did you have to meddle?"

Confused, George looked from one to the other. "I do not understand. Surely you are pleased?"

His father leaned across to pick up the diamonds. "Pretty, are they not?" he asked, turning them this way and that to catch the light. "Very convincing. You would almost believe them to be the real thing. But these are not the Durmaston diamonds, my boy. These are a very clever copy, nothing but paste."

"*What?*"

"We could see that Anne was never going to leave without the diamonds, so we intentionally left them somewhere easy for her to find, so that she would take them and go away."

"The Peacock Room," George groaned. "And you kept me tied to the card table to give her time to find them."

"Exactly. They were quite well hidden, too, though I say it myself. I made a little secret compartment at the back of one drawer, and then, of course, I worried that she might not find it at all and you would get there first and ruin the whole game. But we thought we had managed it when she left so early the next day."

"Do you mean," George said indignantly, "that I went to all that trouble for nothing? For paste jewellery? We had the most appalling time and suffered the most dreadful inn and then got shot at, and it was all for nothing?"

"Inn?" Lady Graham said.

"Shot at?" Sir Matthew said.

"If only you had told me this before!" he cried. "Instead, we spent the night at an inn and then we were held up by real highwaymen and got shot at and Grace's reputation may be ruined and we could have been killed and it was *all for nothing?*"

They stared at each other in horror.

21: Taking A Walk

Sir Matthew was the first to recover his wits. "It seems to me that there is a great deal more of the story yet to be told. You have some explaining to do."

George was still too angry to answer sensibly. He jumped up and paced across to the window. Outside, one of the gardeners was kneeling at one of the flower beds, patiently weeding, in a rhythmic process. A scuffle in the dirt, the weeds pulled free then dropped into the bucket at his side. Lean forward, pull a weed, lean back, drop it into the bucket. Such a simple life, being an under-gardener. Nothing to think about except the next weed, and the next, and the next. Smooth over the earth, stand up, shuffle yourself and your bucket two feet to the left, kneel down and begin again. No worries, no responsibilities, no good friend potentially ruined, no disappointed parents.

George sighed. He moved slowly back to his chair, sat down and took a long draught of brandy.

"Why did you not tell me?" he said tiredly. "All this could have been prevented if I had only known. But you did not trust me with the truth."

"A secret is kept best when no one knows it," his father said quietly. "It was not just you we did not trust with this knowledge, it was everyone. Your mother's grand-mama always wanted her to have the diamonds, but she knew perfectly well that if your Aunt Lilian got hold of them, your mama would never see them, no matter how carefully worded the will may be. So she handed them over many, many years ago. We had a copy made, in case it was ever needed, but the necklace itself was broken up a long time ago. Some of the diamonds went into that very nice set of your mama's, and—"

"Oh, the anniversary set?"

"Correct, although it pained me to allow it to be thought that I had bought it. We had sets made for each of your sisters. The rest of the diamonds were sold to increase Lady Graham's portion, which will also go to the girls, in time. This copy is now all that remains to show what the original necklace was like. I suppose we should have told you the truth, but it amused you to search the house for the diamonds, and it seemed a harmless enough occupation. If we are being perfectly honest with each other, I must confess that I was glad for you to have some project to keep you at home, instead of jauntering here, there and everywhere with those rackety friends of yours, and costing me money with all the scrapes you got into."

"If you would allow me to share the management of the household accounts and your investments, as I have asked many times, perhaps I would have been more contented here," George said. "If you exclude me from all meaningful occupations, you cannot be surprised if I fill my days with purposeless activity."

His father raised his hands. "A palpable hit, my boy. You are quite right, and I should take you into my confidence more. As, perhaps, you should, also? Could you not have told us what you were about?"

"Grace told Miss Bellows," George said, in surprise. "She knew everything we planned."

"Miss Bellows!" Lady Hardy said. "Her mind is too full of her own plans just now."

"She has developed an interest in birds," Sir Matthew said with a smile. "A harmless enough hobby."

"It is not the birds I mind, so much as the amount of time she spends watching them with your brother," she said indignantly.

Sir Matthew only laughed. "They are both of age, Bertram has a very comfortable living as well as some money of his own, and I think they will do very well together. She could not do better, you know."

"*She* could not, but *he* could certainly attract someone a little higher up in the world than a governess."

"And after all these years, he has never before found anyone to disturb his bachelor life. If they choose to marry, let us be happy for them. For myself, I have no wish to talk about Bertram or Miss Bellows when there is a shooting and an inn to be accounted for. Do, pray, enlighten us, George."

So George recounted the whole sorry saga, leaving nothing out, for they knew the worst of it and his father, at least, was not disposed to look harshly on the enterprise. On the contrary, his eyes sparkled with interest, and he let forth an occasional appreciative chuckle. When George came to the description of the real highwayman, his father leaned forward in his chair, muttering "No!" and "Goodness!" from time to time. His mother said nothing, but her lips were set in a thin line, and her hands were clenched in fists so tight that the knuckles were white.

"So it ended well after all," George said, with a tentative glance at his mother's tense face. "Mark Allamont will recover, Mr Wright is gone for good and Grace is safe with her cousin."

"So you saw no one you know at the inn?" his father said.

"Not a soul. Luckily we chose the Drovers' Inn, for we should have been bound to bump into Cousin Anne or her coachman at the King's Arms."

"And you signed in under a false name, which was sensible. But can the Hardys be depended upon, do you think?"

"Lady Hardy is very much minded to assist us," George said. "She has invited Grace to stay with her for another day or two, to add verisimilitude to the story. She will bring her back here in her own carriage."

"And is Sir Osborne of the same mind as his wife?" Sir Matthew said. "There is also the Dowager to consider, and the two sisters."

"Lady Hardy will impress on them the disastrous consequences for Grace if any rumour is spread. The servants, too."

"Hmm. That is a great number of people who know that Grace did *not* spend the night there. We must hope for the best, but George, have you thought of how things might turn out if the worst happens?"

"If you mean do I intend to offer for her, then of course. I know my duty, I hope."

His father's face softened, but his mother gave a low moan. "No, George, no! You cannot marry that… that *hoyden*! Grace Allamont is the wildest and worst-behaved chit it has ever been my misfortune to know. She has no manners and if she ever did one thing as she ought, I would be astonished. If she were as meek as Alice, it might do, since she has a very good dowry, but she is no lady, and you will *not* bring her into this family. I absolutely forbid it."

Before George could gather his thoughts to rebut this tirade, his father's voice cut sharply into the silence. "If you have any regard for this family at all, madam, you will keep such thoughts to yourself. Grace is a lovely, good-humoured young lady, who needs only a little taking in hand from someone more experienced — such as yourself — to make a perfect wife for the boy. Better a lively hoyden than the likes of Alice, who is afraid even to open her mouth in company."

Lady Graham gasped. "You surely cannot approve of such a match, Sir Matthew?"

"Most certainly I do. I like a girl with spirit very well — after all, I married one, did I not? Better by far that George marries Grace than that Miss Dull-as-ditch-water you thought to pair him with."

"Miss Dilworthy's family is impeccable."

"What does that matter when the chit had not an ounce of backbone? Would you rather see him wed to a milksop like that or a woman who can stand up to highwaymen, eh? If this business goes sour and George is obliged to offer for Grace, then he will certainly have my blessing."

"Well, he will not have mine! And if you expect *me* to take her in hand, and undertake all the finishing her mother should have done, then you are much mistaken, sir! I look for peace under my own roof, not a continuous stream of disasters."

"Have it your own way. Primrose Lodge is empty just now, a very pretty little house that would suit them extremely well."

"Primrose Lodge!" she said, her voice rising in tone so that it was almost a squeak. "You have this all settled, then?"

"Nothing is settled," Sir Matthew said, waving a hand languidly. "We must wait and see how matters turn out. If Grace's reputation survives intact, you may yet be spared the horror of having her as a daughter-in-law."

"I shall pray to be spared such a prospect."

Listening to this exchange, his mother angry and his father coldly composed, George found it hard to believe they were talking about him and his future. As if they had any say in the matter! He was of age, he would marry where he pleased. Naturally, he had no wish to disoblige his parents, but he could not accept their high-handed way of ordering his life as if it were nothing to do with him at all.

And then there was Grace. How could he stand idly by while his mother called her a hoyden and a badly behaved chit and, the worst insult of all, no lady? As if Grace were not worth ten — no, a hundred, a *thousand* of any of them. And by God, if he had to marry anyone, he had as soon it were Grace than any other woman alive.

So when his parents finally stopped spitting at each other, George jumped up from his seat. As much to his own surprise as anyone else's, he said robustly, "Pray as you please, Mama, that is between you and the Lord, but you may as well get used to the idea of Grace as a daughter-in-law, because whatever happens, I fully intend to make her my wife."

~~~~~

Grace found Brinford Manor to be a place of the utmost tranquillity. The servants moved about on silent feet, speaking only in whispers. Meals appeared at the precisely appointed time. The inhabitants kept to a rigid timetable of activities, with no room for impulse or a sudden change of plan. At first, this calmness soothed Graces jangled nerves, and the unpleasantnesses and alarms of the past day and a half began to retreat into the recesses of her mind.

This pleasant state of affairs lasted all of two hours, when restlessness reasserted itself. Grace was used to being busy, and at Graham House there had been Alice's lessons to attend or little errands to run for Lady Graham. At home she would be making up baskets of food or blankets to give to the poor. Here, nothing more exciting offered than sitting in the little parlour where Mary kept her household records, watching her scratch away with the pen at her morning lists and letters.

"It is such a fine day, I thought I might take a turn about the garden," Grace said.

"We always take our walk at two," Mary said, head bent over her papers.

"Oh. May I not go earlier?"

Mary raised her head. "Of course you may, if you wish it, but I would ask that you keep to the eastern side of the house only. If Sir Osborne should look out of his window and see you, he would perhaps be concerned to see you out so early in the day."

"It is past noon!"

"True, but walking proceeds at such a slow pace that he feels sure that one must be exposed to the risk of a chill. Two o'clock is late enough to be free of early morning dew and dampness, and too early for any chill from dusk. Even then, one must be well wrapped up." Her eyes twinkled as she spoke.

Grace gave it up, and went in search of some more interesting activity. The Dowager Lady Hardy and the Miss Hardys were not to be found, but the sound of high-pitched children's voices led her to the nursery wing, where the five children of Sir Osborne's heir resided. Here she spent a happy hour reading to the four oldest, to the gratitude of the harassed governess, before a servant came to summon her to attend Sir Osborne and Lady Hardy on their walk.

Sir Osborne was indeed bundled up in greatcoat and scarves, despite the mild spring weather, and he eyed Grace's spencer and muslin gown with alarm.

"You will catch a chill, Miss Allamont, I am certain of it," he said as he offered her his arm. "Do look how sensibly Lady Hardy is attired for this changeable time of year. Although I cannot persuade her to wear a scarf. The throat is so vulnerable, Miss Allamont, and one can never be too careful."

"You are too good, Sir Osborne, but you need not be concerned on my account, for I have never suffered from a chill in my life."

"That was exactly what your father always said, whenever I expressed my concern for him. Always striding about the countryside quite heedless of the damp. And look what happened — he took a chill and a fortnight later he was dead. A dreadful lesson for us all, Miss Allamont. But let us talk of happier matters. How wonderful it is that you are safely restored to us after your terrifying encounter. Two men with pistols! And shots exchanged and you were caught in the middle of it all, yet here you are, as calm as if nothing at all had occurred to discompose you. Yet you must beware of delayed effects, Miss Allamont. You have no dizziness, I trust? No fainting or queasiness? And as to the risk of nightmares — a cup of chocolate before bed is just the thing, and you must ensure the maid warms your bed adequately. Nothing is more fatal for one's repose than a cold bed."

In this gentle way, they walked at a funereal pace the full length of the terrace. They had just turned to begin the return when Sir Osborne was overcome with a fit of coughing and was obliged to retreat indoors with Mr Merton, thus freeing Mary and Grace for a much brisker walk around the gardens.

They had not long returned to the house when Amy and Hope arrived, with Mr Ambleside and Aunt Lucy.

"We went to Graham House, to hear that you were staying with Mary," Amy said, her face anxious. "You have not quarrelled with Lady Graham, sister dear?"

Grace was obliged to give out a very truncated version of events, to the effect that George had taken her out for a drive but the broken axle had obliged them to seek shelter with Mary.

"I liked the idea so well that I asked Grace to stay on for a few days," Mary added in her placid way. "Lady Graham can spare her, I am sure. I have written to her, but there cannot be the least objection."

"Oh no, such an excellent plan, no one could object," Amy said, but Mr Ambleside looked sharply at Grace with the slightest hint of a frown on his face.

As soon as he had an opportunity, he moved closer to Grace and said in a low voice, "Perhaps I am mistaken, but I wonder if there is something left unsaid. Is there any way in which we can be of service to you, Miss Allamont? If you should be in any difficulty—"

"No, no," she said hastily. "Nothing that need alarm Amy, in any event. However, if the subject should arise in company, I should be obliged if you would relate the story exactly as I have described it."

He nodded. "You may depend upon me. Know also that I should be honoured if you would confide in me if you should ever need counsel or aid. I am part of your family now, as Mrs Ambleside is part of mine, and any... any *unpleasantness* that befalls any one of us, falls equally on the rest. So do not hesitate to call upon my services, should the need arise."

"Thank you, sir."

Grace could say no more. Her spirits had begun to rise as she felt that the worst was now behind her and the whole sorry business of inns and broken-down curricles and her wretched reputation could be left in the past where it belonged and be forgotten about. But seeing Mr Ambleside's serious face, she realised that nothing was forgotten and her future still hung by a thread. It was infuriating and dispiriting and worrying, all at the same time.

Worse than that, her foolishness could drag the whole family into disrepute. Why had that never occurred to her before? Reckless as she might be of her own future, she fervently wished no ill on her sisters or their husbands. Belle would not care, perhaps, and Connie was a marchioness and could hold her head high in any society, and Dulcie was far away in Scotland, but Amy! Dear Amy, good, sweet person that she was, would be grieved beyond measure if she knew what had happened or had to see her sister cast out of good society.

And Hope! However much she protested that she should never marry, surely she must have the opportunity. Now, perhaps Grace had blighted her sisters' hopes as much as her own.

Grace sank into the deepest gloom.

22: *Ups And Downs*

Grace was so caught up in her own thoughts that she jumped when Mr Ambleside said, "Your aunt is waving to you. I believe she wishes to talk to you, Miss Allamont."

For a moment, she was almost too upset to move. How could she make insipid conversation when everything was so unsettled? But there were just enough of her father's features in Aunt Lucy to compel her obedience, so after some moments she excused herself from Mr Ambleside and crossed the room to sit by her aunt.

They talked of nothing very much at first — of Liverpool, and her aunt's news from there, which was of no interest to Grace. But then Aunt Lucy said, "I went to see the Allamont family solicitor the other day."

"Mr Plumphett?"

"The very same. At last! He is a difficult man to gain access to. If I were of a suspicious nature, I might think he was avoiding me." She laughed heartily at this. "But I finally got sight of the will, as I have wished for all this time."

Grace frowned. "But I thought we knew all the provisions of the will. There is nothing new, is there?"

"No, but I wished to know the exact wording of it, you know, as it affects Ernest and Frank."

Grace was alert suddenly. "You have had news from them?"

"Regrettably not, but I have learned that there is still time to discover them. I was confused, you know, by the talk of five years and then the Hall goes to the church, but if one of you girls marries one of your cousins before the five years, then the Hall would go there instead. I had all this originally from that Barnett fellow — good Lord, I suppose he is my nephew! And your brother, child. What a dreadful thought, for he is not at all the thing, you know, and his mother worse, for all they pretend to be so respectable now. But then, Liverpool society is not so particular as London. As I say, he told me of the will, but he is not a lawyer and gave me some garbled version of how it should work. But I have it quite clear in my mind now — if the boys are found, then the Hall is theirs, or rather it is Ernest's if he is found, and Frank's if he is found but Ernest is not."

"Yes, that much was always clear," Grace said.

"True. But it is now clear to me also. And the marriage to the cousin will only succeed if neither of the boys is found. What is more, I have clarified the exact date. Five years, the will states. That is five years to the day of your father's demise, and the boys must be found or the marriage must have taken place within that time. If not, then the church takes everything."

Grace was struck by a sudden thought. "What does it mean when it says that the boys must be found by that date? If we should hear that they are alive and living in Scotland, are they found?"

"Ah, you are a smart girl! No, I asked that too, and Plumphett says that they would have to present themselves at his office in Brinchester by close of business on the day before the anniversary of the death. So we have one year and five months, Miss Allamont."

"And do you think you can find them by then?"

"I shall do everything in my power to do so," she said. "Tomorrow I shall set off for Liverpool, for not a moment must be wasted. Let us hope that I am not too late."

Grace was thoughtful after this exchange with Aunt Lucy. She had not thought much about Ernest and Frank for years now. She had been thirteen when they left, and the whole household thrown into turmoil on account of it. Yet within days, their chairs had been removed from the dining room, the bedroom they shared emptied, their books and slates in the schoolroom put away. After that, they were never talked of, and the family closed up around the gap they had left as if they had never existed.

Even when Papa had died, and Mr Plumphett had inserted notices in all the likely newspapers, it had seemed impossible that they would suddenly appear, a few years older and taller, men not boys, and resume their places in the family. She could not even imagine it.

Yet Aunt Lucy had seen them. They had lived with her for two years before something had driven them away again, but in different directions this time. Could she find them? Did she have places to look in Liverpool, or share acquaintance who might know what had happened to them? Did they even know that Papa was dead, and they stood to inherit Allamont Hall and all Papa's fortune? Clearly Mr Plumphett's notices had not reached them, or Aunt Lucy either. So many questions, and no answers. Perhaps they would never know, and in a little over a year the Hall would be turned over to the church. Then Grace and Hope would have to leave their home and move into the Dower House with Mama. It was a lowering thought.

But after this the talk was all of poor Cousin Vivienne, and the succession of physicians who had been unable to ameliorate her condition, and the visitors left soon after, leaving Grace in the lowest of spirits.

How she wished George were there! No matter how bad everything seemed, he always had the power to elevate her mood. He was such easy company, and she had been with him so much lately that she missed him unbearably. It was like a constant itch that could not be scratched. If only she could see him, she was sure she would feel better. And then she thought of the way he had kissed her when they had fallen, and the look in his eyes at the inn. *'I will always take care of you.'* How badly she wanted him there with her at that moment to take care of her. But he was gone, and she had never felt more lonely in her life.

~~~~~

The following day, Mary summoned the carriage to take Grace into Higher Brinford.

"I shall visit the apothecary, for Mr Pym is a dreadful gossip and will be sure to tell everyone that Miss Grace Allamont is staying at the Manor. And the haberdasher and chandler, too, for everyone goes in and out of those two shops. That will spread the word nicely. We shall call on Mr Sidderfin at the parsonage, too. I should like to see Miss Endercott, but I am not sure we have time to go to Lower Brinford today, and tomorrow I must take Mark back to Willowbye, now that he is up and about again. And of course I want to see Mama."

"Is Cousin Vivienne going to die?" Grace asked in a small voice.

There was a long silence. "I will not lie to you, Grace. She is very ill, and nothing has answered. I asked Sir Osborne's physician about the case, for Dr Percival is very modern in his methods and has improved Sir Osborne's health a great deal, but he can give me no assurances."

"Is it because of the coming baby?"

"I believe it is. There are many things that can go wrong. Sometimes they can be recovered from, but not always. The letter that came from Papa yesterday said that Mama has made her peace with God and is prepared for the end, if it should come to that. All we can do now is to pray for her. Here is the carriage coming round. Remember, Grace, smile at everyone. You are perfectly happy, and enjoying a little stay with me, and nothing untoward has occurred."

Grace nodded and followed Mary demurely to the carriage, but she wondered how she would manage to get through the next few days and weeks without misery consuming her. Just three days ago she had been aflame with happiness and excitement, and today all was turned to ashes.

~~~~~

Until George had publicly declared his intent to marry Grace, the thought had not seriously occurred to him. He had found it very enjoyable to have her staying at Graham House, of course, and he had wished that the visit would not soon come to an end. Occasionally it had crossed his mind that Grace was very much the sort of woman he admired, and he hoped that, when the time came for him to marry, he would be lucky enough to find someone like her. And latterly, it had to be confessed, and especially since he had kissed her, his thoughts had become somewhat warmer, and his mind had begun to be filled with a certain face with a mischievous smile. But he had not quite made the obvious leap.

Now that he had, he realised that she was exactly the perfect wife for him. She was so lively and high-spirited that there would never be a dull moment with her. She would argue with him, of course, but better that than a doormat of a woman like the dreadful Miss Dilworthy, for all her impeccable family. Grace would always make him smile, and she was so pretty! How was it that he had never noticed that before?

The question was how to go about the business, now that he had made up his mind, and here he hesitated. His first thought was to rush to her side and declare his love and settle the business once and for all. But Lady Hardy had sent him off from Brinford Manor with the strict instruction to stay away from Grace for a while. *'We want to disassociate the two of you in everyone's minds,'* she had said. *'At all costs we must prevent people from automatically connecting your names together, for then they might start looking into the story more closely. For Grace's sake, do not show her any special attention.'*

He could see the point of it, so he curbed his first instinct and stayed quietly at home, or accompanied his mama and papa on their visits around the neighbourhood, less from duty, it had to be said, than in the hope of encountering Grace. But by the time they went to Brinford Manor, Grace had already left there, summoned home to Allamont Hall by her mama. Miss Bellows had also gone, and Hope had been recalled from the Amblesides' house.

Knowing that she would not be returning to Graham House galvanised George into action. He felt all of a sudden that if he did not declare himself immediately — at once! — he would lose Grace to some scheming fortune-hunter like Wright. There was always one or other of them sniffing around her, smiling unctuously and bringing little posies or books of poetry, as one poor fellow did. Poetry! As if Grace would be impressed by that. None of them had bothered him before Wright, but Grace had never seemed to see the fellow in the proper way, and had smiled at him in such a warm fashion that George had become quite incensed by the odious man. Jealous, he supposed now, with a wry smile, although he had not realised it at the time.

So on the first day after the discovery that Grace had gone home, he made his way to Allamont Hall to secure her hand and his future happiness. He was quite at peace with himself, as he had never expected to be when the time came for him to tie himself for life to a female. With Grace, there was a rightness to it that warmed his heart and lifted him so high up that he almost felt like singing.

It was a fine day for a ride, and on any regular occasion he would have made his way by the shortest route, galloping across the fields, skirting the grounds of Thornside, where Mr and Mrs Wills lived, and then either across Mr Garmin's farm or through Brinmorton Woods. Today he felt the full weight of the step he was about to take, and galloping anywhere seemed too frivolous for the occasion.

Instead, he rode sedately along the road, passing Primrose Lodge, and then on through Lower Brinford. As he rode, he contemplated with delight his life with the future Mrs George Graham, and the possibilities of Primrose Lodge. He had heard his mother talk about the house many times, but had never paid much attention. Now he wondered how many rooms it had, and whether that would be adequate for their needs, and how many servants might be required. He would want to set up his stable, too, and made a mental note to ask his papa where he might order the building of his carriage.

Allamont Hall looked the same as ever, although perhaps there were more weeds growing in the drive than he remembered. But with no man about the place, and Lady Sara away so much, the house was directionless and the servants drifted. Amy had taken an interest in the garden, he remembered, and Belle had had a practical bent that kept the house in order, but with only Grace and Hope left, perhaps no one cared about appearances any more, not even the gardeners.

Inside the house, he was shown at once into the drawing room. He found Grace alone there, her face pale and her eyes puffy, as if she had been crying. His heart jumped at the sight of her, and he wanted nothing so much as to sweep her into his arms and plant kisses all over that pretty face and make her smile again. But he knew he must not. Informality had no place in a proposal of marriage, and he must keep to the conventions on this of all days.

So he bowed and said, "Good morning, Miss Allamont. I trust you are well?"

She gazed at him blankly. "Hello, George. Why so prim, all of a sudden?"

He could hardly say, *'Because I am about to offer for you, and I deemed it appropriate,'* so instead, thinking quickly, he said, "Lady Hardy told me not to show you any special attention, in case people start wondering about us."

"But we are quite alone. There is no one here to see how you treat me."

This was not going as well as he had hoped, and for a moment he was flummoxed. He settled randomly on saying, "Where is everyone?"

"Mama is still at Willowbye, but we expect her later today. Miss Bellows and Hope have gone into the village with Mr Bertram Graham."

"Uncle Bertram? What is he doing here?"

"Courting Miss Bellows, as anyone with half a brain might see," she said. "Oh, do sit down, George. You make the room look untidy, lurking over there by the door."

He could not think of a good reason to refuse, so he perched on a chair some distance away from her, for he was still settled on a formal approach. "Miss Allamont—"

"What is the matter with you!" she cried, jumping to her feet, so that he was obliged to do the same. "I see nothing of you for days and days, and when you do come, you are so altered that I hardly know you. It is not kind in you, George. I am in the most dreadful situation here, where I might at any moment be quite ruined and you could have been cheering me up and making me laugh, as you usually do. Instead, all I get is *'Miss Allamont'* this and *'Miss Allamont'* that, as if we have not known each other for ever. Are we not friends any more, George?"

And to his utter dismay, two great tears rolled down her cheeks. Now George had seen Grace in many moods, angry and nervous, mischievous and sad, terrified and excited, but he had never seen her crying before and he had no idea what to do. He desperately wanted to rush to her and hold her tight until all the tears had gone away, but perhaps that would make everything worse.

"No, no, you must not cry," he said helplessly. "Of course we are friends."

"Are we?" she cried. "Oh, you are hopeless, George Graham!"

She swirled away and strode across to the window, standing with her back to him, but he could see her shoulders heaving as she sobbed silently.

He could resist no longer. In a few strides he was across the room, coming up behind her to wrap his arms around her waist. And, because she was quite irresistible, he bent down to kiss her bare neck, inhaling the flowery perfume that clung to her, feeling the warmth of her body against his, the sweet delight of being so close to her, and every rational thought went out of his head.

"Ah, Grace, you must not distress yourself," he murmured. "This is all for the best, you will see. We shall get married and everything will be wonderful."

She stiffened in his arms. "No."

And with that single word, all his hopes and dreams came crashing down about him.

"No?" he said in astonishment, releasing her.

She turned to face him, her cheeks wet with tears, but her voice was composed. "No. You must not marry me from a misplaced sense of obligation, George. I... I am upset just now, but I shall go on perfectly well, whatever happens. You do not want to marry me, I know that."

"But I do!"

"It is very gallant in you, George, but nothing will convince me. You can offer until your throat is hoarse, but I will never accept you."

"Never?" he whispered.

"Never."

23: Advice

Grace had no idea how she expected George to react to her refusal. Would he be angry or upset? Would he rant and rail at her? That would be all right, for she knew how to deal with him in that mood, and could talk him down from the boughs. She could always make him smile when she set her mind to it.

Her worst fear was that he would talk of love. If he did that, or worse, if he kissed her again... How could she maintain her composure? She could still feel the place on her neck where he had rested his lips — so warm, so soft! Heaven help her, if he kissed her again she would fall into his arms, and that would never do. He must not be allowed to throw himself away because of some stupid sense of responsibility for her predicament. He had told her himself, very plainly, that he had no thought of marriage for many years, and he had never shown the least sign of being in love with her. He had kissed her that time when they had fallen on the stairs, of course, but that was only fun, he had said so himself. And today... but no doubt that was just what he imagined ought to be done when offering for a lady.

He was not in love with her, and she could not bear it if he were to marry her merely from obligation. She could find the strength to refuse him, if only he would not kiss her again. So she held her breath and waited for his reaction.

George turned without a word and stalked out of the room.

She let out her breath all in a rush, then she hurled herself into the nearest chair and cried and cried. She could not explain, even to herself, just why she was crying. After all, she had half expected George to do something foolish like offering for her, and she had already made up her mind to refuse him if he should try it.

And yet...

With all her being she longed to accept him. How feather-brained of her to fall in love with a man who saw her only as a friend. Yet no matter how much she berated herself for her idiocy, the tears kept falling.

~~~~~

Lady Sara returned from Willowbye that afternoon.

"There is no change," she said sorrowfully when Hope and Grace pressed her for news. "I have tried every remedy I know, and the physicians have done their best, but nothing helps. Poor Vivienne! How she suffers. The laudanum gives her some relief from the pain, at least. Grace, will you come upstairs with me while I remove my bonnet and coat?"

"Of course, Mama."

Grace bobbed a curtsy and followed her mother up the stairs, and into her bedroom. Grace could not remember ever being there before, and looked about her with interest. It was an elegant room, light and airy, although the furniture was somewhat dated now and the wallpaper was a little heavy. Perhaps it was the same that Mama had chosen when she first married. But it was not the furniture that drew Grace's eye the most. Over the mantelpiece was a large portrait of Mama — or rather, two Mamas, two laughing beauties side by side, wearing the stiff gowns of a generation ago, their hair powdered, arms around each other's waists.

216

"Aunt Tilly," Grace breathed.

Her mother laughed. "One of them is. Can you tell which one?"

"No! How strange it must be to have another person exactly the same as one. It would be like looking in a mirror."

"Oddly enough, it is not. When I look in the mirror, what I see is not the same as my twin, although I do not know why that should be."

"How could anyone distinguish one from the other?" Grace said.

"They could not, of course, not if we wore the same clothes. But to make it easy for people, we each wore a ribbon around the wrist. Mine was yellow and hers was red."

"But you could have swapped the ribbons," Grace said.

"So we could," her mother said with a smile. "Although that would be very bad, would it not, to deceive people so? Now, Grace dear, come and sit beside me here and tell me how you are, for Mary has told me all about your misadventure and you have been crying, I think."

So Grace told her everything, not excluding George's proposal, and her mother listened sympathetically.

"You were quite right to reject him," she said, when Grace had finally lapsed into silence. "A marriage of that nature — both parties forced into it, resenting it — no, it does not answer. It solves the immediate problem, but in five years, or ten, or twenty...? Better by far to wait for love, however long it takes, for true love will live for all eternity without reproach or diminution. Though it be the tiniest spark, it will never be extinguished, but ready to burst into flame at the least puff of breath."

"Oh," Grace said. "Because you have always told us to accept the first offer that is made, for one man is much the same as another. So you have said many times."

"Have I?" her mother said, but then she laughed. "Perhaps I am mellowing in age, Grace, or it may be that my time at Willowbye has made me philosophical. I have been here too long, I think."

"You have not been here an hour," Grace protested.

"How literal you are! Nevertheless, I believe I must go back to London soon. Now, dear, you must not worry about what has happened, for at the moment there is no rumour abroad about your little adventure. Even if it should become known, I truly believe your credit is good enough to carry you through, and if not, then we shall send you to Connie and her patronage will protect you. Run along, dear. Do ask cook if there is any duck to be had, for I have such a longing for it."

~~~~~

George rode home in such misery that it was fortunate for him that his horse knew the way without guidance, for its rider was paying no attention to his surroundings. After all his high hopes, his future was dashed to pieces and he could not see his way clear to a recovery. There was nothing in Grace's refusal to give him the slightest hope, even with the most optimistic interpretation. That one word — *'Never!'* — could not be more final.

What was he now to do? All his dreams were over, and he had nothing to look forward to but a succession of Miss Dilworthys laid out for his inspection by his mama.

Not wanting to face his mother, he took the horse round to the stables himself, and set about unsaddling and grooming him. Anything to postpone the awful moment when he had to confess that Grace had refused him, and see the look of triumph on his mother's face.

He was so intent on his work that he failed to take notice of the arrival of another horse, until his father's voice cut across his bitter brooding.

"George? We pay grooms to do that sort of thing, you know." Then he caught sight of George's face. "Ah. Leave it for Loxton and come inside."

His father led him in silence to the library, and not until he had poured two glasses of Madeira and they were both seated beside the fire did he say, "You have been to Allamont Hall, I take it. And she refused you?"

George could only nod miserably.

"Of course she did." His father sipped his Madeira, watching George over the rim of his glass. "I daresay you have never courted her properly, have you? Sent her flowers, or written poems about her—"

"Poems! She would think me a simpleton if I attempted any such thing!"

"Well, perhaps you are right about that. Grace is not the romantic sort. But have you ever paid her any particular attention beyond that of commonplace acquaintances? Or given her the least indication that you are head over ears in love with her?"

George took a long breath, but there was no point in prevaricating. "You can tell that?"

His father smiled. "Naturally. I see the way you look at her, and the way you always rush to her side as soon as we rejoin the ladies after dinner. I was not quite sure that *you* were aware of it, to be frank, until you stated so robustly that you planned to marry her, and even then, I could not be sure it was not mere chivalry for a lady in distress. But now..."

"Now I am quite cast down," he said glumly. "She will not have me, and there is an end to it. What on earth am I to do?"

His father raised an eyebrow. "Are you seriously asking my advice?"

"I believe I am," George said, his lips twitching in amusement. "Who would ever have imagined I would reach such a desperate point? But I want Grace more than anything in the world, and I will even ask my own father's advice if it helps me achieve that aim."

Sir Matthew smiled, but shook his head. "I cannot make any promises on that score. But if I were you, I would set about showing her how much you love her."

"How do I do that?"

"Tell her, of course. If poems will not do it, and I daresay you are right on that head, for you know her better than any of us, then tell her openly and sincerely. Tell her how wonderful she makes you feel, and that you cannot live without her. And kiss her, if you get the chance."

"I should like to get the chance," George said, with a half smile.

"There, that is more like yourself. And give her time. Let her know that you will wait for her to be ready, and that you will not go away. I have never understood all these men who offer once and then give up if they are not accepted instantly. If a man loves a woman, he should be prepared to wait as long as it takes, and to ask repeatedly until he gets the right answer. I proposed to your mother five times before she accepted me, you know. If a woman is worth having, she is worth waiting for. So never give up."

"So do you think—" George began, but he never finished the sentence.

A knock at the door heralded the butler. "Beg pardon, Sir Matthew, but—"

And then, barging into the room, her eyes afire and her face red with anger, was Cousin Anne. His expression pained by this breach of protocol, the butler silently withdrew, the door closing with a soft snick behind him.

"Anne. This is a surprise," Sir Matthew said calmly, but as he stood, he moved a little closer to George, as if to demonstrate their solidarity under attack.

"Is it indeed? I should have thought you might have been expecting me."

"You are quite mistaken on that score. But how are you? Have you recovered from your dreadful ordeal at the hands of that desperate band of highwaymen. Six armed men, was it? Or seven? I forget exactly what your letter said. But you resisted so bravely and your coachman saw them off. Was that not how it went?"

If possible, she went even redder, but she lifted her chin defiantly. "Never mind that. It is easy to become confused when pistols are being waved about. It was two men, and I now know the identity of one of them."

"And you have come all this way to tell us of your discovery," Sir Matthew said. "How gratifying. I wonder you did not go straight to the nearest constable."

"I am come to inform you," she said in her haughtiest tones, "that the perpetrator of this wicked deed was none other than *your son!* What do you say to that?"

"Why should you suppose such a thing?"

"Because the leader of the highwaymen called my coachman *by his name!* He knew Cartwright, and therefore had to be a person known to me also. When I mentioned this to Cartwright, he recalled that he had seen George's groom loitering about the inn at Dalbury Cross. Naturally I went there immediately to investigate—"

"Naturally," Sir Matthew said.

"—only to discover that George had been putting up at the *other* inn. And that is not the worst of it."

"Oh, do tell us the worst of it."

"He had given a false name, and was staying there *with a female!* What do you say to that!"

"Why, that George is a grown man, and if he enjoys a little dalliance from time to time, what could be more natural?"

George tried very hard not to laugh, as Cousin Anne spluttered with indignation.

"Well, I had expected better of you, Uncle Matthew! Such loose morals in one so young are not to be tolerated! And there is something loathsome about a man spending his days in respectable society, and his nights in... Well! It is disgusting, and I am very disappointed in you, George. I thought you were too caught up in your silly games with Grace Allamont to have any thought for—"

His father's hand rested briefly on his arm, a warning touch, and George kept his mouth firmly shut, but he could not help his face changing as anger swept over him.

Anne saw it, and at once her face lit up with glee. "Oh ho! So is that the way of it? It was *Grace* you were with? I always thought there was something unprincipled about her and that she would fall into wantonness all too readily."

"I will not hear a word said against Grace!" George burst out. "She is entirely innocent."

"Innocent? When she spent a night at a public inn with a man, and not even a maid to protect her virtue? If indeed she has any virtue to protect."

"Enough!" Sir Matthew said. "You had better leave now, Anne. Grace has done no wrong, and I will not hear a young lady of good standing in society abused in that way. Be assured that you will not be welcome in this house in the future."

She lifted her chin and looked him in the eye, undaunted. "That is just like you, to reject family and protect harlots."

"Family is always welcome. Thieves are not. How many small but valuable items have you stolen from us over the years, and I have let it pass because you were family? Well, no longer. This time you have gone too far. If you had not attempted to steal the Durmaston Diamonds, George would never have set out to recover them from you and we would all have been spared a great deal of distress."

She licked her lips, perhaps wondering how to answer that without admitting her guilt. Instead she said mildly, "The Durmaston Diamonds belong to the Durmaston family. You should never have had them."

"It is far too late for that now. They were freely given to Lady Graham years ago, and the necklace broken up and the diamonds sold or reworked. The necklace you stole was a paste copy."

Her mouth dropped open, and for an instant she was speechless.

"I hope that will teach you a lesson," Sir Matthew said. "However, I am not optimistic."

"How dare you!" she hissed, eyes narrowing. "If you think this is the end, you are greatly mistaken. I shall certainly not come here again, after you have treated me so abominably. But you will find that I am not without friends. No, indeed, I have a great many friends who will no doubt be most interested to hear all about the Drovers' Inn at Dalbury Cross and what went on there. Then we will see whether Grace Allamont is of good standing in society or not."

24: Trouble

Grace had no time to brood over George as she was kept busy helping Mama to pack for her journey to London. That was new, too, for previously Mama had taken the greatest delight in surprising them, simply appearing one morning in her travelling outfit, her coach already sent for. But she had a new lady's maid now, so perhaps she had not yet learned to trust her with such matters. Grace rather liked this mellower version of her mama, who involved her daughters in her doings and invited them into her bedroom and listened without reproach. But it was more than three years since Papa had died, and she supposed that even Mama was now able to throw off the yoke of subservience to a domineering man.

They stood in the hall, Mama adjusting her bonnet and pulling on her gloves, Hope in tears, as she always was when Mama went away and Grace trying to conceal a tear in her fichu. Miss Bellows was nowhere to be seen. But when the sound of horses' hooves was heard, it was not the travelling coach appearing, but a single horseman. Through the open front door strode George Graham, the very last person Grace had expected to see. She blushed and hung her head, but he made his greeting to her mother in the regular way, sounding so entirely his normal self that her head shot up in surprise.

"Miss Allamont." He bowed formally to her, his face serious. "Miss Hope. My lady, I wonder if I might speak to you and the Miss Allamonts on a matter of some importance. I shall be very brief, for I see you are about to set off on a journey, but I have some news that you should hear before you depart."

Dread swept over Grace. What could he have to say that was so urgent, so important that he must needs delay her mother? Was it about his proposal? But she soon discovered that it was worse, far worse. Cousin Anne knew everything, and was determined to ruin Grace's reputation by every means at her disposal.

Grace sat rigidly, barely able to breathe. All her fears were coming true, her world crashing down about her ears and yet Mama and George talked so calmly together, as if it were no more than a small difficulty in the kitchens, a minor irritation.

"Whatever will she do?" Hope whispered. "Grace will be quite ruined!"

"Nonsense!" Lady Sara said briskly. "No one who knows Grace at all will be fooled by the scheming of this devious woman. Our friends will stand by us."

"Must we leave the neighbourhood?" Hope said. "Perhaps we should not go about at all until this blows over."

"Now, that is exactly what we should *not* do," Lady Sara said firmly. "When is the next assembly? A fortnight or a little more, I fancy. We shall attend as usual. Before that, I think we must hold a dinner for as many of our acquaintance as we can. Grace, you must arrange that while I am in London. One week from today, if you please, and tell Mrs Cooper to produce something very special. I shall bring whatever I can from London. And invite everyone - *everyone*, mind. Some will not come, but we will at least know who our true friends are. I shall return as quickly as I am able. Now, there is my coach coming round." She rose from her seat. "Remember - invite everyone, Grace."

~~~~~

While Mama was away, Grace tried her best to carry on just as usual, as Mama had advised, and that meant not hiding away at home, but going about her normal round of outings and visits. She was not quite confident enough to go into the village, except for church, but she liked to go to Miss Firth's school and read to the children, who knew nothing of her disgrace and were always delighted to see her. She found her way there almost every day, even when Hope and Miss Bellows could not go with her, for the long walk through the woods lifted her spirits far more than sitting about with her tapestry. Better by far to be doing something, anything, rather than endlessly waiting for something to happen.

She was on her way home one day after such a visit, and hurrying through the woods rather in the hope that George would be at the Hall waiting for her, when she came upon a man sitting on a stile, head down, as if lost in thought. He was smartly dressed, so she did not quite like to ignore him, but nor was she minded to be drawn into a long conversation, either.

"Good day to you, sir," she said briskly, without breaking stride, and would have been past him and away if he had not looked up at that moment.

"Good day to you, too, Grace."

Oh, that familiar face with the roguish smile and a glint in his eye, the face she had hoped never to see again. "Mr Wright," she said coolly, slowing to a halt. "I had imagined you to be long gone from here."

"So I should be," he said, the smile broadening. "So I intended to be. Yet somehow I find myself drawn here. I wonder what the attraction can be?"

"I cannot imagine, but I suggest you leave at once. There is still time for me to set the constables on you."

He laughed immoderately at this, his lips curled into a sneer, and she wondered why she had ever thought him handsome. There was a displeasing coarseness about his features that was now obvious to her.

"Well, now, that would be an uncharitable act, do you not agree? Especially as your own actions have not been beyond reproach in the matter of stealing diamond necklaces and holding up the coaches of wealthy ladies. If we are to attract the interest of the constables, there might be much I could say on the subject of your cousin Mark, if it comes to that. And we would not wish that, now would we, Grace?"

She could not argue with him on that point. Indeed, she had no great desire to talk to him at all. Annoyed with herself for stopping in the first place, she turned and would have walked on, but he jumped up and stood in her way.

"Now that is downright uncivil of you, Grace. Can we not have a chat for old time's sake? You were not always so unwilling to talk to me. I seem to remember a dinner at Graham House when you were very friendly towards me."

"That was when I thought you were a gentleman. I do not think we have anything further to say to each other, Mr Wright. I suggest you take yourself back to wherever you are staying and leave me alone."

"Very high and mighty these days, aren't we? Yet I don't believe you have anything to be so superior about, not if all I hear about you is true. There are a lot of rumours flying about stuck-up Miss Grace Allamont these days, to do with inns and a certain Mr George Graham and pretending to be married. So you've got no reason to look down on me, have you, young lady? You're no more a lady than I'm a gentleman."

"You leave George out of this," she said hotly. "He has done nothing wrong, and nor have I!"

"Doesn't make any difference, does it?" he said with an unpleasant grin. "People think you have and that's what matters. You'll be ruined and serve you right."

"I shall not stay here to be insulted by you!" She would have flounced past him, but he grabbed her wrist in a painfully tight grasp. "Ow! Let go of me, you beast!"

"Beast, am I?" he said, his face looming within inches of hers. "I'll show you what a beast I am. I warned you what would happen if I ever got you on your own, missy, and now, here you are. If you weren't ruined before, you will be by the time I've finished with you."

Grace trembled at these words, but as much with anger as with fear. She stared at him, hardly believing that this could be happening. How many times had Miss Bellows told her never to walk alone through the woods, because of the Romanies and wild men? She had encountered Romanies more than once, and found them to be friendly and not at all threatening, and she had never yet come across any wild men. Until now.

She was not the type to swoon, and she was too far from any possible rescue to make screaming worthwhile, but there must be some way to escape from this wicked man. Yet he held her fast, and he was a big, powerful man, not someone she could put up a fight against.

"Let me go!" she said, trying to snatch her arm away from his tight grip. "You are hurting me. Release me at once!"

He only laughed, and pulled her closer, his free hand snaking round her waist. "Give me a kiss, Grace, why don't you?"

His hand holding hers was only inches from her face, and with a sudden lunge she bit down on him as hard as she could. With a shriek and a curse, he released her and she grabbed the momentary freedom. Picking up her skirts, she ran.

Behind her, he yelled, "Come back here, you little vixen!" and she heard his heavy footsteps pounding after her.

She knew she could never outrun him. It was almost a mile back to the Hall, and he would catch her long before she reached safety. What she needed was a weapon to fight him off. A heavy stone would do it, and had she been in Farmer Garmin's fields she would have known exactly where he stacked the stones turned over by the plough. Here in the woods there was no certainty about stones, but there were plenty of fallen branches. There was even a log pile of sorts, in the clearing used by the Romanies when they camped here.

As soon as she had the thought she veered off the path and plunged under the trees. Brambles snagged her clothes and more than once she stumbled over the uneven ground, but fear drove her on. Behind her, she heard Wright crashing around and cursing her, but drawing steadily closer.

She burst into the clearing, leaping across the charred stones of the fire-pit in the centre, half buried in fallen leaves. On the far side, the log pile she remembered was no more than a few leftover branches, but it was enough. Picking up one that looked heavy enough to hurt, but small enough for her to wield, she spun round to face her assailant, holding the branch in front of her like a sword.

He rushed into the clearing, then stopped and laughed at her, hands on hips. "Well, you've got spirit, girl, I'll grant you that. It'll make the taming of you even more of a pleasure. What are you going to do with that stick, knock my head off?"

"If I have to."

He laughed even harder, but he did not come any closer. Instead he slowly stepped in a wide circle around her, so that she also had to turn to keep him in view. Already her arms were tiring holding the branch, and she was not at all sure how long she could keep going. All he had to do was wait and he would have the better of her in the end. She wondered if she could provoke him into a rash move.

"Are you just going to prowl around like a cat?" she said. "What, are you afraid to come any closer?"

With a snarl, he rushed her. She swung the branch with all her might, and although he ducked as he saw it coming it still caught him on the shoulder.

In an explosion of rotted wood, it smashed into a thousand pieces, not even slowing Wright down.

With a roar, he was on her, his momentum carrying her backwards and slamming her into the ground, all his weight on top of her. A thousand bumps and rocks and chunks of wood dug into her back and legs, and neither her bonnet nor a deep cushion of dead leaves prevented her head from thumping onto the hard-packed earth. For an instant she could not catch her breath, and felt sure she was going to die there, suffocated by Wright's body. But then he shifted slightly and she gasped, gulping gratefully at the cold air.

"Now I have you," he said softly, and that was more menacing than all his threats.

He wriggled about, then half shifted off her as he tried to pin down both her hands. At once she pushed with both legs, and he shrieked and fell to one side of her. She rolled to her hands and knees, and that was when the miracle happened. One hand landed on something smooth and hard. Her fingers closed around it and lifted it. A rock!

Without an instant's hesitation, she raised it, and brought it down with every ounce of her strength against his head. At once, he fell still.

She did not stop to see if she had killed him. Instead, she scrambled to her feet and ran for her life back through the trees, somehow finding the narrow track that led back to the main path, and then directly for home. She dared not turn around to see if he was following, and although she strained to hear, the only sounds she could distinguish were her own gasps for breath and her pounding feet, rushing through the swirls of leaves. No pursuit could be heard, neither footsteps nor curses.

She reached the gate and made directly across the lawn for the house. Now, now when she was within reach of help, she shouted with all her might.

"Help me! Help! Someone help me, please!"

By the time she had gained the steps, the door was open and there they were, Young and Miller and William and Sir Matthew Graham and Mr Ambleside pouring out of the front door, and a couple of gardeners and a groom running round the side of the house.

"Grace? What has happened?" Mr Ambleside, taking immediate charge.

"Wright... attacked me... woods... hit him. Insensible. Romanies' clearing."

"I know the place."

And then he was shouting orders, rounding up men to go off and find Wright, gathering weapons — guns, even — and people were running here and there in confusion.

And in the midst of the chaos, the second miracle, for there was George, calm and strong and unflustered, his arm around her, helping her, supporting her up the steps. When her legs unaccountably turned to water, he picked her up as if she weighed nothing and carried her into the house.

"Brandy, Mama," he said, his voice sharp. "Or smelling salts."

Then she was in the book room, and George set her down very tenderly on a sofa, with Lady Graham and Hope and Amy bustling round. Someone waved something foul-smelling under her nose.

She coughed. "Good Lord, what are you trying to do to me? That stuff is revolting!"

George laughed, but his mother chased him away. "Outside, George, if you please. You are not needed in here."

Then, when the door shut, she turned to Grace. "Now, dear, tell us exactly what happened, every detail."

So Grace did, sipping the brandy gratefully, and feeling the welcome warmth spreading through her limbs. Several times Lady Graham said, "Yes but did he *hurt* you at all, dear?" and Grace described her bumped head and the tightness of his grip on her wrist, and the rocky ground digging painfully into her back as he lay on top of her, before she finally realised the question that was being asked.

"Oh no, he did not *hurt* me. I... I hit him before... No. I am not *hurt*."

And only then, finally, did Lady Graham sigh and venture a small smile. "Ah, good. A bath, I think, young lady, and some fresh clothes, for you are quite covered in mud. Hmm, I believe this pelisse is beyond all hope of mending. Come along."

Outside in the hall, they found George waiting forlornly on a bench. He sprang up when he saw Grace.

"Are you all right? Mama, is she all right?"

"She will be as right as ninepence when she has had a good soak in the tub."

"Thank God! They will catch him, Grace, and he will be hanged or deported and not trouble you again."

But that was just what did not happen, for when the pursuing party arrived at the Romany clearing, there was nothing there but a torn bonnet and a blood-stained stone. Her attacker had escaped, and when enquiries were made in the village, it was reported that a man answering his description had boarded the public coach to Brinchester, and from there, it was later discovered, he had bought a ticket to Liverpool. Wright was gone for good.

25: The Assembly Rooms

A bath, a hearty dinner and a good night's sleep saw Grace somewhat restored, and thankful to have escaped with no more than a few bruises. Her nature was not one which tended to dwell on the unpleasant, but her spirits were low at this time for a number of reasons. Although she had suffered no lasting ill-effects, she could not help reproaching herself for placing her reputation and her very life at risk. Her foolish independence and childish willfulness had led to both her recent misadventures, and she was determined to do better. She had the examples of her mother and her sisters to guide her. She would be good from now on! If only it were not too late for remorse.

The attack served one useful purpose, for it caused all her neighbours to rally round her. Amy and Mary came almost every day to see her, and the drawing room was always full to overflowing with friends, shocked by so vicious an assault within the neighbourhood, and by one formerly accepted as a gentleman. In the matter of Grace's reputation, the reports they brought were less hopeful. Cousin's Anne's innuendos had spread far afield, and so Grace's spirits sank lower and lower. As for Hope, she was in even more despair than Grace herself, and Mama had reverted to her distant self. There was no comfort in any of them.

George was her staunchest supporter during this time, and her greatest friend. He came every day and sat quietly talking about normal things — his horse, his friends, an interesting item in the newspaper, or amusing tales of his valet, who had no great opinion of George and told him so often. *'I used to valet for the third son of a duke!'* George would mimic, in a high, lisping voice. *'How I am come down in the world!'* He always cheered Grace up. He made no reference to marriage or proposals, and said nothing that she could interpret as the words of a lover. She should be pleased, she knew, for it showed that he had accepted her refusal and given up all thought of marriage. But no matter how many times she told herself that was a very good thing, she always felt low afterwards. Her future was bleak indeed without George — her splendid, gallant George, the man she loved with all her heart.

The dinner was more successful than Grace had dared to hope. The dining room was full and Grace was almost overcome by the good wishes that surrounded her.

"That Miss Durmaston is a nasty piece of work," old Mrs Donborough declared forthrightly. "I never believe the half of what she says, and when she spreads such lies about dear Miss Grace, she may expect me to cut her when next she comes into the neighbourhood."

"If ever she dares to come this way again, she will not be staying under *my* roof," Lady Graham said with pursed lips.

It was heartening, but the assembly at Brinchester would be the greatest test, Grace knew. Such events were the province of the burghers of the town, and the gentry and a few of the nobility from a wide swathe of the country areas of Brinshire, and her well-wishers from Lower and Higher Brinford formed a very small portion of the whole.

The day of the assembly arrived, and Grace was utterly miserable.

"Must we go, Mama?" she asked for the hundredth time.

"We must," her mother said in implacable tones.

How many times had Grace entered the assembly rooms at Brinchester, her heart filled with joy at the prospect of a long evening of music and dancing and a hearty supper? Now all she felt was dread. Yet when they were announced, only a few heads turned to look at them. No, to look at *her*, of course, the hussy who had so far forgotten all sense of propriety as to stay at a common inn with a man, and quite unchaperoned.

She had not taken many steps into the room before she realised that the dowagers were whispering behind their fans. Perhaps only a few people knew her shame so far, but by the end of the evening everyone would know it.

"Head high," her mother whispered. "And smile. Always smile."

How difficult it was! Yet she must do it. Smile! And smile again! They settled themselves in their usual seats — smiling! — and Grace looked about her for the usual stream of eager young men rushing to claim her or Hope for the first dance. No one came. Smile, smile, smile and try not to notice the whispering, the covert looks, the fans raised to hide the shocking words being transmitted from person to person. One young man, one of Hope's admirers, set out towards them, only to have his mother call him back. Keep smiling! But it was so difficult, and Hope looked about to cry. How Grace longed to have her mother's aristocratic serenity. Nothing ruffled her. Grace lowered her head, quite unable to keep up the pretence a second longer.

A pair of elegant shoes appeared before her, with above them two shapely legs in stockings and satin knee-breeches.

"Might I have the very great honour of your hand for the next, Miss Allamont?" George said.

When she raised her eyes, he was smiling down at her with a warmth that made her quite fluttery.

"Oh! Oh, yes! Thank you!"

And then, to her delight, he took the empty seat next to her and rattled away in the most reassuring manner. She had no idea what he said, and answered quite at random, but he seemed not to mind. When the music began for the next dance, he led her out onto the floor quite unselfconsciously, and in no time she found herself chatting away to him as easily as ever. Dear George! She could not imagine what she would have done without him this last fortnight.

"I am so glad you did not go away!" she said to him impulsively as they waited their turn to go down the set.

"Go away?" he said. "Why on earth should you imagine I would do that?"

"Oh, I just thought... after... after what I said, that you might not want to see me again."

"You must think me very poor spirited if you imagine I would just creep away. I meant what I said, you know. Every word of it."

For a moment her breath caught and she could only stare at him. There was an intensity in his eyes that made her tremble.

"Our turn, Grace," he said, holding out his hand to her. "Oops, not that way."

"I beg your pardon, sir," she said, as she stood on someone's toe. It was so difficult to mind her steps when George was holding her hand, and looking at her in just that way, as if he could not take his eyes off her. Provoking man!

By the time George returned her to her mama, their party had grown larger. Amy and Mr Ambleside had arrived, Sir Matthew and Lady Graham were talking to Lady Sara and, shortly afterwards, Sir Osborne Hardy and Mary were announced.

"Sir Osborne was so incensed by these scurrilous rumours that he insisted on coming himself to dance with you," Mary said.

"Oh dear! I do hope his health will not be set back by it. He looks very pale."

"I think his outrage has strengthened him," Mary said with a smile. "He is better today than I have seen him for some time. And the weather is so dry just now. It is dampness that most affects him, you know, but I shall not allow him to dance more than a set or two, nevertheless. I cannot have him becoming over-tired. Ah, look, here is the Willowbye contingent."

With the addition of Belle and Mr Burford, James and his wife Alice, Hugo and even Cousin Henry, Grace was now surrounded by her family. She noticed also that many from Lower and Higher Brinford who did not usually attend were also there, making a point of greeting the Allamonts. Yet still no one from outside their immediate circle came to greet them. It was very lowering. There would be no shortage of dance partners for Grace and Hope, but standing up with one's sister's husband or a cousin was not at all the same as having young men from the whole of Brinshire falling over themselves to secure a dance.

But then a commotion around the entrance turned heads, and a hush fell upon the room.

The liveried announcer banged his staff. "The most honourable the Marquess of Carrbridge, the most honourable the Marchioness of Carrbridge, the Lady Harriet Marford, the Lord Reginald Marford, the Lord Humphrey Marford, the Lord Augustus Marford, the Lord Montague Marford, the Lord Gilbert Marford," he intoned.

The gasp that ran round the room was audible.

"Oh, *all* of them," George breathed. "How absolutely splendid."

"*Connie!*" squealed Grace, and tore across the ballroom to hurl herself into her sister's arms. "I had no idea you were coming!"

"It was a surprise to us, too," Connie said, gently disentangling herself and straightening her headdress. "But a cousin of Lord Carbridge wrote the most outrageous letter to him, and nothing would do but for him to come at once. We made the journey from Drummoor in two days, changing horses everywhere, and I have never been so rattled about in my life. We arrived but two hours ago, and of course all the hotels and inns were full and we had to descend on an old school friend of Reggie's, whose mama is not at all pleased, I can tell you! But here we are! And we made sure to bring partners enough to keep you on your feet all evening."

"You are so kind! And I am so glad to see you!" Grace cried, hugging Connie so fiercely that the headdress was in grave danger of being dislodged altogether.

After that, things went on charmingly, for the good people of Brinshire had no willpower to resist the patronage of a Marquess, and declared themselves satisfied that there was no truth whatsoever in the despicable rumours being spread about regarding Miss Grace Allamont, and had they not always said so?

"Save the dance before supper for me," George murmured in Grace's ear before she was swept off by Lord Humphrey for the cotillion, after the most exciting argument between three of the Marquess's brothers for the right to claim her hand. She danced and twirled and even remembered the steps, most of the time, and none of her partners grew impatient when she went wrong, so her smiles came quite naturally this time. But as she danced, her eyes often found themselves resting on a certain gentleman, not dancing himself, but seemingly content to watch her enjoying herself.

When he came to claim her for the supper dance, and bestowed on her that warm smile, she placed her hand in his with a singing heart.

"Hello again, George."

"Would you mind if we do not dance after all?" he said. "A glass of champagne, perhaps?"

She nodded, for she hardly minded whether they danced or not, so long as she was with him.

He led her up the stairs to the supper rooms, but instead of turning aside into one or other of them, he led her on, past the card rooms and down to the far end of the corridor and round the corner.

"Where are we going?" she asked, her heart beating faster.

"You will see."

Then he pulled open a door and pushed her inside.

It was dark, with just a little light emanating from a grill over the door, and an overpowering smell of beeswax.

"What is this place, the housemaid's cupboard?"

"Oh, probably. One of my friends discovered it a year or two back when he was trying to steal kisses from a young lady. But when they emerged and found all of us waiting outside, Lord, was her face red!"

"Are you trying to steal kisses from me, George?" She held her breath, not sure whether he would laugh it off or look at her in that way again, the look that made her knees shake and her heart flip over in the most exciting manner.

He looked her full in the face. "Oh Grace! If only I had the right! I just want to talk to you, alone. You are always surrounded by your friends and relations, and admirable as that is, I have things to say that cannot be said in public."

"Oh," she breathed.

"I want you to know…" he began, and then, with a little groan, he closed his eyes and rested his forehead against hers. "Oh, Grace, how you torment me! I had such a fine speech prepared, and now it has flown out of my head." He moved away from her, head tilted on one side. "So beautiful, so adorable, so maddeningly enticing!"

"Oh!" she said again, gazing up at him in rapture.

"I meant what I said, you know. About *wanting* to marry you. I am going to try very hard not to… to harass you, but I will not go away or give up or anything of that sort. Because if I am very patient, maybe one day you will fall in love with me too, and then I shall be the happiest man in the world, and I can cherish you for ever."

"Oh, I should so like to be cherished," she whispered.

"My sweet Grace, I love you to distraction, and I—"

She put one finger on his lips. "Do you mean that? Truly?"

"Every word."

"You did not just offer for me from a sense of duty?"

"Not in the least. I have been so miserable since that day! I want to marry you more than I have ever wanted anything in the world, but that word — *never*! Dear God, you cannot imagine how much it has tortured me. But I can wait for you. Heaven knows, you are worth waiting for, dear, beloved Grace. Do you think—?"

"Stop talking and kiss me."

His intake of breath was audible, but he needed no second invitation. He leaned towards her and pressed his lips on hers and she lost herself in his warmth, his strength, his love that wrapped itself around her like a blanket.

When they parted, both breathing heavily, he murmured, "Shall we elope? Run off to Scotland to get married? I can organise things in a couple of days, I expect."

She laughed, burying her head in his coat. "Oh George, that would be so much fun! But it seems to me that our wilder impulses have not turned out too well lately." She looked up at him shyly. "Perhaps we should begin our married life more circumspectly. Besides, I should like to be married in my own church, with Mr Endercott officiating, and Cousin Henry to give me away, just like my sisters."

"It shall be exactly as you wish, my love." And he smiled down at her, a smile of heart-stopping adoration.

~~~~~

Lady Graham wished to hold a small entertainment to celebrate the engagement of her only son. Her idea of a small entertainment being a dinner for sixty people followed by a ball for several hundred, a certain amount of planning was required. Therefore Lady Sara was invited to spend a day at Graham House, so that the two ladies might combine their ideas.

But that very morning, even as the Allamont ladies waited for the carriage, a groom arrived from Willowbye bearing the saddest of news, for Cousin Vivienne had died.

"Oh no!" Hope wailed. "Poor, poor Cousin Vivienne! I prayed so hard for her, and to no avail."

"Perhaps your prayers were answered," her mother said sharply. "Surely you prayed for her to be relieved of all pain and the sorrow of illness, and now she is in a better place far beyond the weariness of the world."

"She is with God, that is true," Hope said. "But still, it is such a grief when anyone dies."

"It comes to us all, in time," Lady Sara said more gently.

"The grief is with those left behind," Grace said. "Poor Cousin Henry! How he must feel it. I know she left him for all those years, but once she returned they were very happy together, I think."

Her mother gave her a curious look. "Happy? Perhaps, but I do not think he will be inconsolable. However, this is a blow, Grace, for we must go into mourning for a while, you know, and Lady Graham's careful plans must be delayed perforce. Not long, perhaps, for Vivienne was only a second cousin, but one would not wish to be neglectful of any observance, especially at the moment, when there are still those who would spread foul rumours about."

"Oh, certainly," Grace said at once. "But perhaps we should not go to Graham House today?"

"Lady Graham will wish to know at once, and there is nevertheless much that may be done. I daresay we can still have you married by the autumn, without the loss of more than a couple of masked balls. And then, Hope, it will be your turn to find a husband."

"I believe I shall never marry," Hope said in a small voice.

The carriage arrived just then, and as Lady Sara swept down the steps to where it waited, Grace said quietly to her sister, "You must not mourn the loss of Mr Burford for ever, Hope. There are any number of young men in the world who are perfectly charming and eligible." Not that Mr Burford had been either of those when he had been so desperately in love with Hope. A blushing, stammering curate, with hardly a hundred pounds to his name — yet Hope held his memory dear.

"I do not care about charm or eligibility," Hope said. "I want a man who will look at me the way Mr Burford once did. The way George looks at you, sister."

Grace was forced to concede the point.

When they arrived at Graham House, Lady Graham was not at all dismayed by the news. "Well, I am sorry for her family, but it is a blessing for the lady herself. Such a dreadful affliction! But this is not such an unexpected event, so I have kept it in mind from the start. Only a few adjustments are needed to our arrangements, I wager. Lady Sara, will you join me in my parlour? We shall not need the rest of you. Go and walk about the gardens for an hour or two, for it is such a fine day today. Lady Sara and I will do all the work while you enjoy yourselves." But her eyes gleamed with pleasure at the prospect of such enjoyable work.

Obediently, the ladies fetched bonnets and gloves, and the gentlemen canes, and out they went into the sunshine, Sir Matthew, Mr Bertram and Miss Bellows, Hope and, hand in hand, George and Grace.

"At least your mama is quite happy about everything now," Grace said. "I thought she would be so angry with us."

"Lord, so did I! When we emerged from that cupboard at the assembly rooms, and there they all were, outside the supper room, I wanted to curl up into a ball like a hedgehog."

Grace giggled. She could laugh about it now, but at the time it had been terrifying. But it had taken Lady Graham precisely five minutes to veer from annoyance to resigned acceptance to planning every detail of the happy couple's wedding. Within two days she had drawn up lists of balls and dinners and card parties for the summer, culminating in a grand autumn ball before the wedding itself, and had whisked them off to look at Primrose Lodge, negotiating very agreeable lease terms with the agent.

By walking very slowly, they soon managed to drop far behind the rest of the party.

"Come on," George said. "If we are quick, we can cut through here, make a little detour and still catch them up before the coach house."

With a delighted laugh, Grace picked up her skirts and ran, following George through the shrubbery, across the sundial lawn and into the woods on the far side. Then, right in the heart of the trees, he stopped.

"There! What do you think?"

"About what? This oak tree?"

For answer, he pointed upwards.

"Oh, a tree house!" she cried, clapping her hands together delightedly. "Was it yours when you were a boy?"

"It is still mine," he said with a smile. "Here, there are steps cut into the trunk on the other side. Can you climb up, do you think? Hold the rope rail tight! I should not want you to fall and break your neck."

She scrambled up without difficulty, her skirts bunched in one hand. "I suppose you are looking at my legs," she said, as she reached the platform.

"They are very shapely legs, well worth looking at," he said, grinning up at her.

She turned, looking at the house with its sturdy wooden walls, a proper door with a knocker and curtains at the windows. Painted over the door, she read *'Larkwood'*, *'George's House'* and *'No admittance to girls'*.

"It is lovely, but I am not allowed in," she said sadly.

"Not yet, but just wait a moment."

He disappeared inside, and emerged a moment later with a small bucket and a thin paintbrush. In a very few moments he had amended the signs. Now it read, *'George's and Grace's House'* and *'No admittance to others'*.

"Now you may enter," he said, making her a sweeping bow.

There was not much furniture inside, just a worn chaise longue, and a card table with mismatched chairs.

"This was my retreat as a boy," George said. "Somewhere safe I could hide away when I was in trouble, when Mama was cross and Papa was disappointed in me. Later on, I came here with my friends sometimes, somewhere where the servants could not spy on us, and we could get drunk and play cards without any disapproving looks. I suppose if I had been that way inclined, I would have brought girls here, too. But now I want to share it with you, and only you. It is not going to be easy for either of us to settle down and play the respectable married couple and be responsible for our own house and servants and babies and so forth. There will be times when we just want to escape from it all for an hour or two, and then we can come here and be free again, just for a little while."

"You are getting very wise, George," Grace said seriously. "I cannot decide whether I love you most as wild George or as wise George. Wise George is very dependable and will make an excellent husband, I fancy, but I should be sorry to lose wild George altogether."

"I doubt he will ever vanish completely, for look how cleverly he has managed to get you quite alone and defenceless here, so that he can kiss you to his heart's content."

His face alight with love, he opened his arms to her and she walked into them in perfect contentment.

Thanks for reading!

If you have enjoyed reading this book, please consider writing a short review on Amazon. Would you like to know more about the Allamont family and their friends? The next book in the series is **Hope: The Daughters of Allamont Hall Book 6**. You can read Chapter 1 at the end of this book.

A note on historical accuracy: I have endeavoured to stay true to the spirit of Regency times, and have avoided taking too many liberties or imposing modern sensibilities on my characters. The book is not one of historical record, but I've tried to make it reasonably accurate. However, I'm not perfect! If you spot a historical error, I'd very much appreciate knowing about it so that I can correct it and learn from it. Thank you!

About the books

The Daughters of Allamont Hall is a series of six traditional Regency romances, featuring the unmarried daughters of Mr William and Lady Sara Allamont. When their father dies unexpectedly, his will includes generous dowries for the sisters, but only on condition that they marry in the proper order, the eldest first.

Book 1: Amy
Book 2: Belle
Book 3: Connie
Book 4: Dulcie
Book 4.5: Mary (a novella, free to mailing list subscribers)
Book 5: Grace
Book 6: Hope

About the author

I write traditional Regency romances under the pen name Mary Kingswood, and epic fantasy as Pauline M Ross. I live in the beautiful Highlands of Scotland with my husband. I like chocolate, whisky, my Kindle, massed pipe bands, long leisurely lunches, chocolate, going places in my campervan, eating pizza in Italy, summer nights that never get dark, wood fires in winter, chocolate, the view from the study window looking out over the Moray Firth and the Black Isle to the mountains beyond. And chocolate. I dislike driving on motorways, cooking, shopping, hospitals.

Any questions or comments about the series? I'd love to hear from you! Email me at mary@marykingswood.co.uk.

Acknowledgements

Thanks go to:

My grandparents, Henry and Hannah Austin, who named their four children Amy, Constance, Ernest and Frank, and thereby inadvertently inspired these books

My good friends at AC (you know who you are!) who provided me with advice, support, encouragement and kicks up the backside, hand-holding and hugs, laughs and tears, woo chickens, tacos and tubesteak

My beta readers: Clara Benson, Mary Burnett, Marina Finlayson

Last, but definitely not least, my first reader: Amy Ross.

An extract from Hope - Chapter 1: A Marriage Of Convenience

Hope watched dispiritedly as the agents made their farewells to her mother. They were very respectful, almost obsequious to her, bowing as low as they could without falling over, every sentence milady this and your ladyship that. Nevertheless, the task they were charged with could not but be deeply unpleasant to everyone. To have people crawling all over Allamont Hall, measuring, inspecting, looking under carpets and behind paintings, and silently assessing the value of the property was unspeakable.

The pleasure in their eyes as they moved from room to room was clear to see. Allamont House was a splendid property, built in the grand style common in the last century, with well-proportioned formal rooms and all the facilities required for living in the country. It was perhaps a little old-fashioned now, but nothing that some slight refurbishment could not ameliorate, and with fine pleasure grounds and woodlands. Yes, no doubt the agents could not believe their good fortune in having such an admirable property fall into their laps like a ripe plum.

As soon as they had left, Lady Sara whisked upstairs to her sitting room. She was presently in one of her cold, withdrawn moods, and who could blame her? She must be as downhearted as Hope this summer. In just three months from now, they would be thrown out of their home, and mother and daughter would be obliged to move to the Dower House, and what comfort would be theirs then?

Hope saw Hugo watching her, his face as dark as hers must be.

"Come," he said, with a flick of his head. "Have a glass of ratafia, or something stronger, if you prefer. Nothing else to do but drink and be sorrowful together."

She followed him into the book room, once a cheerless place devoid of ornament or picture, where she and her sisters had recited their lessons or read from the Scriptures or translated a passage of Greek under her father's hawk-like eyes, trembling with fear of his disapprobation. He was long gone, and since Hugo had taken over the management of the Hall, it had become a warm, friendly room, books and papers and rolled-up maps scattered on every surface, and his three dogs lolling in front of the fire. Hugo was no more than a distant cousin, but he and his family were their only relatives who lived nearby.

"I still do not understand why they need to measure everything so soon," she said for perhaps the fiftieth time. "Why could they not wait until October? For the church cannot have the Hall before then, can they? They must wait the full five years for the terms of Papa's will to take effect, surely?"

"They cannot have possession, that is true," he said, pouring ratafia for her and Madeira for himself. "They have to wait until the very last day, because there is always a small possibility that one or other of your brothers will turn up to claim his inheritance. But October is a difficult time of year. Houses are much easier to sell in the summer, when people may travel more easily to inspect a property. The Bishop wants to hold an open day for prospective buyers to look around before the weather turns bad, and to do that the occasion must be advertised widely, and to do *that* they must know the exact numbers of rooms of each type, and their proportions, and the size of the linen cupboard and so forth. And then there is the value of the estate. Someone is to come next week to inspect the accounts, to determine the exact income from the tenants and holdings."

"You can tell them that to the penny."

He smiled then. He was an odd looking man, far too thin, dark of hair and eye, handsome, she supposed, in a melancholy, brooding sort of way, but his strange little lopsided smile gave his face a quirky charm.

"They will not take my word for it," he said, with a lift of one shoulder. "I am not to be trusted, it seems, since I have a personal interest."

"I suppose that is understandable." Her voice trembled slightly, her tears not far away. "Oh Hugo, this is so horrid! I do so wish we could stay in the Hall."

She could have bitten her tongue for her foolishness, for his face lit up eagerly.

"You do not have to leave it, Hope, you know that. Marry me, and we can keep the Hall. You would not even have to change your name. Should you not like to be Mrs Hugo Allamont, the mistress of Allamont Hall? For I tell you honestly, I should very much like to be Mr Hugo Allamont, the master of Allamont Hall."

How many times had he made the same speech, or some variation of it? And all because of a casual line in her father's will — if the long lost sons could not be found, then any of the three cousins could inherit if they married one of the daughters. Hope was the last of the daughters now, for all her sisters were married. And Hugo was the last of the cousins, since James was married and Mark had gone off to Scotland to become a teacher.

"I should not mind being mistress of Allamont Hall," she said, as she had told him so many times. "I already am, in many ways, for Mama takes no interest in the household. And you have already taken the role of master here, and we are most grateful to you for that. But I am not sure whether I want to marry anyone at all. Although," she added punctiliously, "it is most obliging in you to offer, Hugo, and if I were minded to marry at all, you would be my first choice."

He raised an eyebrow. "So it is not my person in particular that repels you but the very notion of marriage? Your sisters are all happily wedded."

"Oh yes, and no one could be more delighted for them than I. But they were lucky — they each met a man who adored them and looked at them with fire in his eyes. I was so fortunate as to experience that once, long ago, and I cannot settle for less, Hugo. I cannot marry a man who does not look at me in that way. And then — there is your mama," she added in a low voice. "I do not want to die because of a baby growing wrong."

"I can understand that," he said seriously. "Poor Mama! How she suffered at the end, when even the laudanum began to fail her. And many women die during the birthing of a baby. It is a terrible, dangerous business."

"Oh yes! I have not forgot poor Mrs Wills! Such a tragedy, and Mr Wills so grief-stricken."

They were both silent for a while, Hope sipping her ratafia and nibbling a bonbon, and Hugo rubbing the ears of one of his dogs.

"You know, Hope," he said suddenly, leaning forward in excitement, "there is a way around this. We could marry but not... erm, not be husband and wife, if you see what I mean."

"How could we be married but not be husband and wife… oh!" She blushed crimson. "You mean, no bedroom… erm, happenings."

"Exactly! A marriage solely of convenience. So long as we marry before mid-October, and there is no sign of Ernest and Frank, we would inherit the Hall. What do you say?"

"But then there would never be a man who would look at me with fire in his eyes," she said, her voice quivering.

He sat back in his chair, defeated. "Will you at least think about it?"

"I cannot see that my feelings will be any different tomorrow or next week or next month."

He sprang to his feet, to the alarm of the dogs, and paced restlessly back and forth. "Then our only hope is to find Ernest and Frank. We still have time, and there must be a way. I cannot believe they are dead!"

She looked up at him warily, knowing his fidgety moods of old. "Aunt Lucy from Liverpool is trying to contact them. That is where they were last seen, so surely that is the best place to search."

He spun round, his face alive with enthusiasm. "You are absolutely right! Liverpool! But she is merely asking here and there. We need to broadcast our situation more widely. An advertisement, that is what we must put out. There must be newspapers in Liverpool."

"When Papa died, Mr Plumphett posted notices in all the newspapers, I believe," she said.

"Oh, Plumphett! He is such a pompous old fool. I am sure he is a good enough sort of solicitor for common matters, but he drew up this will of your father's in the first place. I hold him entirely responsible for the extraordinary nature of parts of it."

"I daresay he only wrote what Papa told him to," Hope said. "No one could change Papa's mind when he was set on a certain path."

Hugo laughed then, and stepped over the dog to take his seat again. "Of course you are right. Perhaps I should talk to Plumphett before I do anything, to understand what was attempted to discover Ernest and Frank. Still, another try at advertising can do no harm."

~~~~~

"Hope, I should like you to come down to the Dower House with me tomorrow," her mama said one evening as they drank their tea after dinner. "The refurbishment is almost complete now, so it will be the perfect opportunity for you to choose your bedroom."

"Must I? The very thought of moving there is so lowering. The weather is so fine, I had hoped to begin my sketch of the northern aspect."

Hope hated these evenings when the two of them were alone. Often Hugo stayed for a night or two when he was busy on estate business, and then he would play cribbage with her, or sing while she played the pianoforte. Occasionally he read poetry to her, for he had a fine voice for such recitations. But when he was not there, and she and her mother were alone together, Hope had the darkest vision of their lonely future in the Dower House.

Lady Sara set down her cup. "You are very sentimental about this house, Hope. All the drawing of this angle and that is well and good in its own way, and a perfectly acceptable accomplishment for a young lady to pursue, but it does not do to become too attached to any place. Few people are so fortunate as to reside in one house from the cradle to the death bed. October will see us settled in the Dower House, whether you will or no, and it is as well that you become accustomed to the idea."

"Indeed, I am accustomed, Mama, but I need not like the change. Having lived all my life in the Hall, every room, every chair, every picture has memories for me."

"They cannot all be good memories, surely? Your father was a harsh and intolerant man, with few redeeming qualities."

"Mama!"

Her mother sighed. "There is little point in pretence. He was an evil man in many ways, and we all suffered at his hands. I was glad when he died, I will not lie about it, and Allamont Hall has few happy memories for me. Perhaps you were luckier, although I cannot say. Your father had the raising of you and your sisters, and I knew little of what went on the nursery. He refused to let me see you, did you know that? Each of you was lifted from my arms when you were but three days old, and taken away from me. I was permitted an hour with you on Sundays, that was all, until you were old enough to eat family dinners with us." She picked up her cup again. "But this will not do. Your melancholia is afflicting me also, Hope. Ugh, this tea is cold."

"May I fetch you another cup, Mama?"

"Thank you, Hope. You are a kind girl, even if I deplore your sentimentality."

"To regret leaving one's home of many years is surely something more than sentimentality, Mama. I shall not complain when we are in the Dower House, but I cannot but feel the loss keenly."

"I wonder you do not marry Hugo, then, if you feel so strongly about it," her mother said.

Hope shuddered. "That would be to give up all possibility of a marriage for love."

"Sometimes I despair of you, and your sisters were just the same. Love — that is all you young people think about these days. You read too many novels, I think. Love does not answer, Hope. It never has. Such a flimsy, insubstantial emotion, liable to blow away at the first puff of wind. Men are wicked creatures, every one of them, and not worth giving one's heart to. Take their money and position in society, if you must, but do not look for happiness in marriage."

Hope was too depressed to answer.

~~~~~

The Dower House was a pretty enough little place, Hope had to concede. Built at the same time as the main house, which it greatly resembled in style, the outer appearance was reassuringly familiar, even if it felt tiny by comparison. Outside, piles of detritus from the renovations still littered the drive and buried overgrown bushes masquerading as flowerbeds. Inside, the bare wooden floors echoed hollowly in every empty room, and the air smelt violently of freshly cut wood and distemper.

"This is the dining room," Lady Sara said. "The ceiling still needs work, but the size is adequate. We shall be able to seat fourteen, or sixteen at a pinch. And this will be the drawing room. The aspect is not what one would wish, but we must make do. And through here is the morning room."

"It is very dark," Hope said.

"It is. I fear that massive tree on the lawn will have to go. It must have been pretty enough once, but now it is too monstrous for words. Now, upstairs we have four bedrooms. This one is mine, but you may choose any of the others that you wish. Then the other two will be for a guest and your companion."

"Companion?" Hope said in a faint voice.

"Of course. You will need a companion for those times when I am away."

"Might I not stay with one or other of my sisters, or with Cousin Mary?"

"You cannot constantly be packed up and dispatched to this house or that like a piece of luggage! Far better to stay quietly at home. I will advertise for a companion for you, or perhaps I might ask Miss Endercott. She knows everything that goes on in the neighbourhood, and will be sure to know just the person. Such a pity Miss Bellows left. I must say, it was most inconsiderate of her to go off and marry like that. At her age too! What can be more ridiculous than a middle-aged bride?"

"It was an excellent match, Mama, and she could not keep Mr Graham waiting indefinitely, just so that she might chaperon me about when you are not here. But perhaps if you were from home less, or... or if you were to take me with you..."

Her mother turned her gaze full on her daughter, her still-beautiful face alight with merriment. "I do not think that would answer! If you find your situation difficult, Hope, you have brought it upon yourself by refusing some very eligible offers for your hand. Your father gave you an excellent dowry, your accomplishments are adequate, you dance well and you have enough looks to appear to advantage in company. You would be nothing special in London, but here you may have had your pick of young men any time these last three or four years. Yet here you are, two and twenty and still unwed. If you dislike the prospect of living in the Dower House, then the solution is in your own hands. You may marry tomorrow if you please. I could name half a dozen young men who would be delighted to win you."

"To win my dowry, you mean," she said. "That is all that interests them. They court me with glib words and promises, but they care nothing for me."

Her mother shrugged. "I am tired of this fruitless discussion. You may return to the house while I talk to the builder."

Hope needed no further prompting. She could barely wait to be outside again, out in the clean air, untainted by paint or plaster or the sound of hammering. As she walked up the drive, she came upon Hugo, supervising one of the gardeners who was pulling weeds out of the gravel. He stood up at once, and, waving the man to continue, fell into step beside her.

"Hope? Are you all right?"

"Could anyone be all right who is expected to leave all this behind?" She waved an arm to encompass the western face of Allamont Hall, mellow in the summer sunshine. "The Dower House is so tiny, Hugo! I shall suffocate there! And Mama is not planning to stay at home any more than she does now, so I must have a companion, she says. A stranger to spend my days with — what could be more dreadful."

"Well, if you have to spend your life with a stranger, you would do better to marry one, for then you would at least have your own establishment."

Hope was much struck by this thought. "That is true! A husband, even if one knows him well, is still a stranger in many ways. I recall Connie saying something of the sort — how Lord Carrbridge liked things to be done in a certain way, and she felt quite lost at times."

"I daresay Marquesses are trickier to deal with than plain old Misters," Hugo said. "But I am no stranger — you could marry me and know exactly what you are in for."

"I am not so sure," she said seriously. "I know that you enjoy kippers for breakfast, and prefer claret to Madeira, and that you like your dogs and your horse better than most people, but I do not think one can ever know what sort of husband a man will be until it is too late."

He stopped then, turning towards her, his face eager. "But if one has known him for years and years, has seen him grow from boy to man, and at his worst as well as his best — surely that is enough of a guide? You could say then with a great deal of confidence that this man would be a good husband. You cannot deny it, Hope. You know I would make you a good husband, none better."

She was taken aback by his intensity, and tried to laugh it off. "Well, you do not beat your dogs so that is a promising sign that you would not beat me."

He grabbed her arm, and would have said more, but abruptly he released her and spun away. "Ah, Hope, if you only knew how alike we are! We both despair to leave Allamont Hall. Yet you will not take the obvious step."

"Do not tease me about it, Hugo. We have time still, and something may yet happen to change our situation."

They walked on in uncomfortable silence, Hugo with his head lowered. She could not tell whether he was offended, but she had no wish to cause another outburst so she made no attempt to find out.

In the entrance hall, the butler, housekeeper and footman were huddled together, whispering. They sprang apart as Hope and Hugo walked in.

"Miss Allamont! Mr Allamont!" the butler began, then stopped, flustered. In his hands, he held a newspaper.

This was so unlike him that Hope said, "Whatever is wrong, Young?"

"It is the newspaper, Miss. There is a notice..."

He folded the newspaper and placed it on a silver salver, presenting it to Hope with a bow. Hugo snatched it and vanished into the drawing room.

"Really, Hugo!" she cried, following him. Then she saw his face. "What is it? Tell me the worst! Has something terrible occurred?"

"It is the church's notice about Allamont Hall. There is to be an auction in October, and a viewing day next month. We will have people trampling all over the house, and poking about in the bedrooms, and disrupting the kitchens."

"Oh no!" She took the newspaper from him, but her tears fell so fast that the words blurred together. "Oh Hugo, what are we to do?"

He wrapped his arms around her and rocked her gently. "If you hate this as much as I do, then marry me, Hope. Marry me and we can put a stop to this once and for all."

Her head shot up. "Yes!" she said fiercely. "I cannot bear it, so yes, I will marry you, Hugo."

END OF SAMPLE CHAPTER OF *HOPE*

.